MIDNIGHT REIGN

MIDNIGHT REIGN

BOOK SIX

KRISTEN MARTIN

Black Falcon Press

To those fighting their own demons –

may you vanquish the darkness

with the force of a thousand suns.

PRONUNCIATION GUIDE

CHARACTERS

Arden: Ar-den

Rydan: Ry-den

Darius: Dare-ee-us

Aldreda: Al-dray-duh

Cerylia: Sur-lee-uh

Braxton: Brax-ten

Xerin: Zer-in

Nevaeh: Neh-vay-ah

Dulot: Doo-low

PLACES

Trendalath: Tren-duh-loth

Sardoria: Sar-door-ee-uh

Vaekith: Vy-kith

Orihia: Or-eye-uh

Ipcea: Ip-see

Chialka: Key-all-kuh

Miraenia: Mur-ay-nee-uh

Lonia: Lone-ee-uh

Lirath: Leer-ath

Eadrios: Ay-dree-os

OTHER

illusié: ill-oo-see-ayy

magick: ma-jik (magic)

Caldari: Kal-darr-ee

Cruex: Crew

Vaekith Mountains
Drakken Isle
Rovie
Volkharn
Miraenia
Trendalath
Declorath
Crostan Islands
Ipcea
Athia
Sunngate
THE LAND
AERID

rath Cave
Eadrios
Sardoria
Woods
Eroesa
Chialka
Orihia
Thering Forest
Isle of Lonia
OF
on

MIDNIGHT REIGN

ARDEN ELIRI

EMBERS LICK THE sides of the pyres in honor of our fallen Caldari.

Opal Marston.

Felix Barlow.

Except, unlike Opal, Felix's body still hasn't been recovered. Nor has the soul gem Cerylia informed us of.

Angry tears prick my eyes as I recall the events from Midvale—how I'd foolishly and mistakenly murdered the man I'd shared a bed with. The way he'd looked at me as the light had left his eyes, the last thing he'd ever see . . . *me.*

Betraying him in the worst way possible. Heat builds within my body, a stark contrast to the snow falling around me.

Having known them the longest, Estelle stands on the dais, delivering her eulogy. How desperately I want to listen to her beautifully curated words, but there's only one repeating in my mind over and over again. *Murderer.*

The irony isn't lost on me—attending my victim's funeral. It hadn't been intentional. Quite the opposite in fact. When I'd brought my blade down upon his chest, I'd done so because it'd been Darius I'd hoped to strike down. That's who I'd seen, thanks to the immaculate work of the Caster. In more ways than one, he's just as at fault as I am for Felix's death. Not that it matters to him in the slightest.

Why should it?

I'm briefly pulled out of my guilt-induced thought spiral as Estelle finishes her speech and leaves her post at the dais. The flames dance against a backdrop of snow-capped mountains and, if it weren't for the morose setting of a funeral, the view would be one I could look at for hours on end. I lift my gaze to the mid-afternoon sky, catching Rydan's stare along the way. He mouths a question we both already know the answer to.

Are you okay?

No. Absolutely fucking not.

If there's one thing giving me any glimmer of hope, it's that, before his untimely death, Felix's soul was extracted and placed inside a soul gem by none other than my aunt. How the soul gem came to be in her possession is, quite frankly, a mystery to me, but what isn't a mystery is who has it now.

Xerin Grey.

Seeing him at Midvale, standing side by side with Darius, was enough to make my stomach turn. Trusting him hadn't come easy and I suppose now, in hindsight, that was for a reason. Despite his sister's many defenses in his favor, the look of disgust on her face that day had said it all. As much as we might think we know someone, all we ever really see is the surface—what *they* want us to see. Xerin expertly hid behind a cleverly constructed mask, one we all failed to recognize.

Even those closest to him.

The fire is still burning bright when I realize I'm the last one standing outside. When everyone had left and returned indoors, I haven't the slightest clue. I shiver as the chill of evening air wraps itself around me, the lights to Sardoria castle flickering in the near distance. I gaze at the setting sun, dreading the next visit that's about to take place: to the infirmary to see my father. Not that he can actually *see* me, since he's still unresponsive.

Yet another reminder of how badly I've fucked up.

At least he's still breathing, still has a pulse.

The reminder does little in the way of consolation, yet I've told it to myself every night since arriving here.

I sigh, leaving the pyres behind as I head toward Sardoria castle. I'd much prefer to visit my father alone this evening, but Haskell is hell-bent on making sure that doesn't happen. Not because he doesn't trust me, but because he wants to be there for me and for our father. I find his persistence in the matter both incredibly endearing and downright infuriating.

I've only made it a few steps inside the castle walls when my brother appears seemingly out of nowhere. "Is it that time already?"

I give him a dubious look. "It would appear so, seeing as you're lurking in the shadows, waiting for me."

He brings a hand to his chest in mock offense. "That would imply that I have nothing better to do."

"Than visit our father?" I shoot back.

He narrows his eyes, then says, "Touché."

We begin to climb the stairs to the fourth floor, walking in silence as we have every night prior. There comes a point in every family when all there is to say has been said and all that's left to do is sit with your own thoughts, no matter how awkward or inconvenient. Luckily with Haskell, it's never been either.

The fourth floor is quiet, save for the bell tower chiming in the distance. How it's already midnight is beyond me. I glance at Haskell, knowing he's thinking the same thing.

"I'm surprised you haven't asked for an update on my travels." He waggles his brows at me. "Then again, I suppose there's nothing new to report."

"Figures." I sigh. "Although, if I were Darius and Xerin, I wouldn't want to be found either."

"Certainly not with the current condition of their ranks being nonexistent and all."

I make a sharp left down the hall that leads to the infirmary. "I wouldn't exactly say *nonexistent*. I'm sure there's still a Savant or two out there somewhere."

"Did we not witness the same obliteration at Midvale?"

"We did." I pause. "But if Xerin and Darius were able to escape, who's to say a few of the others didn't as well?"

"But you saw the bodies—"

"It's not like I was keeping track," I counter. "I was a bit preoccupied." *With our dying father*, I want to add, but decide against it. I push open the door to the infirmary, its familiar creak both welcoming and looming. At first glance, it seems all of the Healers have retired for the evening, as should be expected seeing as it's so late—but then I hear the clinking of glass vials. In the far back corner, I can see the shadow of a woman behind a curtain. There's some rustling, the knocking of wooden trays, and the opening and closing of cabinets before she draws the curtain back and steps out from the workstation. Our sudden presence must come as a shock because she nearly drops the tray she's carrying.

"Lords, I didn't hear you come in," she says with a nervous smile. "You gave me quite a fright." She shuffles a few of the fallen items around on the tray before returning her attention to us.

There's something about the way she looks at me that sets me on edge. There's a hint of recognition in her gaze, but I'm certain I've never met this woman before in my life.

"I'm Edith," she goes on to say as she adjusts a gold pendant that's looped around her neck. "I take it you're here to see our one and only patient."

I lock eyes with her, trying not to be distracted by the intricate design of her necklace, but it's hard not to take notice. It must have cost a fortune. She toys with it again before saying, "A wedding gift. From my husband."

"You must be new," I say, bringing the focus back on her. "We've been here every night to see our father and not once have we seen you attend to him." I angle my head at his bed across the room.

Edith hesitates. "I'm not new, no, but this *is* my first night shift in the infirmary." She crosses the room, making sure to take a path that comes nowhere near Haskell or me.

I follow her warily, motioning for my brother to trail behind me. I can't help but notice the small metal tin in the center of the tray. "What's that?"

Edith looks from me to the tin, then wets her lips. "A healing salve. My own recipe." She removes the lid, dipping her ring finger into the yellow balm before gently working it into each of my father's temples. "It's primarily used to stimulate the mind, although it's particularly effective on victims of the casting variety." She purses her lips, shaking her head before adding, "Disillusionment is nasty business and can take months, if not years, to fully restore one's faculties, as well as overall sense of reality."

Having been a victim of the Caster's attacks more than once, the statement should give me cause for concern, but it actually does the opposite. I've got a pretty good grip on reality, as unfortunate as it may be.

"We didn't see the other Healers use a salve," Haskell notes.

"Perhaps they should have," she retorts. "His progress would be much further along." Edith leans back to assess her work before adding some of the salve to his lips.

I study her closely—the wrinkles lining her eyes and mouth, the strands of gray poking through waves of chestnut, the way her shoulders hunch even when she's standing upright—and realize that she's likely more seasoned in her profession than I've given her credit for.

"What's your prognosis?" I demand.

She regards me with inquiring eyes, no doubt making her own judgment about me. "It'll take time, but eventually, he'll wake."

It isn't what the other Healers have said—far from it, actually. Their outlook on the matter has been rather grim, but Edith doesn't need to know that. Something tells me it wouldn't affect her belief in the matter anyway.

"How long?" Haskell asks, taking the next question right out of my mouth.

Edith shakes her head. "It's hard to say."

"Ballpark it," I challenge.

She narrows her eyes, irked by my tone. "No longer than two months, no earlier than two weeks."

She says it with such conviction that I find myself questioning if such a timeline truly is plausible. "And this healing salve of your own making . . . it'll do the trick?"

She pockets the tin with a hasty nod. "As long as it's administered daily in the proper quantity, preferably at night." Her eyes dart around the room as if she expects an interruption of some sort. "If for any reason I'm not here or happen to be reassigned to another shift, you must see to it that the patient receives the proper dosage."

The statement lacks confidence and the way her voice falters near the end makes the conviction I felt just moments prior disappear altogether. I exchange a wordless glance with my brother, but he doesn't seem to pick up on my uneasiness. "Who do we speak with about having you as our father's primary Healer?"

My mouth drops open. He can't be serious.

There's a brief glimmer of victory in the old woman's eyes, but, based on this interaction alone, I'm guessing she wouldn't be caught dead beaming with such pride. "You are Queen Jareth's niece and nephew, are you not?"

"We are."

"I have it on good authority that as long as you request such a thing, it will be so."

Before I can voice my growing concern, my brother says, "Consider it done. We'll see you tomorrow evening, Edith."

She grins with satisfaction. "I look forward to it."

Haskell gives Edith a small wave before abruptly grabbing my arm to lead me out of the infirmary.

"What was that all about?" I hiss.

He waits until we've cleared the doorway before asking, "How do you mean?"

"You heard the other Healers," I huff as I tear my arm from his grip. "We have four other opinions that say the chances of our father ever waking up are slim to none."

He stares at me in disbelief. "And now we have one that says otherwise—*and* with a time frame, no less. Two to eight weeks is promising."

"It may not be realistic, Haskell." I hate the contempt that's crept into my voice, but I can't shake the bad feeling I have about Edith.

"It has to be." His breath shudders. "He has to wake up."

And that's when it becomes clear to me. He's desperate. Desperate for answers, for results, for *hope* . . .

"I know." I sigh, feeling a wave of crushing guilt all over again. "But we need to prepare for the possibility that this might be it. That we met *and* said goodbye to our father in nearly the same breath."

"I can't accept that." He shakes his head before turning a lethal gaze on me. "And you shouldn't either."

The shame I feel is near suffocating as he stalks down the hall without another word. I swallow the lump forming in my throat as I glance back at the door to the infirmary. *This has to work.* Because if it doesn't, I'll never be able to forgive myself for what I've done. And I have a sinking feeling that my brother won't either.

RYDAN HELSTROM

THESE SAME STEPS are the very ones he'd fled down in a snowstorm much like the one he finds himself in now. Discovering he's illusié feels like a distant memory. Yet being here, back in Sardoria, only emphasizes both the shock and disgust he'd felt that day. Fast forward to now, he couldn't imagine his life as anything other than an Ignitor.

Rydan takes a long drink from the canteen he'd swiped from the kitchen. He'd managed to fill it with verdot with no one being the wiser, despite the many eyes that'd been nearby. The stealth of a seasoned assassin comes in handy, no doubt.

There's something about the chill in the air, the falling snow, and the absolute silence around him that makes the wine taste even more delectable than if he were sitting inside. The peaceful moment ends too soon, however, when he hears the sound of footsteps approaching the castle doors. In the cover of night, Arden slips through the entrance seemingly undetected—that is, until she's spotted.

"Well, this is awfully familiar," she jokes as she walks over to where he's sitting. "Except last time, if memory serves, you could hardly stand the thought of being here, around *our kind.*"

He takes another swig of his drink before offering the canteen to her. "How times have changed."

"Indeed." She sighs, taking it from him, then proceeds to sit next to him on the snow-covered bench.

"Any word on your father?"

"Nothing worth mentioning." She drops her gaze to the ground, shaking her head. "Although there *is* a new Healer in the infirmary named Edith. She's started administering a salve that should help."

Rydan turns his head to look at her. "That's big news."

"It will be if it works out when all is said and done."

The despondence in her voice is crushing. He reaches out beside him to squeeze the top of her hand. "If there's anyone who can pull through, it's an Eliri." Her eyes meet his and he gives her a firm nod. "Don't forget, I've seen it with my own two eyes."

"Seen what, exactly?"

"How damn resilient you are." He briefly averts his gaze, wishing he hadn't responded so quickly. "I'm sure your father is no different."

"You'd better be right." She takes another drink from the canteen before handing it back to him. "Looks like you'll need a refill soon."

"Nah," he says, setting the leather piece beside him. "I just needed something to take the edge off."

She arches a brow. "Do tell."

"It's the crescent fire." He drums his fingers against the bench, the snow silencing the sound. "Now that I have it in my possession, I can't help but feel like I should know how to use it. There's so much pressure—"

"From whom?"

He hesitates, unsure as to how to answer. "No one in particular, I guess. But knowing that we have the capability to destroy the very thing keeping Tymond in control . . ."

She nods in understanding. "It feels like a missed opportunity."

"Exactly." He blows out a long breath. "And when your father mentioned the crescent fire at Midvale, it felt like things were finally coming together, like he could teach me how to wield it—or, at the very least, point me in the right direction." He stops, realizing how insensitive he sounds.

"And then I had to go and fuck it all up."

"That isn't what I meant."

"I know." She stares off in the distance, detached. "It doesn't make it any less true, though."

The disappointment in her voice is palpable. He's temped to close the distance between them, but something about the moment feels off. Grief lingers in the air, dark and heavy—for what could have been, for what *might* be.

"There's no telling what Stanton knows," he says, making sure to use the present tense. "But *someone* has to know *something* about the crescent fire and how to wield it."

Arden scoffs. "Honestly, our best bet was probably at Midvale, but I doubt we'll be headed back there anytime soon."

Rydan hesitates before asking, "Has your aunt mentioned anything about the Archmage?"

"Besides the fact that Haskell was able to transport her body back here?" Arden shakes her head. "I wouldn't be surprised if she decided to hold a modest ceremony in her honor."

"Why is that?"

Arden shrugs. "From what I've gathered, Cyfrin was a private person. Not to mention, they have a history."

"Don't we all?" He doesn't realize he's said it out loud until he catches Arden grinning at him. The moment is humbling knowing that her feelings lie elsewhere, with someone who currently isn't even alive . . .

Technically speaking.

"I wonder if my father knows anything about soul magick," Arden muses, as if she can read his every thought.

"I wouldn't be surprised if he did since he intentionally entered the Medial—something none of us even knew existed. I bet he's just overflowing with knowledge and lived experience—" He immediately stops talking when he catches the somber expression on her face.

"This salve . . . it has to work, right?" she whispers. "I mean, if it doesn't . . ."

"Then we'll find another Healer. We'll keep trying." He gives her an affirming nod. "We just have to be patient."

She cracks another smile, but this one doesn't reach her eyes. "Which is something we're both oh so skilled at."

"What better time to learn?"

She rolls her eyes before pushing herself off the bench. "Well, while you're practicing patience, I'll be getting my hands on every book I can find that mentions soul magick."

"I take it another visit to the library is in order?" His cheeks burn as he recalls their last encounter at one of the many Midvale libraries.

"Care to join me?"

"Seeing as I have my own research to do, that would be wise." Grinning, he takes her outstretched hand and follows her into the castle.

DARIUS TYMOND

DARIUS STANDS AT the stern of the ship, mesmerized by the cerulean sea thrashing beneath him. Xerin had made it clear that flying into the Crostan Islands on dragon-back wouldn't fare well with the locals. In fact, any indication of illusié ability may as well be a death wish, but he's willing to take that chance if it means finding new recruits to build his numbers back up again. Whatever Arden had channeled that day in Midvale had swept through his ranks like the plague, leaving little to his name.

Trendalath isn't exactly safe either—not without the Cruex or the King's Guard to protect him. While the Mallum may possess copious abilities, he's more concerned with having the option to communicate with the entity, an option that's no longer available to him without his staff. Darius grits his teeth as he recalls the memory of Queen Jareth and his once loyal advisor baiting him, knowing full well that he would have caved had Xerin not been there.

He's pulled from his thoughts as the Shaper joins him at the stern, propping his elbows on the wooden railing. "You haven't left this spot in hours."

Darius lifts his gaze from the roaring waters below. "It isn't the largest ship to wander. Honestly, I expected better."

"Of course you did," Xerin sneers. "But when things don't go according to plan, we have to improvise. You should know that better than anyone."

Darius refuses to respond to such petty nonsense. He turns his gaze back toward the sea, a distant coastline coming into view. How he'd ended up in this situation is beyond his comprehension. He'd had so many assurances— from the King's Guard, the Cruex, the Savant, the Mallum, Xerin himself—but none of that had mattered when it came down to it. Cyrus had played him like a fiddle and the Eliris had unleashed such astonishing power—it's a wonder he'd made it out alive.

This isn't the first time he's been left with nothing. In fact, he's rather familiar with the feeling. But no matter how many times he tells himself it's a fresh start, he can't help but feel like he's failed. His reign has been tumultuous at best, and it doesn't seem to be improving anytime soon.

"We'll be arriving shortly," Xerin barks, interrupting his thoughts. "I think it'd be wise for you to get some rest once we disembark."

Darius shakes his head. "There's too much to do."

"It's late and only getting later," Xerin counters. "Those on the island don't take kindly to those who keep late hours."

Darius studies him closely before raising a brow. "For a place known for its seclusion, you sure seem to know a lot about its inhabitants."

"I get around," Xerin says plainly. "As a Shaper, the same old same old grows rather tedious after a time."

"But why there, of all places?"

Xerin smirks. "Why not?"

Darius doesn't return the smile, just shifts his gaze back to the coastline. "Let's hope the accommodations are decent. I'm going to need it if I plan to get any rest."

"Fortunately for you," Xerin boasts, "I know just the place."

XERIN GREY

T H E   W A Y   H E   sees it, Midvale had been a disaster. Not only had Darius failed in using the Mallum to gain all illusié abilities, but he'd seemingly ignored the request to target those who mattered most: the Caldari. He's known for some time that he's had his work cut out for him, but to this degree? He never could have imagined.

After dropping Darius off at a discreet seaside inn at the edge of the Crostan Islands, Xerin's making his way inland, alone. He hadn't bothered telling the king his plans regarding his whereabouts because, quite frankly, he doesn't need another catastrophe on his hands. And, lately, where Darius goes, disaster seems to follow.

The journey inland is smooth, although the roads are worn and more traveled than he remembers. The towns he passes by have certainly seen better days—shingles dangling from rooftops, doors boarded up with wood that's near rotting, cobblestone that's no longer raised but run haphazardly into the ground . . . *ah, paradise.* But for the outcasts who reside here, this had been their only option. Cut off from Aeridon, from the world. Forced to succumb to a grim fate.

Xerin stops at a fork in the road, turning left at the wooden stake in the ground toward Bellmoor. The town of Kilshade lies in the opposite direction and, if he has no luck at the former, that's where he'll go next. It's been some time since he's traveled by foot, but using his abilities here would only draw unwanted attention—and mark him as a potential threat. Making enemies certainly isn't on the agenda.

Much to his surprise, the foliage grows denser, lusher, and more colorful the closer he gets to town. He's even more surprised to find that the upkeep of the small village itself is near impeccable, far from the memory he has from his last visit. The buildings are intact with the same bones as before, but appear to have received a thorough washing, a fresh coat of paint, and new hardware on the windows and doors. The planters outside the windows point to a woman's touch, which can only mean one thing. His old friend has kicked the bucket, putting his wife, Thora, in charge.

Not the best news for him, seeing as Thora never particularly liked him. But the chances of her recognizing him now are low, so he might have a shot.

There's only one way to find out.

Unlike the haphazard road before, he follows the pristine cobblestone path to the center of town until he reaches a familiar cottage with a magenta-stained door. He unlatches the lock to the fence surrounding the property, all the while rehearsing in his head how to greet a woman he hasn't seen in years. As he approaches the door, it suddenly opens, and a young woman steps out. Xerin stops in his tracks, taking in her features—the elongated nose, the deep-set cheeks, the wide amber eyes—and quickly realizes that this must be their daughter.

She sets eyes on him, looking both perturbed and intrigued. "May I help you?"

Xerin clears his throat, unexpectedly overcome with nerves before saying, "I'm an old friend of your father's. Is he in?"

She arches a brow, eyes wary, then looks him up and down. "I'm not sure *friend* is the appropriate title. Because those who knew him are well aware of what he suffered through."

Xerin nods apologetically. "I take it he's no longer with us."

She casts her gaze at the ground. "For some time now."

"And your mother? Thora?"

The use of her mother's name has her looking back up at him. A semblance of trust flickers in her eyes. "The same affliction, I'm afraid."

"I'm sorry to hear that." It's a lie, but it's the appropriate thing to say in this situation. "I don't believe I got your name."

"That's because I didn't give it to you."

Xerin tries to hide his smile. "Care to indulge me?"

"Alyna."

"It suits you." It's the first thing he's said this entire conversation that he actually means. "It's nice to meet you, Alyna."

"And you are?"

"Xerin Grey."

"And how did you know my parents?"

It should be a simple question to answer, but his history with the Wilmotts is rather complicated—and lengthy. She must sense his trepidation because she narrows her eyes as she says, "Riddle me this. If they were alive, would your showing up here be a welcome surprise or not?"

"I wish I could say," Xerin answers wistfully. "My relations with your father were as good as they get, but your mother . . ."

She cracks a smile. "My mother was tough to win over. Even as her daughter, I had to fight for her affection and approval. I quickly learned that it was an impossible task."

"We share a similar upbringing then," Xerin muses. "I, too, had difficulty winning the affection of my mother."

"It makes for a lonely childhood."

"That it does." The compassion in his voice is genuine and, for a moment, he briefly forgets why he's come here. Not wanting his stare to linger, he glances past her shoulder at the door. "I take it it's just you, then. No siblings?"

"Is it that obvious?"

"I mean it as a compliment." He makes a sweeping gesture with his hand at the fence and the town sitting just outside of it. "I don't know how you've managed to bring Bellmoor to its prime, but here we are. I never thought I'd see the day."

"It just needed a woman's touch, I suppose."

Her response is an echo of his exact thoughts the moment he'd stepped foot into the quaint, charming town.

"So, Xerin Grey," she says with a sly smile, "what business with my family brings you to Bellmoor?"

"If I'm being honest, it's a rather peculiar request—something I'm not sure you'd even be open to."

"Try me," Alyna challenges.

Even though there's no one around, Xerin lowers his voice. "It has to deal with the likes of illusié."

Alyna's face pales. "I can assure you, we have no business discussing anything related to illusié. You'll find that the residents of Bellmoor feel the same way."

"That's exactly why I've come. The king and I have been working tirelessly to rid Aeridon of all illusié."

"Using a magickal entity," Alyna points out. "Yes, I'm well aware."

"If there were a way to rid magick without the use of magick itself, we would have found it. Believe me when I say, this is it."

"And pray tell *why* this would interest my father? Or me, for that matter?"

"Because, if we play our cards right, there's an opportunity for redistribution of illusié abilities. For everyone in Bellmoor, in Kilshade—across the Crostan Islands as a whole." He can tell by the way her pupils dilate that he's playing to her ego. "Imagine being the leader of such a movement."

A sad smile stretches the length of her face. "As promising and idealistic as that sounds, I'm not sure the people of the Crostan Islands would welcome such an opportunity, or even be open to exploring it."

"What's the alternative, then? To remain hidden and secluded from Aeridon for the rest of time?"

Alyna shrugs nonchalantly. "It's worked in our favor thus far. What you're suggesting would only bring strife and chaos to the island—something we've managed to successfully avoid all these years."

Xerin raises his hands, backing off. "All I'm saying is that as beautiful as Bellmoor is, perhaps you wouldn't have to stay here. You could return to Aeridon—to the ease, simplicity, and pleasures of life. With the added bonus of illusié abilities, of course."

He can see the wheels turning in her mind as she considers the truth of what he's just said. The residents of the Crostan Islands may have adapted and adjusted to their current way of life, but that doesn't necessarily mean it's the life they would have chosen for themselves. The manual labor, limited resources, and lack of purpose in the way of contribution can only go on for so long. It's human nature to want more, to ask for more—and that's precisely the offer Xerin is making.

Alyna studies him closely, no doubt trying to find holes to poke through his logic, but there are none. "How likely is this to happen?"

"That depends on one thing," Xerin replies, "which is the willingness of the people of the Crostan Islands to side with Trendalath."

"By *side with*, you mean fight with."

"To a degree, yes. Redistributing the wealth of illusié is no minor task."

"I never assumed it was." Alyna chews on her lower lip. "I suppose I could hear your proposal in full before making a final decision." She turns back in the direction of her front door before saying, "Not out here, though. The last thing we need is an eavesdropper. And we don't have much time, maybe fifteen minutes at most."

"Not to worry," Xerin says with a smile as he follows her to the door. "That's all the time I need."

CERYLIA JARETH

SHE SHOULD CONSIDER herself lucky having gone from one advisor to two, but the stark difference between the two men's ideologies hasn't gone unnoticed—and the effects are starting to wear on her.

"I've said it once and I'll say it again. Trendalath has some of the best Healers known to Aeridon." Cyrus stabs at the slab of meat on his plate, further emphasizing his tone. "Just say the word and I can have them here in a day, maybe less."

"Right, because that's exactly what we need. To bring the enemy to the frontlines." Delwynn gives him an exaggerated eye roll. "Our Healers will suffice, thank you very much, just as they have for years."

Cyrus brings the utensil to his mouth, ripping the meat from it like a barbarian. "With Stanton's affliction, time is of the essence, more so than ever before." He waves his fork in the air. "If your Healers were any good, they'd have found a solution by now."

"Any good?" Delwynn echoes in disbelief. "You don't know the half of what they've accomplished, the illnesses they've treated—"

"But what have they *cured*?"

"Enough," Cerylia says quietly, resting her hands on the table. "That's quite enough." The men fall silent, save for their obnoxious masticating. "Indeed, we are running out of options," she muses with a faraway gaze.

Delwynn pushes his plate away from him before looking at the queen. "Your Greatness, you can't possibly be considering such an alternative?"

Oh, but she is. It may be a hard truth for her to swallow, but it's what Dane would have wanted for his brother—for *her* brother-in-law—who'd somehow managed to stay alive long enough to see another day outside the Void, no matter how short-lived it'd been.

"We must do anything and everything we can to see that Stanton makes a full recovery." There's no need to justify her response. The men at her table know full well the implications if he doesn't. "If that means recruiting some Healers from Trendalath, then so be it."

Delwynn bows his head in disappointment. "I've already voiced my concern, but I feel I must do so again. I strongly advise against this course of action."

Cerylia shoots him an icy glare. "Well, until you provide us with another feasible option, this course of action is the only one to take."

A dish clatters in the distance, drawing the table's attention. A meek young man with freckles splashed across his nose and unruly blonde hair lifts his tired gaze from the mess on the floor. He doesn't say anything as he begins to back away toward the door, as if suddenly invisible and not at fault.

"And who, might I ask, are you?" Cerylia questions.

Mid-step and mouth agape, the man stares at the queen.

Cerylia rises from her seat, her impatience at an all-time high. "Tell me your name."

"I'm just the assistant," he murmurs as he picks at the gold stitching on his white tunic. "I'm nobody."

"Assistant to whom?"

"Edith." His reply is firm and unwavering, unlike his first impression.

"The new Healer," Delwynn says with a nod. "Who happens to hail from Miraenia and not Trendalath," he points out.

Cerylia deigns to acknowledge his pettiness, refusing to take her eyes off the young man's face. "Is that true?"

"Yes, I've lived there my whole life. My family ran a successful apothecary business until . . . well, until the Tymonds took over."

Until they killed my husband and left me with nothing, Cerylia wants to say, but instead remains silent, maintaining her composure.

The man clears his throat. "It's been brutal. The trade embargoes. The lack of food, water, supplies . . . I'm surprised half the town hasn't dropped dead by now."

"I'm terribly sorry to hear that." Cerylia bows her head, meaning every word. "If there's one thing the Tymonds excel at, it's withholding what isn't rightfully theirs."

Her statement seems to spark just enough trust for him to finally introduce himself. "Name's Gabriel Thomason."

"It's a pleasure to make your acquaintance." She gives him a warm smile. "How about we get you a fresh plate and you can update me on Sir Eliri's status?"

Gabriel's hazel eyes grow wide at the request, as if he never could have imagined having an audience with the queen. "I would be honored."

Cerylia swipes her goblet from the table, joining him at the buffet-style table but not before turning over her shoulder to address her two advisors. "Be a dear and clean this up, would you?"

Delwynn looks at her as if she's completely lost her mind but doesn't argue. "Right away, Your Greatness."

Knowing it'll keep them occupied for a time, she links her arm in Gabriel's and walks him to the table. "Now, would you prefer pork or veal?"

KRISTEN MARTIN

BRAXTON HORNSBY

"ARE YOU SURE you can't stay?" Braxton stands at the entrance to Sardoria castle with one hand on the door, the other holding Hanslow's bag. "We've only just arrived."

The old man's eyes twinkle. "My dear boy, you and I both know that I don't belong here."

Braxton nods, the truth of the matter sinking in. "But what if Athia isn't what it once was?"

"I don't expect it to be."

A fitting answer only Hanslow could give. "Where will you go? How can I find you?"

"I'll be around." He winks. "Might I remind you that as the town's primary innkeeper over the years, I'm owed a lot of favors—many of which I never got the chance to redeem." He clears his throat before reaching for the bag Braxton's holding. "Now, hand it over. And no further questions. I'm already going to be late enough as it is."

Braxton sighs, reluctantly handing him the overstuffed bag. "Can I at least ride with you to the docks for a proper sendoff?"

"No need for that," Hanslow quips with a superfluous wave of his hand. "You'd think you were my mother with all this coddling."

It's meant to be a joke, but the words sting. Hanslow was the closest thing he'd had to a father figure he actually looked up to. Leaving him behind in Athia at the mercy of the Savant was one of the hardest things he'd ever had to do.

The guilt's eaten at him ever since.

Braxton tries to keep his voice from cracking. "If Athia's taken a turn for the worse, I do hope you'll consider returning to Sardoria. You're always welcome here."

"You're really pulling out all the stops, aren't you, kid?"

"Wouldn't you, if you were in my shoes?"

"Fair point." Hanslow grins. "Correct me if I'm wrong, but you've fared just fine without me."

"I lost my abilities, got kidnapped by my father, *and* fell into the Void—"

"—and you're alive to tell the tale," the old man finishes.

Braxton shrugs. "I suppose I can't argue with you there."

Hanslow opens his arms wide before pulling Braxton into a firm embrace. "I'd only serve as a distraction. If you're going to go head-to-head with your father, you'll need to concentrate."

Braxton nods as he pulls away. "You're right, as per usual."

"I know." Hanslow winks. "Go on now. Head inside. Don't make this any harder than it needs to be." He throws his bag over his shoulders, then mounts the chestnut mare Cerylia had acquired just for him from a stable near the port. "And keep an eye on Avery, will you? From one Herbal Alchemist to another, drafting selphinium tonics is nasty business." He shudders.

"I don't think you're giving him enough credit."

"That may be so. Regardless, *someone* needs to know what that boy's been up to." He shrugs. "Who knows? It may come in handy one of these days."

"Coming from you, I don't doubt it," Braxton says with a grin. "You have my word."

"Very well. I've delayed my departure long enough," Hanslow says with a small wave. "I'll be seeing you. Hopefully sooner rather than later."

He gives his old friend a nod before turning toward the steps that lead back to the castle. Hooves meet pavement and when Braxton glances over his shoulder one final time, Hanslow's already at the forest's edge before fading from view altogether.

ARDEN ELIRI

O F   A L L   T H E books shelved in Sardoria's massive library, I'd assumed there'd be at least one that would cover soul magick in depth, but no . . . not so much as a mention. It's one thing to seek the knowledge of something, but having it and not being able to apply it? Well, it's probably worse than not knowing about it at all.

Rydan had given up hours ago, opting for some solitude after an unexpected outburst amongst the quiet of the archives. It seems not being able to apply the knowledge of the crescent fire is getting to him. At least I'm not alone.

I heave a loud sigh, shelving yet another let-down. Disappointment lingers as I walk to the arched window that overlooks the courtyard. A blanket of white covers the ground, the benches lightly dusted with snow. The urge to call it a night and retreat to my chambers is tempting, but I remain at the window, caught in a sort of daze between fantasy and reality. My gaze spans beyond the castle borders to the treetops lining the Roviel Woods. I can't help but think of Felix.

If he isn't really gone, then where is he?

In some liminal space between life and death?

It's unanswered questions like these that haunt me. My lower lip trembles, tears pricking my eyes. I blink them back and clear my throat, hoping it'll magically fix how I'm feeling, but the relief is only temporary.

Like most things these days.

Below, a familiar figure comes into view, momentarily drawing my attention away from my thoughts. I'm about to knock on the window in the hopes that he'll hear me when Braxton suddenly stops walking. He lifts his head, his ice-blue eyes staring straight at me. Although it's unnerving, I motion for him to join me. He nods, giving me a meager thumbs up before disappearing behind the castle's double doors.

I remain at the window, not bothering to turn around when I hear the library doors open and footsteps approach. He joins me at the window without so much as a hello. I can tell from his silent demeanor that he's just gone through something heavy. Another look out the window has me following a trail of hoofprints in the snow.

He's just said goodbye.

I swallow, choosing my words carefully. "Do you want to talk about it?"

He sighs, then shakes his head. "Not necessarily."

Instead of retreating, I decide to respond lightheartedly. "Good. We've had enough news in the less-than-fortunate category as of late."

But Braxton doesn't seem to hear me as he spirals further into his misery. "Why does it feel like everyone I love would rather leave?"

"Hey," I say, reaching for his hand. "I'm here. I'm not going anywhere. And neither are the Caldari."

He smiles, but it doesn't reach his eyes. "I think I'm going to lie down for a few. I've been up since early morning helping Hanslow pack . . ."

I pretend like I don't hear the way his voice cracks when he says the old man's name. "Right, of course. Get some rest."

"Was there a reason you called me up here?"

"Nothing that can't wait until later."

He gives me a genuine smile this time. "I hope you find whatever it is you're looking for," he says, eyeing the library's many shelves as he makes for the doors.

"Me, too," I murmur. "Me, too."

⁓ ⁓ ⁓

For now, I've decided to call it quits on the research front. The more dead-end books I flip through, the more time I feel I've wasted. I finish shelving the books, returning them to their rightful places when I hear shuffling from behind one of the rows. Suddenly on high alert, I crouch, peeking around the end of one of the shelves. Vira's on the other side, running her fingers along a few of the spines.

I straighten before rounding the corner and greeting her with a soft wave. Her wide eyes and half-smile indicate she thought she was alone. When she'd slipped in, I haven't the slightest idea, but perhaps this happenstance will render itself fortuitous. I haven't had a chance to confront her about her brother since everything that had transpired in Midvale . . . Although the look on her face *then* pointed to her knowing just as much as the rest of us—which is next to nothing.

"Do you have a minute?" I ask in the lightest tone I can manage.

"Not really," she replies, keeping her gaze fixed on the shelves. "Seeing as I'm only here on Rydan's behalf."

"Understood. But this is important."

She sighs, dropping her head. "If it has to do with my brother, I'll tell you what I told Cerylia, Estelle, and Avery. I've had no part in any of it. I'm just as baffled as the rest of you."

"Understandably so." I chew on my lower lip, treading lightly. "But you know him better than anyone. And while the others' questions are probably centered around what he's doing suddenly siding with King Tymond, mine isn't." I draw in a breath, hoping it'll steady my voice. "I want to know what he'd want with Felix."

Vira studies me for a moment, then shrugs. It's so nonchalant—as if we're talking about something mundane, like the weather. "Your guess is as good as mine."

"Why have Cerylia extract his soul? Why not just . . ."

"Leave him for dead? Like you did?"

I bite back the venomous remark sitting on my tongue and instead say, "We were searching for help—both Haskell and I."

"Did you ever consider that perhaps you should be *thanking* Xerin?" The question drips with disdain. "Without him, Felix would be just as you left him." She blinks, her expression cold and unforgiving. "Dead."

Knowing this conversation isn't headed anywhere productive, I begin to back off. "You might be right. But fleeing with the soul gem certainly isn't a good look."

"And killing your boyfriend is?"

I know the only way out of this involves taking the high road, but that path is becoming less and less viable the longer this conversation carries on. "Enough with the insults, Vira. When you're ready to talk, you know where to find me." I turn to leave, not bothering to acknowledge her final snarky remark.

"Well, Eliri, I hate to break it to you, but you'll be waiting a long, *long* time."

RYDAN HELSTROM

RYDAN'S MINDING HIS own business when Vira suddenly storms into their chambers. She's mumbling something under her breath and while he can't catch the entire string of obscenities, it only takes him one guess as to who's got her so worked up.

"I take it you've just returned from the library?"

She's so wrapped up in her rage that his voice seems to startle her. The way she looks at him indicates she had no idea he's been sitting there the entire time, listening to every word.

"The nerve of that girl," Vira huffs, cheeks reddening. "I honestly don't know how you can stand to be around her—in the Cruex or otherwise."

"Years of practice," Rydan jokes. She shoots him a warning glance. He clears his throat, his tone turning serious. "What happened?"

"Let's just say she's made her position on my brother quite clear."

He falls silent, wishing he hadn't asked. Because in the grand scheme of things, if it's Xerin they're talking about, he's likely to side with Arden. He's seen too much, knows too much . . . but there's no changing the subject now.

"I know he isn't the most reliable among us and that he's made some poor choices, but that doesn't mean we should exile him. If anything, he needs our help now more than ever."

It's a complete one-eighty from what she'd said in Midvale after seeing that Xerin had sided with Trendalath. Rydan resists the urge to point out everything wrong with her statement and instead just nods his head. "I'm sure Arden's just looking for answers. We all are."

Vira whirls on him, eyes blazing. "Of course. You *would* take her side."

"Whoa there." Rydan leans back with his hands raised. "I'm not taking sides. Just stating a fact."

"She can never do wrong in your eyes, can she?"

The question angers him more than it should. "I could say the same about you and your brother."

"We're family," she seethes.

"So is Arden."

The disgust on her face is palpable. "Just because you grew up together, trained together, and lived under the same twisted fucking roof doesn't make you family—"

"Maybe not by blood, but when your family history is entirely unknown like mine is, forgive me for clinging to the only semblance of *family* I've ever known."

Embarrassed, she drops her gaze, well aware of her misstep. "Rydan, I didn't—"

"You didn't what? Mean to upset me? Belittle my entire life experience?" he scoffs, knowing full well he should stop before he says something he'll regret, but the words keep coming, rendering him completely unhinged. "Instead of using Arden as a scapegoat, perhaps you should take a good long look in the mirror and consider *who* you're defending and *why*. Because I can count, on more than one hand, several instances where your brother didn't own up to his word. In fact, he went against it."

There are tears lining her eyes, but now that he's started, he can't seem to stop. "In the meantime, I refuse to surround myself with ignorance and denial. I'll request that Delwynn assign me to a different room." He gives a flourish of his hand. "These chambers are all yours, Vira."

She shakes her head. "You stay. I'll go."

Before another word can be uttered, she stalks out the door and slams it shut behind her.

DARIUS TYMOND

THERE'S A STARK contrast going from freely roaming Trendalath castle and its surrounding territories to hiding in a room at an inn on some no-name island. Xerin had assured him they'd be safe here, but the greeting he's received from the locals has been far from welcoming. Suspicious eyes seem to follow him wherever he goes, and even the barkeep who'd rented them the room hesitated in doing so. For what's supposed to be a fresh start, it feels like exactly the opposite.

Darius isn't one to hide, but he's frequented the inn's doorside service more times than he cares to admit. He rings a bell, it alerts the staff, he informs them of what he needs, and it's dropped right at his door. Minimal interaction, minimal complication. He's convinced himself that laying low is in his best interest . . . at least until Xerin returns. Which had better be soon because the inn's menu is growing stale, much like the view.

A clang in the hallway indicates his next meal has arrived. He waits for the sound of footsteps to fade before opening the door to find a tray of thinly sliced meats, bread rolls, a variety of potatoes, and a vegetable stew. It'd sounded appetizing when he'd ordered it, but looking at it now, much less so. Nevertheless, he removes the tray from the ground and carries it into his room.

He's just starting to cut into the meat when the lock clicks. In walks Xerin, who's no longer wearing a chip on his shoulder but appears rather pleased instead. His nose turns up at the overwhelming scent filling the room. "You couldn't have eaten your meal downstairs with the rest of the patrons?"

"I don't do that in Trendalath. Why would you expect I'd do it here?"

Xerin sighs, taking the seat across from him. "Because we came here to rally support for Trendalath. To build our numbers. That's pretty difficult to do when you're holed up in a room where no one can find you."

"Perhaps I don't want to be found."

"Then we should just leave," Xerin replies sharply, "because being here is a waste of time if you're not willing to do your part."

Darius brings the fork to his mouth, chewing slowly. "I haven't had to rally support in the past—"

Xerin scoffs. "It wasn't ever required because the people of Trendalath feared you, feared for their *lives* if they didn't obey. Since the Crostan Islands is sovereign, you don't have that kind of power or effect here."

Harsh as it may be, it's the truth. Darius wrinkles his nose. "And if I can't garner the support we need?"

Xerin reaches across the table for a utensil before stabbing at one of the round golden potatoes. "We always knew that was a possibility. Fortunately, we're a step ahead, thanks to me."

"How did you—?"

"Let's just say I have connections and favors owed to me and leave it at that. The town of Bellmoor has agreed to ally with us. Kilshade, too."

He's unfamiliar with the area but, regardless, this isn't the news he'd expected. It's better.

"Great. So our work here is done."

Xerin raises a brow. "Not even close." He glances at the wall to check the time. "Now, finish your meal. There's someone I'd like you to meet."

XERIN GREY

ALYNA DRUMS HER fingers against the wooden table, studying both Xerin and King Tymond with startling intensity. From what Xerin has gathered so far, she seems less than impressed with his choice of comrade . . . as if he'd had a choice.

They're tucked in the back corner of the inn's tavern so as to stay out of sight from the locals—at least for the time being. Alyna had agreed to ally with them on one condition: that she meet Darius first. But based on the way this meeting is going, they may lose her support altogether.

"If I understand correctly," she says, interrupting Xerin from his thoughts, "your first priority is to retrieve the staff."

"Yes," Darius affirms, twisting the amethyst ring around his finger. "We believe it's currently in Sardoria."

Alyna's face pales. "With Queen Jareth?"

The immediate shift in her demeanor has Xerin feeling concerned. He's about to mention that the staff could be in Cyrus's possession, but the last thing they need is for Alyna to question why the king's advisor, who's been loyal for decades, suddenly betrayed his solemn oath. Anything that puts Darius's character into question should be avoided, so he keeps his mouth shut.

"Sardoria should be rather easy to access. I hear Queen Jareth lets just about anyone in these days."

If Xerin could palm his forehead without their guest noticing, he would, but it'd be yet another thing that'd only raise more questions—and distrust. He forces a smile, trying to do damage control. "I think what King Tymond is trying to say is that Queen Jareth is accepting of both illusié and non-illusié."

"And you aren't?" Alyna challenges.

Xerin catches himself holding his breath as he waits for Darius's response.

"Not when it's a threat to my reign."

Alyna smirks. "Fair enough."

"What other questions do you have for me?"

Having come prepared, Alyna reviews the small piece of parchment she'd brought with her, the tip of her quill drifting down the page until she stops near the bottom. She clears her throat, then fixes her gaze on Darius. "How can I be assured that the distribution of illusié abilities will actually occur in the manner in which we've agreed?"

Darius joins his hands together before setting his elbows on the table. "I take it my word isn't enough?"

Alyna scoffs. "I'm afraid not."

Knowing he needs to answer before Darius does, Xerin replies, "Retrieve the staff and we'll allow you to keep it as collateral."

Darius whips his head toward him, fury blazing in his eyes. "I wasn't aware the staff was up for negotiation."

Xerin levels a steely gaze at him. "Seeing as your carelessness caused it to no longer be in your possession in the first place, I would say that, yes, it *is* up for negotiation."

Darius gives an adamant shake of his head. "We never agreed—"

"Is there a problem?" Alyna interrupts. "If you'd rather retrieve it yourself . . ."

"No." Darius sighs. "It'd be too risky on our behalf."

"So, you *are* willing to hand over the staff? Your line of communication with the Mallum?"

Darius croaks out a hoarse "yes".

"We have a deal, then." She sets the quill down before digging in her satchel. "I know just the person for the job."

Xerin can't help but be taken aback as she retrieves a human skull from her bag and places it in the center of the table. "And this person is . . . dead?"

"Of course not," Alyna says, taking the steak knife from her napkin before positioning it over her open palm. "But you should know that here in the Crostan Islands, we bind our agreements with blood."

CERYLIA JARETH

WITH EACH VISIT to the infirmary to check on her brother-in-law, Cerylia hopes it'll somehow be her last. While the physical progress appears to be slow-going—nonexistent, actually—the Healer has assured her that the salve is working exactly as it should.

To her and every other visitor, though, Stanton can't wake fast enough.

She settles in at his bedside, book in hand, and flips to the marked page. She begins to read, her eyes flicking up every so often to check that he's still breathing—which is absurd, but the act alone gives her some semblance of control.

The room falls darker as the sun begins to set. Cerylia stifles a yawn before closing the book and setting it on the bedside table. The lantern flickers as she shifts its position to the back, the dim lighting casting an eerie glow on Stanton's face. In this lighting, he almost looks like . . .

Her heart nearly leaps from her chest.

Don't go there.

But she's mesmerized as she stares at the face of a man who looks so much like her late beloved.

Dane.

Her eyes well with tears at the sight, one she never wants to tear her gaze from. She reaches for his cheek, lightly brushing her fingers over the cold skin. "Wake up," she whispers, her voice cracking. It's the same thing she'd said at his burial site every week since their final farewell— something he never got to hear.

Grief unlike any other pulls her under, the tears breaking free. Knowing it's pointless to try and compose herself, she lets them fall. Her palm remains on his cheek, the heat from her body warming the skin underneath. A familiar feeling overcomes her, one she's usually able to control, but something about it feels different this time.

Dangerous.

Like she's slipping . . .

Her peripheral grows fuzzy, but, even with her vision lacking, she's acutely aware that she's no longer in Sardoria.

She's also aware that she's now an observer—and that she's observing a much younger version of two brothers.

"Is that all you've got?" Dane shouts as he runs through the woods.

A competition is afoot.

To her left, a lanky boy appears, striking jade eyes on full display. There's no mistaking it's Arden's father. He's out of breath as he dodges a fallen tree branch, nearly tripping over it. "Hey! Wait up, would you?"

His plea goes unheard as Dane takes off down an unmarked trail. It's nearly sundown, the wind whistling through the trees as if to say "bad idea".

Dane never was the cautious one.

Stanton arrives at the trailhead, squinting into the looming darkness ahead. Cerylia does the same thing in the hopes that she'll catch a glimpse of Dane, but there's no movement or sound, save for the rustling of the trees.

"Dane, this isn't funny!" Stanton yells. "We need to head back."

A twig snaps in the distance. Stanton shifts his stance to one that looks like he's about to bolt. But instead of Dane emerging from the trees, it's a tall, muscular man who looks to be nearing his mid-fifties. Stanton takes a step back, raising his hands into fists as if he'd be able to fight him off.

"Where's my brother?" he demands. It's a surprise his voice doesn't shake.

The man chortles. "What are you talking about?" he asks in a voice that certainly doesn't match his body.

Stanton's eyes grow wide as the realization sinks in.

"It's me!" the man shrieks. "Your brother!"

"Dane?" He looks the man up and down. "What happened to you?"

"What do you mean?" As he walks closer to Stanton, the difference in their height becomes abundantly clear. "Oh . . ."

"How did you—?" Stanton starts, hardly believing his eyes. "*Who* are you—?"

Dane rushes over to the still water pond, gazing at his reflection. "Don't you recognize me? I'm the man from the village yesterday!"

Stanton joins him at the pond, narrowing his eyes for a closer look. "The Elemental?"

Dane studies his hands, turning them over before directing them at the pond. Stanton jumps back as frost spreads from their feet all the way across the surface.

"Does that answer your question?" Dane asks, clapping his hands together in glee.

"It's your illusié ability," Stanton whispers. "You're a—"

"Shifter!" Dane finishes. "I'm a Shifter, brother!"

The concern in Stanton's eyes is evident, but he doesn't say anything further.

"Just imagine the things I'll be able to do, the people I can be, the abilities I'll have access to!" Unable to contain his excitement, he spins in a circle and throws his hands into the air.

"Only for a short time," Stanton murmurs, but Dane's too caught up in his frenzy to hear him.

"Once I learn how to control it, I'll be unstoppable. Imagine what I could get away with—and no one would be the wiser!"

Stanton finally finds his voice. "Being a Shifter isn't something to be taken lightly, Dane."

Dane levels a steely gaze at him. "I never said it was."

"You sure are acting like it."

"Just because your abilities haven't manifested yet doesn't mean you need to take your grievances out on me."

"That isn't what I—"

"Save it," Dane scoffs before stalking off in the opposite direction. "The least you could do is *pretend* to be happy for me instead of pointing out all the ways I'll misuse what I've been given."

To that, Stanton has no reply. He hangs his head, keeping his distance as he follows after his brother.

Cerylia pulls her hand back, clutching it as if she's just been electrocuted. She stares at her brother-in-law, unable to shake one particular phrase from repeating itself over and over again in her head.

All the ways I'll misuse what I've been given.

It isn't so much the verbiage he'd used that has her concerned, but his use of the future tense.

I. Will. Misuse.

Cerylia leans back in the chair, pondering. Perhaps she hadn't known her late husband as well as she'd once believed—a thought that will keep her staring aimlessly out the window well past midnight.

BRAXTON HORNSBY

HE ISN'T SURE why the queen has willingly granted him permission to take the staff for a short time, but he's glad she obliged. He's also glad that the trust between them hasn't been broken, seeing as the mission she'd sent him on to retrieve his father's ring had ended in disappointment. And an unexpected capture. Regardless, they seem to agree upon who the real enemy is, which is all that truly matters.

Perplexed, Braxton turns the staff over in his hands, trying to recall exactly how his father had used it at the jaded spring. Both the ring and the staff are connected to the

Mallum, this much he knows—without one or the other, his father's power is immensely weakened. Which begs the question . . . what is so special about this damn staff?

Two minds are better than one and, as if she's read those very thoughts, Lane comes waltzing into the small study reserved for traveling scribes. It's a room Cerylia's assured him isn't used often, since most of the scribes were either murdered or executed in the days leading up to Tymond's reign—because who in their right mind would want a history of events recorded knowing they'd only shine them in a poor light? Especially as the new reigning king?

"I still can't believe Cyrus found the nerve to steal the staff." Lane takes a seat across from him at a wooden desk with wobbly, uneven legs. "To think, your father's loyal, trusted advisor, of all people."

"I, for one, am happy he did and that he unbound himself from the Tymond curse. He deserves to be surrounded by people who actually give a shit about him."

Having only heard one thing, Lane raises a brow. "The Tymond *curse*?"

"Just a figure of speech," Braxton says, waving a hand flippantly in the air. Although he's often wondered if there's some truth to it—it would certainly explain a lot—but he isn't willing to admit that out loud.

"So," Lane says, eyes flicking between him and the staff, "what are you hoping to do with it?"

Braxton shrugs, feeling defeated. "I'm not really sure. Right now, I'm just looking for clues, I suppose."

"What kind of clues?"

"For starters, what it's for, how to use it, why it's so valuable to my father . . ." his voice trails off as he sets the staff on the desk between them.

"Well, we know from Cyrus and Cerylia that it's a form of communication with the Mallum, so that's something."

Braxton nods. "And if Cerylia is correct in her assumption that the amethyst ring is used to summon the Mallum, then we have two key pieces of information at our disposal."

"So, the ring is used to summon the Mallum while the staff is used to communicate with it," Lane affirms. She opens her mouth as if she's about to say something else, then seems to change her mind.

Braxton has a feeling he knows what she was about to say. "But what you and I saw at the spring—that interaction felt . . . *personal*."

She looks him square in the eye. "You took the words right out of my mouth."

"It has to be more than just commands and orders," Braxton thinks aloud as he sizes up the staff. "Something about what we saw feels almost . . ." He searches for the right word but can't seem to find it.

"Intimate," Lane finishes. "If you ask me, your father's connection to the Mallum goes far beyond some random entity he calls forth to do his bidding." She begins to reach for the staff, then pulls her hand back. "Pulsing," she murmurs. "It's like he's attached to it somehow—as if it were a second pulse to him."

Braxton leans back in his chair, deep in thought. "What if—?" He stops himself, shaking his head.

"What?" Lane presses. "Tell me."

Braxton closes his eyes, gathering his thoughts. "What if we took the staff and went to the jaded spring to see for ourselves?"

"But we don't have the ring," Lane points out, a fact he's well aware of.

"I know. But I'm wondering . . . since both Arden and I have confronted the Mallum, maybe we don't need the ring to summon it. Maybe the staff is enough."

Lane looks at him like he's just grown two heads. "I feel I need to remind you that your confrontation with the Mallum resulted in a devastating loss of your ability to deviate."

Another fact he's well-aware of.

"And didn't it alter Arden's ability to heal? Leaving her with a mess to sort out?"

"It's hard to say. But this is the only lead we have . . . and it's a good one."

Lane sighs. "It's too bad Cerylia would never allow it— going to the jaded spring unsupervised, that is."

Braxton gives her a sly grin. "Who says she has to know?"

ARDEN ELIRI

"I CAN'T BELIEVE I let you talk me into this,"
I say, giving Braxton a pointed glare from my seat on the
horse.

The mare he's riding, which is one of three that Lane
impressively summoned, trots next to me, keeping pace as if
its life depends on it. Braxton meets my gaze. "It didn't
exactly take much convincing."

Before I can respond, Lane, who's a few paces ahead of
us, calls over her shoulder, "It's just up ahead, to the left!"

Snowflakes dust her ebony hair, shimmering in the
fading daylight. I grip the reins, noting that my leather gloves

are slick with melted snow. I brush them against my cloak one at a time, not realizing just how much has fallen during our travels through the Roviel Woods. I was worried that without Rydan's occasional igniting of what he's deemed the *ring of fire*, we'd be frozen to the bone, but the temperatures seem to be rising the farther west we travel.

Thank the lords for that.

When we finally reach the bottom of the Vaekith Mountains, its steep ascent is the first thing that comes into view. "You mean to tell me that a horse-drawn carriage made it up *that?*"

Lane turns over her shoulder, grinning. "Well, when you say it like that . . ."

"It does look steeper than I remember," Braxton muses. "Are we sure this is the right entrance?"

"The one and only."

Braxton furrows his brows. "If you're sure."

"The snow has a funny way of altering our depth perception," Lane explains as if she's been here hundreds of times. "I'm positive that this is it."

"Now that that's settled," I chime in, "perhaps we should stop wasting time and get moving."

"Better to waste a little time down here than hours in the wrong spot up there."

Well, I can't argue with that. Using the reins, I gently nudge my horse in the right direction, making sure to follow closely behind Lane. Braxton falls in line behind me. The journey uphill is anything but quick. My hands, lower back, and legs ache from having to keep myself firmly planted in position during the long, steady climb. There isn't much relief in the way of flat landings, and I can tell the horses are growing weary of the trail.

When we finally arrive at the gates, we breathe a collective sigh of relief. I take my time dismounting, careful to not accidentally twist a ligament on the way down. Every inch of me feels frail and exhausted—the last thing I need is an injury that keeps us from doing what we came here to do.

We tie the horses to a nearby tree, then approach the gates. I'm not the only one who's disappointed to find that they're locked.

"Shit," Braxton mutters. "We certainly didn't plan for this." He brings the staff closer, waving it around like it's a magic wand.

"I don't think it works like that," I offer, sarcasm dripping from my tone. "We need to find another way in."

As soon as I say it, the unthinkable happens. I'm pulled away from the gates, away from Braxton and Lane, away from the Vaekith Mountains altogether. It's a familiar pull, one I've experienced before . . . when I'd landed in a memory that wasn't my own. I find myself in a similar situation now in that it isn't mine, but it *is* the memory of someone I'm quite close to—and who happens to have traveled here with me.

Braxton.

I watch as a bystander as he reads through a piece of parchment—one I've seen before. *The note from his mother.* Except in this view, the note looks different. While the words are unclear from this angle, I can tell that some of the letters are printed and others are scrawled in an obvious fashion. Braxton had shown me the note, but what had it said, exactly?

Before I can consider this any further, the room spins, and I land in yet another memory in Trendalath castle. This one is brief as Braxton kneels by a small chest in his late mother's room with a speculor in his hands. Another spin and I'm dropped into a place I know all too well: the Daegrum Chambers. Unlike the other two memories, Braxton isn't here. His father is.

The same speculor I'd just seen Braxton holding has somehow made its way into Darius's possession and is now being locked away in a plush, velvet-lined box. The miniature sphere gleams against the burgundy fabric as Darius closes the lid and secures the lockbox with a brass-plated skeleton key. I wait to see if he's going to take both items with him when he does the unexpected. He returns the small box to its original position in the cupboard, then walks across the room and hangs the key on a hook on the wall. There must be ten other keys hanging on similar hooks, but there's no mistaking the one that opens the lockbox.

Just as I'm starting to wonder what'll be shown next, my surroundings begin to fade and a recognizable sensation creeps up the back of my neck. A dense black mist swarms my feet and legs, the hissing and whispering building in intensity.

Arden, the Mallum whispers. *Do you see now?*

I shiver, not knowing to what it's referring.

"I see, but I'm not sure I understand."

A low chortle. *Ask the Tymond boy.*

Before I can respond, I'm launched back to the gates of Volkharn with both Braxton and Lane staring at me, their mouths agape and eyes wide. I lose my balance as I try to regain my bearings and end up falling right on my ass. They rush over to help me, no doubt just as confused as I am.

"Where the hell did you go?" Braxton demands as he grabs me by the arms and pulls me to my feet. "We've been trying to snap you out of some bizarre trance for the past ten minutes."

"Ten minutes?" It'd felt like only seconds. "It was the Mallum."

At its mention, Lane jumps away from me as if I've somehow been contaminated or worse, persuaded to do its bidding.

"But we didn't even make it inside the gates," Braxton insists. "And you weren't even holding the staff."

"We don't have time to worry about the logistics," I say, recalling each piece of the memory. "Oddly enough, the Mallum showed me . . . well, *you.*"

"Me?" Braxton crosses his arms. "What about me?"

"The note your mom left you . . . the speculor you found in her room—"

"I only told you about one of those things."

"I know."

When I don't elaborate further, he says, "What exactly did it show you?"

"Where your mother's speculor is hidden." I click my tongue against the roof of my mouth. "Or, more precisely, where your father hid it."

"Which is?"

"In the Daegrum Chambers."

"Hang on a second," Lane interjects. "If Darius is nowhere to be found, then that means Trendalath is uninhabited. Which also means we can retrieve it."

Braxton shakes his head. "There's just one problem. Only the Savant can access the Daegrum Chambers. And seeing as all the Savant were taken out at Midvale—"

"All but one," I correct, trying not to reel over the fact that the fate of this mission might come down to the Caster.

"Or maybe two," Braxton whispers, clearly remembering something that I don't. "Wasn't Stanton in the Savant?"

The folded portrait of the Savant I'd discovered long ago flashes across my mind. The man with the gold pocket watch and uncanny features similar to my own. Stanton. My father.

"Once upon a time, yes, that may have been so; but I think it's safe to say he's no longer a part of the Savant. Not to mention, he isn't exactly conscious at the moment."

A bout of silence falls over us as the realization of what this means sinks in.

"So, what I'm hearing is the Caster, who's likely the most unhinged and unpredictable member of the Savant, is our only option?" Lane looks between us for confirmation.

I grimace. "That would be correct."

"Well, this just became infinitely more challenging—and annoying," Braxton says as he runs a hand through his damp hair. "Unless. . ."

I lock eyes with him as we both have the same epiphany, simultaneously saying, "Cyrus!"

Lane grins. "The king's advisor *and* senior member of the Savant. There's no way he doesn't have access."

"Unless Darius revoked it after their encounter at Midvale," I point out.

"With what time?" Braxton counters. "He fled the moment he could."

"We need to get back to Sardoria," Lane says. "One of you needs to talk to Cyrus. The trick will be not letting Cerylia catch wind of this."

With a plan forming, we turn away from the gates and head back toward the trees where we'd left the horses. Lane's a few paces in front of us as Braxton tugs on my arm, then whispers, "My mother's note, my mother's speculor . . . of all things, why would the Mallum show that to you?"

I shrug, handing him the reins to my mare. "I don't know," I say as I mount the horse, "but I'm guessing it's up to us to find out."

BRAXTON HORNSBY

THE DEBATE AS to who is going to approach Cyrus has somehow resorted to the childish game of rock, paper, scissors. Best of three and so far, he's losing.

"I said it once and I'll say it again," Braxton mutters as he gears up for the final round. "My relationship with Cyrus is subpar at best."

Arden scoffs as she lays her hand flat, choosing paper to cover his rock. "As the son of the man he was advising, I'd say you have a leg up on the Cruex."

"Ex-Cruex," Lane corrects, her smile widening. "And that's game."

"One more round?" Braxton pleads, his gaze darting between them. "He's going to say no. Or worse, offer to come with us. Or even worse, let Cerylia in on our plans."

Arden shakes her head. "No can do. We beat you fair and square." She extends her hand to Lane in a low-five. "Looks like the Cruex haven't lost their touch."

"*Ex*-Cruex." Lane makes the correction once more with a sigh.

"Right," Arden says with a sheepish grin. "What can I say? Old habits die hard."

Braxton runs a hand along his jaw, his gaze drifting from the two women in front of him to the door that leads away from the comforts of his room and into the halls of Sardoria castle. They'd only been back for about an hour, giving him little to no time to settle into their newly formed plan, let alone the flawless execution of it.

"You want me to go talk to him *now*?"

"What, like you have anything better to do?" his cousin counters.

"Yeah, like make sure I don't blow the one shot we have to do this?" he shoots back.

In an effort to diffuse any further tension, Arden scoots forward on the bed, placing herself between them. "Solid points on both accounts. But the more pressing issue is just how long Trendalath will be empty for."

Damn her for being right.

"Fine," Braxton says with a huff. "I'll go, but I'm not making any promises. And if this all goes horribly wrong, the blame falls on you two. Are we understood?"

Lane gives him a mock salute. "Yes. Now stop stalling."

"And you're certain, after all your time spent in the Cruex, neither of you saw one of the Savant enter the Daegrum Chambers?"

"Out of our jurisdiction." Lane shrugs.

"I wasn't even aware of the Savant until *after* I'd fled Trendalath." Arden rises from the bed and walks to the door, opening it to dismiss him. "But the son of the king and his advisor can surely put their heads together to remember *something*."

Braxton grinds his teeth. He swipes his cloak from the back of the armchair and throws it over his shoulders. "I'll let you know what I find out," he mumbles as he walks out the open door.

"We'll be here," Arden calls after him before slamming the door shut in a fit of laughter.

The relief they must feel. He'd be laughing too if his only job was to sit and wait for their return. He follows the light of the sconces down the long hallway, turning left, then right, his anxiety climbing the more scenarios he runs through. He's about to make another right which will take him to the wing where Cyrus, Delwynn, and Cerylia's chambers are located when an idea strikes him.

There's one other person in this castle that spent just as much time in the Cruex as Arden. Someone who followed his father's orders and commands as if they were as essential as breathing air. Who wouldn't dare compromise a mission regardless of its complexities. If there's anyone other than Cyrus who might know something, it's him.

MIDNIGHT REIGN

Braxton stops mid-step, veering left down the hall that leads directly to Rydan's chambers.

RYDAN HELSTROM

HE'S JUST STARTED to drift into a peaceful sleep when a knock sounds at his door. Rydan groans, pulling the covers over his head. He presses his face into the pillow as the knocking grows louder.

"Go away!" His words are muffled but loud.

"I know it's late," a familiar voice says from the hallway, "but it's important."

Surprised, Rydan sits upright, throwing the covers off of him. What is Braxton doing knocking on his door? The floorboards creak as he walks across the room in just a pair of wrinkled trousers, not bothering to make himself decent.

He opens the door, squinting into the brightly lit hallway. "What's so important that it requires waking someone up at this unlordly hour?"

"Shit, you were asleep?"

"I was well on my way," Rydan mutters, motioning for him to enter.

Braxton obliges. He surveys the room, no doubt looking for Vira.

"Don't worry, we're alone." Rydan flings the door shut.

"Vira isn't here?"

Rydan squeezes the bridge of his nose. Vira is the *last* thing he wants to discuss right now. "She's requested that she have her own room." Braxton looks like he's about to ask for details, so Rydan quickly adds, "Personal reasons."

"Oh," Braxton utters with a nod, catching the hint to not press further.

"So, what brings you to my humble abode at such a late hour?"

Braxton works his jaw as he removes his cloak and takes a seat in front of the small hearth. "It's random. But I have a question about your time in the Cruex."

Rydan joins him, trying to ignore the uneasy feeling washing over him. "What about it?"

"There's something I need to retrieve from Trendalath, but it's in the Daegrum Chambers."

Rydan angles his head. "But only the Savant have access to the Daegrum Chambers."

Something resembling a hint of smile flashes across Braxton's face, but his tone doesn't change as he says, "Exactly. Except I was never privy when it comes to *how*."

This is what he'd been disturbed from sleep for? Rydan stares at his guest, irritation mounting. "The serpent on their robes. It's illusié-encoded." Which he admittedly hadn't known at the time, otherwise he probably would have fled the Cruex much earlier. King Tymond's hypocrisy is unmatched, a realization he could only have outside of the castle walls.

"The serpent stitched on their robes unlocks the door to the Daegrum Chambers?" Braxton asks, clearly seeking confirmation that he's heard correctly.

"That's what I just said," Rydan snaps. "I'm going back to sleep now. You can see yourself out."

"Thank you," Braxton says as he gathers his cloak and hurries for the door. "You just saved my ass."

"Wouldn't be the first time." Rydan waves him off as he clambers back into bed.

XERIN GREY

THE MEETING WITH Alyna hadn't gone as smoothly as he'd hoped, but the outcome couldn't have been better. Darius had signed the blood oath without question, while Xerin had stood idly by, a mere observer to the one decision the king will come to regret.

Something he's currently oblivious to.

It hadn't taken much to persuade Darius to visit their new allies—the towns of both Kilshade and Bellmoor—and after a short rendezvous to the latter, Darius has indulged in more than a few glasses of mead. Xerin sips from his mug, watching the Trendalath King make his rounds, his inebriated state undoubtedly providing a false sense of confidence.

Good. It should make what he has planned a lot easier.

Darius glances at where his companion is sitting before barreling across the tavern, mead sloshing violently onto the well-worn floor. "This . . . was a great idea," he slurs, raising his half-empty mug. "Cheers to you, Sir Grey. We just might be victorious after all."

Xerin bites his tongue, forcing a smile. "Why don't we head back to the inn? Big day tomorrow."

"But there are still so many people I have yet to meet," Darius says, stifling a belch. "You dragged me all the way out here—"

"And now I'm dragging you back," Xerin argues through clenched teeth. "Unless you'd prefer nausea to be a key component of our day tomorrow, I suggest you heed my advice."

This seems to sober him up a little. "And I thought you were the fun one."

"I wonder what gave you that idea," Xerin murmurs, guiding him toward the exit.

Darius turns to face the patrons of the tavern, a parting remark surely forming on his lips, when Xerin yanks him by the arm and out the door. The last thing he needs are witnesses to the king's exact whereabouts. Arriving at the tavern had been one thing, but it's their exit that must be discreet—which is proving difficult with the king's boisterous demeanor.

Xerin's pleased to find that the crisp weather is keeping people indoors. Even though there's no one loitering nearby, Xerin leads Darius down an abandoned alleyway in the direction of the barracks. Alyna had been kind enough to lay out an incredibly detailed map of the Crostan Islands for him during their first meeting, of which he'd tirelessly searched for the dungeons. He hadn't been able to pinpoint their precise location, but the oubliette he'd found instead was much more promising, and actually near perfect for the execution of his plan. It seems an odd choice to build it near the barracks, but to each their own.

After much stumbling and adjusting outside of the tavern, they finally reach the barracks, the oubliette coming into view. In his inebriated state, it's unlikely the king will remember that Xerin gave him a nice little shove into the small, but rather deep, pit. Anyone who may stumble across it would soon learn that the king had been out all night celebrating at the tavern, libations included. The conclusion, then, is quite simple: he fell.

Having knocked his head on the way down, the king is silent as Xerin drags the giant metal cover across the opening of the oubliette, the air holes allowing for little light from the overheard street lanterns. The immaculate execution of his plan has Xerin grinning the whole way to the docks before shaping into the man he'd so shamelessly betrayed. There can't be two identical kings running around Aeridon, now can there?

75

DARIUS TYMOND

THE SOUND OF neighing horses and carriage wheels rolling over cobblestone has never been so irritating. Or so loud. Groaning, Darius shields his eyes from what little light is pouring in overhead—but in his current state, it may as well be the sun. The floor beneath him is cold and damp, and he momentarily worries he'd somehow fallen asleep in his own filth . . . but the reality of where he's at is far worse.

His mouth is dry, body weak, mind fuzzy, which is arguably the worst combination given the dire straits he now finds himself in. He lifts his gaze skyward, trying to make sense of where he's at. Overhead, there appears to be some sort of cover, and if the sounds that woke him are any indication, then he's below street level . . . *underground.*

"Shit," he murmurs, pulling himself upright on two shaky legs. His head feels like it's on fire. His stomach threatens to hurl its contents at his feet. His joints throb and ache. Yes, he'd partaken in the enjoyment of some beverages the night prior, but had he gotten so belligerent that he can't recall the events of the evening? Namely how he ended up in a dark, dank, atrocious-smelling pit?

Upon further examination, it's clear that this isn't just some hole in the ground, but an oubliette. A *prison.* The likelihood of the cover being removed for anyone to trip and fall into is slim to none, especially with what he's come to learn about the towns within the Crostan Islands. The residents are careful, meticulous, and have a profound respect for one another.

If only that respect could be extended to him.

Footsteps cross overhead, giving him a flicker of hope that perhaps his time down here will meet its end. He cups a hand around his mouth before shouting, "Hello? Kind sir! Madam! I'm stuck down here."

Quiet murmuring and the shuffling of feet are his only response.

"Hello?" he calls out again, trying to hide the desperation in his voice. "I would appreciate some help!"

A hazel eye appears in one of the air holes. It squints before being quickly replaced by crooked, yellowing teeth. "I reckon you ain't supposed to be in there, but how would I know if that's the truth or not?" The voice is gravelly and the way he whistles through his teeth when he talks tells Darius he's probably been around for a while.

Darius changes his tune. "If I came across someone trapped in a hole, I'd surely want to help them."

The man guffaws. "Well, say I believe ya and help ya out only to be told you're ransacking the island?"

Yet another odd question that gives Darius pause. "Do you mean to tell me that people are thrown in here for stealing?"

"Among other things." The man clicks his tongue, then spits something wet, likely tobacco, onto the ground. "If you're a thief, and I help a thief, I wind up with the same punishment. Real risky on my part, ya see."

"But I'm not a thief," Darius says, feeling like he's talking to a wall. "In fact, if you help me out of here, you'll see that I'm the last person who would need to steal."

"Why is that? You rich or somethin'?"

Darius takes a calming breath. "I'm King Tymond of Trendalath."

There's a long stretch of silence before the man finally says, "So, you're a liar *and* a thief?"

However the village idiot came up with that conclusion is beyond him, so he simply says, "I assure you I am not."

"You stole Trendalath—"

Oh, lords help him.

"—and just lied about it."

"I'd hardly call fighting and winning a battle for the throne *stealing*."

"I would," the man sneers. "In fact, aren't you the very reason we were all sent to the Crostan Islands to begin with?"

Somehow this conversation has gone from bad to worse.

"We didn't quite meet your standards as citizens of Trendalath, did we? So, instead of helping us, you had us shipped off with the promise of a new beginning—one you said you'd helped provide for but never did." As if he's suddenly turned scholarly, he continues, "In fact, wasn't one of your first trade embargoes put in place against the Crostan Islands?"

Admittedly, not one of his finer moments.

"And now you're stuck in a pit with no way out in the very place you swore you'd never step foot in," the man sneers. "If ya ask me, I'd say you're exactly where you belong."

Before Darius can respond, the man spits at the hole he was talking into, the glob landing on the king's fine leather boot. Darius tries to shake it off, but the sticky substance doesn't budge. The smell of discarded tobacco fills the air.

Well, at least he'd been right about one thing.

CERYLIA JARETH

RIFLING THROUGH DANE'S study used to bring her so much grief and despair, but ever since that night in the infirmary, all Cerylia feels is rage.

Pure unadulterated *rage*.

I will misuse I will misuse I will misuse

She can't seem to shake the phrase no matter how hard she tries. Day in and day out, it haunts her, lurking in the darkest corners of her mind, waiting for the opportunity to strike when she's weakest.

The man she'd married was honest.

The man she'd married had integrity.

The man she'd married was *good* at his core . . .

But that lords-damned phrase has her rethinking everything, revisiting everything, *reliving* everything. She'd never wanted to reduce Dane to a mere memory of a tragic past, but perhaps that's exactly where he belongs.

The thought is sobering.

Much to her chagrin, there's nothing remarkably noteworthy in the drawers she's opened thus far. Stacks of parchment, half-used inkpots, fraying quills . . . hardly worth her attention. She checks the bookshelves next, pulling the texts out one by one and flipping through them. She even goes so far as to shake them out over the floor, expecting *something* to fall out, but nothing does.

The chaise lounge is next. Dust flies off the pillows as she takes hold of them, nearly ripping one at the seams as she feels around for an undisclosed object. *What* object exactly remains unknown, but her intuition only heightens the more she searches.

She's mid-tirade, cursing at inanimate objects, having forgotten she'd left the door open a crack when Delwynn pokes his head in. "Your Greatness . . ." His eyes grow wide at the sheer destruction that's unfolding at his feet.

Cerylia stops momentarily to observe the chaos around her—chaos *she's* created. She doesn't bother to look at Delwynn as she buries her face in her hands and lets out a gut-wrenching scream. At the sound of his fast-approaching footsteps, she holds her hand in the air, palm upright. The footsteps cease.

"Your Greatness," he whispers carefully. "Let me help you. Please, I beg of you. It pains me to see you in such a state."

Slowly, Cerylia raises her head, her next outburst cresting like a wave. Her entire demeanor softens, however, as she looks past Delwynn to the portrait hanging above the door. It's crooked. She'd entered through that very door with caution—the same door that'd previously been locked for years prior—so there's absolutely no reason why that portrait shouldn't be hanging straight.

Cerylia pushes herself to her feet, dodging the many piles of disarray around her as she clambers toward the door. The portrait is too tall for her to reach, but instead of doing something sensible like moving a chair or the desk to stand on, she grabs a nearby fire poker and jabs at the portrait until it comes crashing to the floor. Without another moment's hesitation, she kneels, turning the frame over to discover exactly what she'd suspected.

Patchwork.

Using a hairpin to pick at the seams, she debates whether she should just rip the patch off altogether, but refrains from doing so to avoid damaging whatever's underneath. When she's finally able to neatly remove the patch, it takes her a moment to process what she's found.

Because it's something she's familiar with.

Something she's seen before.

Cerylia raises the object into the light.

A soul gem.

KRISTEN MARTIN

ARDEN ELIRI

TRENDALATH FEELS MUCH smaller than I remember, which isn't all that surprising. I stand at the entrance with my brother and Braxton, the weight of our shared bloodline heavy on all of our shoulders. We'd recruited my brother to transport us to Trendalath, knowing we'd need a quick turnaround to return to Sardoria before Cyrus notices his chamber key is missing. Lane had decided to sit this one out—the less people to transport, the easier it'd be on Haskell, she'd pointed out. Not to mention, there's less room for error.

The entrance to the castle is an eerie sight. There are no guards stationed. No footprints in the shallow layer of snow. No angry crowds clamoring at the gates. No sign of life at all.

As if it's been abandoned.

"This way," Braxton says, leading us around back to a hidden entrance. "Just in case any of the staff decided to stay. Their rooms are at the front of the castle."

Haskell and I nod, quietly ducking into the vine-ridden alcove and through the door. It's just as abandoned in here as it is out there.

"Some loyalty," Haskell scoffs. "Your father really knows how to pick 'em."

"Call him my father again and I'll start calling him your uncle," Braxton says with a menacing glare.

While technically true, it's a fact none of us like to be reminded of. I step between them to diffuse the tension. "Let's stay focused. If I remember correctly, Cyrus's room is—"

"This way," Braxton cuts in, banking left. "Follow me."

We venture across the castle, trekking past corridors I haven't been down in what feels like ages.

"Is it strange? Being back here?" Braxton tosses the question over his shoulder as if we're the only ones in the castle. I suppose, at the moment, we are.

"Strange, yes," I answer. "But more unsettling than anything else."

Having not run into a single soul on the way up, we reach the door that leads to Cyrus's chambers. Braxton removes the key from his pocket and inserts it into the lock. It clicks and just like that, we're in.

"This almost feels too easy," Haskell murmurs as he follows us inside.

I agree, but I don't dare say it out loud. Wouldn't want to jinx it.

Cyrus's room is minimal and orderly. In fact, it hardly looks lived in—the bed is made, the blankets are folded, the dishes are neatly stacked in the glass cabinet. The only tell is the pair of boots haphazardly thrown underneath the table, but other than that, the room is spotless.

Braxton opens the armoire to reveal a sparse selection of clothing. At least it'll make the cloak easy to find . . . and it does. The serpent is like a shining beacon, unavoidable, even if we hadn't been looking for it. He removes the cloak and puts it on, then fastens the small button at the top.

"There, that was simple," he says with a grin.

Which means now it's time for the hard part: stepping foot inside the Daegrum Chambers.

BRAXTON HORNSBY

THE DOOR UNLOCKS without a hitch. Braxton doesn't bother to shed the cloak as he walks into the Daegrum Chambers. A brief glance over his shoulder makes him aware that Arden is no longer following him.

"Hey," he says as he hurries back over to the door, "is everything okay?"

She drops her gaze to the floor. "I hate this room."

Braxton nods in understanding. "As you should."

She slowly lifts her head, her gaze locking on the ornate cabinetry in the back. She points a finger. "It's that one."

Braxton turns to see what she's pointing at. "And the key?"

"It's a brass-plated skeleton key. It should be hanging on a hook on the wall."

Braxton back-peddles into the room. "There must be a dozen keys on hooks and half of them are brass."

Arden sighs. "It's a skeleton key, it looks . . ." Her words trail off as she searches for an accurate description. "You're going to make me come in there, aren't you?"

"I mean, I can try them all if you'd rather go that route. One of them is bound to fit."

She shakes her head. "That'll take too long. We've got to return Cyrus's key before he notices it's missing."

He shoots her a sympathetic glance. "Then, yes, you will need to come in here."

Making fists at her sides, Arden reluctantly steps into the room and whirls around to face the wall housing all the keys. She scans each one until she spots the key that matches the one from the memory she'd witnessed.

Braxton watches as she removes the *last* key he would have suspected. He extends his arm out to her with his palm open, waiting, but Arden makes a beeline straight for one of the back cabinets. "You don't have to open it. You can wait out there—"

"It'll be faster if I do it, since I know exactly where everything is and what we're looking for." She reaches inside the cabinet, pulling out a small, locked box. "See?"

"Right you are. Meanwhile I'll just stand here and look pretty," he jokes.

"That might just be your color," she quips. "Okay, in all seriousness though, let's open her up."

Braxton joins her as she inserts the key into the lock. The speculor inside is exactly as he remembers it. "There's something in here my mother wanted me to see," he says, raising the miniature sphere into the air. "Something my father desperately wanted to hide."

"And you have no idea what that might be?"

"If I knew all my family's secrets, we certainly wouldn't need to be here right now."

"Valid point." Arden surveys the room with furrowed brows. "We need to leave everything as we originally found it." She proceeds to close the box before returning it to its spot in the cabinet. "Cruex training 101," she adds with a wink. "And then we need to take the speculor to the spring to see what it contains."

"But the gates," Braxton says glumly. "They're locked."

"Oh. Right," Arden says as she hurries to replace the key on its hook. "Then I suppose that leaves us with the option of using an Extractor . . ."

"Of which we only know one."

Who just so happens to be the very person they're trying to keep this from.

Cerylia.

"There is another option," Arden says, chewing on her bottom lip as if she's just remembered something. "In the Archmage's office, tucked away in an alcove behind her desk. A cheval glass. It's supposed to display the contents of speculors."

"Do you know how to use it?"

Arden's shoulders slump. "No," she admits. "But it may be our only shot if we want to keep Cerylia in the dark. At least for now."

Braxton ponders their limited options. "You really want to go back there? After everything that happened?"

Her silence speaks volumes.

"Allow me to rephrase. Are you *ready* to go back there?"

"I don't think I'll ever be ready," she says quietly. "But if we don't uncover what's in that speculor, Cerylia won't be the only one kept in the dark."

"To Midvale, then?"

Arden takes a shaky breath. "As much as I want to say yes, I think it's best if we sleep on it."

But Braxton already knows no amount of sleep will change her mind. Regardless, they're going to have a lot of explaining to do upon their return to Sardoria.

XERIN GREY

XERIN TEARS THROUGH the skies in his preferred form, that of a dragon, using the dense clouds as cover. At this speed, he's bound to make great time, as long as any and all disruptions are kept at bay. It's risky, this plan he's concocted, but waiting around has never been his strong suit.

Was ridding himself of Darius in such a crude manner necessary? Probably not—but on the off-chance Darius happens to find himself back in Trendalath at the same time Xerin's shaped as him, well . . . that's one disruption he can prevent altogether.

He's now the oubliette's problem.

The Great Ocean is eerily calm for such a cloud-filled night. The impending storm heading due north should have hit the area he's flying through by now, but it's dry as a bone, as if all the moisture's been leeched from the air. It's remarkable to think of all he's learned about the weather in his many years of shaping into different creatures. The ebbs and flows, the cycles and seasons, the harmony of it all . . . somehow, it just works. Every year, every season, time and time again.

He soars over the Roviel Woods, continuing his flight path to the snow-capped mountains of Sardoria. As it should have done miles ago, the air thickens, the temperature dropping considerably. His scales repel the budding humidity as he continues to fly through the cloud cover, his destination coming into view.

While rendering the Veil, and subsequently Midvale, useless was completely necessary, it's also come with added benefits. Namely that it's put everything and everyone in one place: Sardoria. The staff, the crescent fire, Stanton . . .

As he'd promised Alyna, he intends to leave the staff for her to retrieve as a gesture of goodwill, but as for the other two? Those are for him to carry out.

The crescent fire being in Rydan Helstrom's possession in the first place is incredibly dangerous—something he'd done everything in his power to evade by *hiding* it in the Void. But, of course, Braxton had to go and ruin that plan— something he'd severely overlooked after the Mallum had absorbed his deviating abilities. It'd been the perfect hiding place . . . until it wasn't.

That leaves Stanton. How he's survived for this long is truly astounding. Leave it to him to find a loophole and capitalize on it. It's the Eliri way, after all. Arden is living proof of that. But Stanton, who's already incapacitated, won't be alive for much longer if he has anything to do with it. One Channeler is all he needs—any more than that becomes a serious threat, jeopardizing everything he's worked for.

The castle is in plain sight now. Searching for the perfect place to land, he spots a clearing on the outskirts of the forest. With a hefty flap of his wings, he dives out of the clouds and straight for the treetops. Hail begins to pelt him from every angle, making the descent less than pleasant, but at least he's a dragon and not its rider. Otherwise, he wouldn't live to see tomorrow, having plummeted to his death and all.

The heavy layer of snow cushions his landing. He dreads what comes next—shaping back into his human form—especially in weather like this. But if he continues any farther as a dragon, he'll knock down every plant and tree in sight, essentially turning the small clearing into an open field. Staying hidden is his main priority, so he goes with the more painful option: braving the cold without the proper attire.

Fortunately, the castle is straight ahead and once he finds himself on the cleared path, the wind seems to die down, making it slightly more bearable. He hurries to the west side of the castle, to an entrance within an alcove that few know about. He's pleased to find that a small fire has been lit in the hearth near the door, no doubt by the stablehands to keep the area warm upon their return.

He pushes the door open, poking his head inside to ensure he's alone. His first order of business is to determine which wing of the castle Stanton and Rydan are occupying.

Shouldn't be too difficult.

A servant scurries by but not quickly enough. Xerin reaches for him and pulls him in, snapping his neck with startling ease. The poor lad falls limp in his arms, giving Xerin the perfect angle to study his features, his stature, his attire, before shaping into him. No one the wiser, he stuffs the body into a closet near the scullery before heading to the main kitchen. He approaches the footmen carrying an array of dishes before saying, "I've been tasked with assisting the butler in delivering Sir Helstrom's meal."

The footmen look at each other and shrug, handing over one of the covered platters. "Much obliged," Xerin murmurs as he rushes over to where the butler had just exited with a full cart in tow. He follows closely behind until the movement in front of him ceases.

"Bertrand," the butler says. "Weren't you assigned to service the east wing this evening?"

"I've been reassigned," Xerin answers in the most neutral voice he can manage.

"By whose orders?"

"Why, the queen herself."

The butler looks him up and down but doesn't proceed with further questioning. "Come along, then. I've got nearly double the rounds to see to this evening."

"Why is that?" Xerin asks before he can think twice about it. If there are unexpected visitors, that could very well thwart what he has planned.

"The Healers have double the appetites, it seems, when really their eyes are bigger than their stomachs, if you ask me."

He didn't, but it's too late for that now. On the upside, perhaps he can get the butler to expand upon what little information he's already given. "Our rounds include the infirmary?"

"Mine always do, although they're the last stop." The butler pauses, then shakes his head. "Disheartening to say the least, seeing that poor fellow just lying there, unconscious, completely oblivious to the goings-on of the world around him." He tisks softly. "It's a shame it's the queen's brother-in-law, too. If it were me, I'd just want to go peacefully. No tonics, no salves . . . just allow Mother Nature to do exactly as She intends to."

All Xerin hears is that Stanton is still incapacitated, which should make taking him out for good much easier than he'd originally anticipated. "Where to first?"

"Are you always this inquisitive?"

Xerin clamps his mouth shut, glaring at the back of the butler's head. The last thing he needs is to raise suspicion.

They climb the stairs to the top of the west wing first, covering the entire floor before moving to the one below it.

His irritation grows with each door that opens to reveal someone other than Rydan. Then again, each failed door is an opportunity to further devise an outcome he'll be satisfied with.

Xerin lifts the back of the cart once more as they wind down the next set of stairs, wondering how the butler has previously managed to successfully make his rounds *without* assistance. The movement serves as enough of a distraction for him to swipe the master key ring from the top of the cart. They arrive at the next door, knocking before announcing themselves.

"Sir Helstrom?" the butler calls from outside the door.

Finally. Not wanting to appear too eager, Xerin waits patiently, but there's no answer.

"Odd," the butler murmurs. "Sir Helstrom never misses a meal." He looks at the platter in his hands, perplexed. "We'll have to circle back once we complete our rounds."

"No need," Xerin says. "I'll gladly wait for Sir Helstrom to return." The butler opens his mouth, surely with some shrewd retort, but Xerin quickly says, "Isn't that what I'm here for? An extra set of hands, should you need them?"

The butler considers the proposal, then somewhat begrudgingly hands over the platter. "I can certainly cover the rest on my own."

Xerin nods, bringing the platter close to his chest before pressing his back against the wall adjacent to the door. "Send my best to the others."

The butler lifts a brow but seems to shake off whatever thought's just entered his head. He rolls the cart to the next door, keeping a close eye on Xerin as he delivers the next meal. Xerin stays put, not daring to make any sudden movement until the butler's rounded the corner to serve the next corridor.

He blows out a long breath, then sets the platter on the ground at his feet. He checks left, then right, before deeming the coast clear. His form as Bertrand is beginning to fade, so he needs to remove himself from sight as soon as possible. He matches the numeral on the door to the one on the key, entering the premises undetected. He's pleased to find that the room is indeed empty and swiftly shapes into Darius before scanning every surface for a sign of the crescent fire.

If his assumption is correct, he has less than one hour before his form as the king begins to fade as well—an unfortunate side effect of his ability he's only recently been privy to. Regardless, it means he'll have to work fast.

He starts his search at the bed, looking under it, behind it, on top of it, but the crest isn't there. The armoire is next as Xerin tears through drawer after drawer, rifling through the various contents within. Still no crest. The desk also proves to be fruitless as the cabinets are too small to even hold such an item. He drops to his hands and knees, searching underneath the furniture when the sound of embers crackling draws his attention. His gaze first lands on the lit hearth before tracking to the door where one undeniably angry Ignitor stands.

"On your fucking feet," Rydan growls, flames dancing at his fingertips. "Now."

RYDAN HELSTROM

KING DARIUS TYMOND.

In *his* chambers. Caught off-guard and woefully unprepared, by the looks of it.

Rydan clenches his jaw as Darius slowly rises to his feet. He doesn't raise his palms in the air in surrender, nor does he look threatened, which is all the more infuriating.

"You have some nerve showing up here," Rydan sneers, his harsh tone indicative of everything he's feeling. "I should have ended your life when I had the chance."

Darius smirks, tilting his head in a way that's uncharacteristic for him. "And yet you hesitate, even now."

Rydan advances, trying to control his temper. "Do not test me," he seethes. "Or you'll be charred to a crisp long before you can utter another word."

A quiet laugh. "Perhaps a visit from our dear friend is needed to remind you of your place."

"The Mallum, the Cruex . . . there's always someone else to do your dirty work for you." His body heats with intensity. "Go on, take my igniting abilities, you coward. I can still just as easily kill you with the Cruex training you so graciously provided. You'll have a longsword cleaved through your neck in no time."

The king ignores the very obvious threat. "You know why I'm here." He walks across the room, his movements stilted, disjointed. "You've always been level-headed. What if we were to make a trade?"

Rydan tries to hide the shock on his face. First and foremost, Darius would *never* "make a trade". It simply isn't in his nature. Secondly, the king would never refer to him as level-headed when his time in the Cruex had proved otherwise. Even still, Rydan decides to play along—the longer he can do so, the more time he'll have to discern who the imposter is.

"What kind of a trade?"

Darius stops pacing. "You know very well what kind of a trade," he snaps. "You have something I want."

Rydan knows he's referring to the crescent fire because it's the only thing of value in his possession that the king would want. "And what are you willing to trade for it?"

"Knowledge. Information."

Rydan studies the king's movements, each observation making him feel more unsettled. Could it be Clive casting an illusion around him? Or another Savant who somehow made it out of Midvale?

"What information could you possibly have that I would want?"

A lupine grin snakes across the king's face, his eyes narrowing as he whispers, "Your family."

It was the last thing he'd expected to hear—namely because the *real* King Darius Tymond knows absolutely nothing about the Helstrom family or its origins. This he'd made abundantly clear during his time in the Cruex to the point where Rydan had finally given up and ceased his search altogether.

But this person, whoever they are, claims to know something, making it all the more crucial for him to uncover the truth behind the mask. He's about to ask how the king would like to proceed with the trade when the door, which he'd left slightly ajar, creaks open. Rydan whirls around at the noise, somewhat surprised to find Vira standing there.

"I was just passing by, hoping to . . ." her voice trails off as her eyes track to the window. "Was that a bird that just flew out the window?"

The pit forming in Rydan's stomach grows even deeper as the realization takes hold. It wasn't Clive. Or another member of the Savant. It was Xerin. Xerin . . . who's on the hunt for the crescent fire. Who's also claiming to know what happened to Rydan's parents. Honestly, he wouldn't put it past him—the Greys are some of the oldest illusié around.

Rydan turns back from the window, not knowing what to do next. He can't tell Vira what's just happened. What are the chances that Xerin's own kin would believe such an outlandish story? Not at all, if history decides to repeat itself, which it so often does. Whether that's a good thing or a bad thing remains to be seen.

CERYLIA JARETH

CERYLIA PLACES THE soul gem in the center of a small table, looking between the only two people she trusts with such information. Delywnn. And Cyrus.

"Is that what I think it is?" Delwynn whispers, drawing closer to the object in question before pulling away as if it's about to implode.

"It most certainly is." Cerylia tries to keep her tone even, steady. "I found it in Dane's old study. It was . . . hidden."

"Hidden?" Delwynn echoes. "But no one's been in there since—"

"I'm well-aware."

Delwynn clamps his mouth shut at her harsh tone.

"Is it even remotely possible that it's your husband's?" Cyrus asks carefully. "If the door to his study has been locked all this time as you say it has, then there's only one logical answer: that Dane put it there years ago."

Cerylia gives an adamant shake of her head. "Dane didn't mess with soul magick—*wouldn't* mess with it."

Cyrus angles his head. "How can you be so sure?"

Her hesitation speaks volumes, and she knows it. Because, if she's being truly honest with herself, she *isn't* sure. Far from it, actually. After what she'd witnessed in the infirmary, in that extracted memory of Stanton and Dane— well, she's questioned everything about her relationship with her late husband ever since. The one person she was supposed to know everything about—weaknesses, flaws, troubles, secrets . . . perhaps she'd barely even scratched the surface.

It's a devastating thought.

Thankfully, Delwynn picks up on how distraught she is and changes the subject. "Regardless of where it came from or how long it's been here, we have a responsibility to set the soul within free."

"If there's even a soul within to begin with," Cyrus murmurs.

"You think it's an *empty* soul gem?" Delwynn challenges.

"It very well could be. As of right now, we know hardly anything about it."

"That isn't entirely true," Cerylia counters. "I can tell you, with absolute certainty, that there *is* a soul contained in this one."

Her two advisors stare at her, dumbfounded.

She sighs, not wanting to relive that fateful moment with Xerin at Midvale. "When I managed to extract Felix's soul, his gem had a sort of ethereal glow to it, much like this one." She picks up the small object for emphasis. "Although this one does seem dull. Muted, almost."

"Which means?"

Cerylia looks to Delwynn. "I wish I knew." She shifts her gaze to Cyrus. "Any thoughts?"

"None," he answers despondently.

"That might just be a first," Cerylia muses as she pockets the gem.

"Have you ever extracted from a soul gem before?"

"*From* a soul gem?" She shakes her head. "Never. Soul magick is risky enough as it is. Such a feat would likely require the presence of two Extractors."

"Or a Channeler," Cyrus says, the wheels in his mind clearly turning. "And we just so happen to know of two, although only one is conscious at the moment."

"*Arden*?" Cerylia asks with wide eyes. "While I love my niece dearly, she isn't practiced enough to handle such a delicate matter."

"That doesn't mean she couldn't be."

Cerylia pinches the bridge of her nose, suddenly questioning her decision to rope her advisors into this. "The *time* it would take—the practice, the skill level . . . it just isn't feasible."

"So we just . . . do nothing?" Delwynn asks in disbelief.

"For now, there isn't much we can do." The finality in her tone signals the end to their conversation. Without further prompting, Cyrus and Delwynn take their leave. Cerylia buries her head in her hands, wishing she could somehow erase finding that soul gem. She doesn't need another reminder that, once again, the fate of so many things rests in her brother-in-law's hands.

DARIUS TYMOND

FUNNY HOW THE one thing he's able to do is of absolutely no use in this damn pit but holds immense power above ground. Paired with him no longer having the staff, the Mallum may as well be just another form of fog passing by.

Darius kicks at a small pile of pebbles, wondering how much longer he'll have to be down here. It's been days since his last human interaction and while it hadn't exactly gone as he'd hoped, at least *someone* had been made aware that he's stuck down here—even if that person just so happened to despise him.

The lack of sustenance—food, water, sleep—is starting to get to him and actually has him rethinking the dungeon conditions at Trendalath. He's never known what it's like to go hungry, to feel starved, to consider doing things *so* out of his nature that he hardly even recognizes himself. He'd hit a low this morning when he'd seen a rat scurry by and had chased it, salivating at the mouth, just to fail at catching it, thereby knocking himself back to his senses.

Kings feast on only the finest delicacies. They do not *chase* their meals—and they certainly don't have *rat* on the menu. If only that were enough to stave off his insatiable hunger.

His surroundings are briefly illuminated by a flash of lightning as thunder rolls overhead, signaling the onslaught of a very heavy storm. He gazes at the tiny air holes above him, hoping that just enough water can make it through to quench his thirst without leaving him to drown. Never has he been so concerned about the weather than he is right now.

Darius pulls his cloak tighter, the amethyst ring snagging on the fabric. If only the Mallum could somehow get him out of here, but even such a dangerously powerful entity has its limitations. For now, all he can do is sit and wait for the storm to pass . . . and hope he doesn't wither away in the process.

RYDAN HELSTROM

HIS ENTIRE CONVERSATION with Vira had passed in a blur. He'd brushed off the bird incident as if it were nothing, even though it's a very big *something*. She'd given it her best effort to smooth things over and, in her mind, she probably thinks she has, but nothing could be further from the truth. He'd been too preoccupied thinking about Xerin parading around as the king, on the hunt for something that doesn't belong to him.

When she'd finally retired to her own chambers, the first thing he'd acted on was retrieving the crescent fire from underneath the floorboards. Clearly, the only way to keep it safe is on his person, so he grabs some leather straps from an old satchel and fastens them in such a way so that he can mount the crest on his back, underneath his clothing. The metal is surprisingly hot on his skin, so he adds an additional layer of clothing between it and the crest. Thankfully it's winter, so his bulky clothing shouldn't garner unwanted attention.

His restless nature getting the better of him, he decides to go for a walk around the castle. The need to clear his head is an understatement. The halls are mostly empty at this hour save for the few servants scurrying about, collecting discarded meal trays. His stomach growls, a timely reminder that he hasn't eaten and wouldn't dare trust Xerin to handle his food, so he makes for the kitchen in the hopes that he can scrounge for leftovers.

He's pleased to discover that the long table filled with assorted fruits, meats, breads, and cheeses hardly looks touched, so Rydan takes it upon himself to make a plate. Less and less of the castle residents and staff seem to want to partake in communal dining, but Rydan doesn't mind in the slightest. The quieter, the better.

A full plate in hand, he turns toward the overwhelming seating selection. He's about to sit at the nearest table when a slight movement at the back of the hall grabs his attention.

It would appear he isn't alone after all.

He makes his way toward the back, first noticing the sky-blue robe the young man is wearing. A Healer. And, if memory serves, the small white patch on his left breast pocket indicates he's still in training as an assistant.

Rydan approaches him with caution, keeping recent events at the forefront of his mind. "Care if I join you?"

Mid-bite, the Healer looks up from the text he's reading and smiles. "Not at all."

Rydan sets his plate down before sliding onto the bench. "I take it you also missed dinner?"

"Not on purpose, I assure you." He glances at Rydan's near overflowing plate. "It seems I'm in proper company."

Rydan lifts his glass in solidarity, eyes traveling to the splayed open book. "Reading anything interesting?"

The young man sighs. "Only if you find poorly written accounts of history interesting."

Rydan smirks. "Can't say that I do."

"Smart lad." He takes a bite of his roll, then wipes his hand on a neatly folded linen before extending it in a proper greeting. "Name's Gabriel Thomason."

"Rydan Helstrom," he says, shaking the Healer's hand. "You work in the infirmary?"

"I'm assisting Edith with a very special case—"

"Right, Stanton Eliri," he finishes for him. When Gabriel gives him a quizzical look, no doubt wondering how he could possibly know that, Rydan quickly adds, "I'm well-acquainted with his daughter, Arden Eliri."

The Healer sighs. "I take it you're here for an update?"

"Not unless it's any different than what she's already told me."

"Which is?"

"That it takes time."

The Healer drops his shoulders in relief. "It's a slow process. Believe me, we all wish it were faster."

Rydan nods in mutual agreement. He ladles some soup onto his spoon, nearly spitting it out the moment it hits his tongue. "Serving soup cold should be a crime," he murmurs as he raises his ignited hand to warm the bowl.

Startled, Gabriel jumps back in his seat, eyes wide with astonishment. "You're . . ."

"An Ignitor," Rydan says, the flames slowly dissipating.

Gabriel shakes his head, then whispers, "Draconian."

Suddenly feeling exposed, Rydan stops what he's doing and folds his arms over his chest. "How could you possibly know that?"

"Your blood, it's . . ." Gabriel's voice trails off as he searches for a better choice of words. "It's your heat signature."

"My heat signature?"

"I can see it. Not just yours. Everyone's," he clarifies. "It's my illusié ability and the reason I chose the healing arts."

His answer takes the edge off, but not entirely. "What do you know of the Draconian bloodline?"

"What don't I know? It was my main course of study at Midvale." Gabriel grins. "I bet the other Ignitors run for the hills the moment you come near."

Rydan arches a brow. "Why would they do that?"

"Your ability supersedes that of other Ignitors. When you wield fire, it weakens the igniting abilities of those around you."

His mind immediately goes to Avery. "And what if, hypothetically speaking, I did not possess this knowledge and were to perform a ritual with another Ignitor?"

Gabriel blanches. "They'd certainly fall ill for some time—weeks, months, *years*. As for their abilities, they'd be woefully diminished."

Rydan stares at him, hardly believing his ears. It would explain why Avery hasn't felt well ever since they performed the ritual for the fallen illusié together. Had Rydan known the repercussions, he never would have involved himself in the first place.

"Everything all right?" Gabriel studies him. "You look like you've seen a ghost."

Wanting to keep things hypothetical, at least in Gabriel's mind, Rydan quickly shifts the direction of the conversation. "Did your studies at Midvale happen to include a family tree?"

"Several," Gabriel affirms. "You're a rare breed, but I take it you already know that, don't you?"

Rydan sets his fork down, saying a small prayer to the lords above. "Not to bore you with the details of my less-than-normal upbringing, but I never knew my family and have been searching for years for anything I can find on them—"

"Last name's Helstrom, you said?" Gabriel ponders aloud. "I knew it sounded familiar. I'd be glad to recreate a rendering of your family tree for you, if you'd like. It might take a few days since I'll need to revisit my notes and all, but it shouldn't take long."

Gratitude swells in his chest. There are no words to accurately convey how much this complete stranger's kindness means to him so he just says, "Thank you."

Gabriel raises his glass. "To the Helstrom family name."

Rydan mimics the motion. "To forging friendships in the unlikeliest of places."

"Hear, hear," the Healer echoes.

Rydan takes a swig of his verdot, much preferring celebratory drinking over any other kind.

ARDEN ELIRI

I CAN PONDER the options as much as I want, but it doesn't change the truth of the matter: we'll probably have to bring Cerylia into the loop on this and soon. If the cheval glass was damaged during the attacks and Midvale turns out to be a bust, we'll have no choice but to depend on her to extract whatever memory is inside that speculor—and if it was important enough for Aldreda to hide from her husband, who knows what valuable information it contains? What questions it might answer?

Knowing better than to travel all the way to Orihia on little to no sleep, we'd returned to Sardoria for the night.

Juniper joins me on the bed, nuzzling into the collection of blankets I've surrounded myself with. I give her a loving scratch behind her ears and, just as she's about to make herself at home on my lap, there's a knock at my door. I sigh, reeling at the thought of having visitors—until I hear the voice on the other side.

"Open up," Rydan says. "I know you're in there!"

He doesn't have to tell me twice. I gently set Juniper down, then rush to the door and usher him inside.

"What's the rush?" he asks, looking around the room as if he expects to find an emergency of some sort.

"There's no rush," I assure him. The truth is, with everything on my mind, I can only handle one guest at a time, so whatever open-door policy I'd abided by in the past is no longer relevant.

"How's your father doing?" Rydan makes himself comfortable at the edge of my bed, leaning over yet another heap of blankets to pet Juniper. After he's had his fill, he looks to me and pats the space next to him.

I stay rooted in place and fold my arms over my chest instead. "I highly doubt you knocked on my door at this hour to talk about my father."

He runs a hand along his jaw. "You're right, although I *am* curious. And the news I have is somehow related."

"I'm not sure I follow."

He pats the space next to him again. "Come. Sit."

"I didn't realize I'd been reduced to the respect level of a mutt." I arch a brow. "Perhaps if you try asking nicely . . ."

"Arden," he interrupts. "Please, just sit the fuck down already."

I bristle at his tone but oblige. "Well, at least you said *please* this time."

Even though he rolls his eyes, it doesn't deter his enthusiasm in the slightest. "I suppose I'll start with the good news first."

"I didn't realize there was bad news."

"There isn't, I don't think. It's more of a confirmation than anything else."

"Let's hear it."

Rydan places a hand on my knee before giving it a light squeeze. "I'm about to uncover my family history."

"What?" I say, unable to hide both the shock and confusion in my voice. "How? From whom?"

"Gabriel."

My mind goes blank. "Who?"

"You know. Gabriel. The Healer's assistant in the infirmary."

It takes me a moment to process. "So, if I understand correctly, you're trusting that someone you've only just met somehow miraculously knows about your family?"

"And you're trusting someone you've only just met to cure your father of his ailments?"

He's got me there. Damn him.

"Long story short, Gabriel is not only a Healer, he's able to see heat signatures. He knew I was Draconian. *Me*, a complete stranger."

I arch a brow, impressed. "Makes for a fantastic Healer, I'll give him that much."

"As I was saying," Rydan continues, "Gabriel studied Draconian bloodlines during his time at Midvale. He said he'd review his notes before rendering a copy of my family tree."

I can tell by the way his voice tapers off that he's nervous. I place my hand over his and smile. "This is exciting news, Rydan. You're finally going to know who your family is. Who your parents are. What happened to them—"

"If they're still alive." It's spoken quietly, as if saying it any louder might jinx the possibility.

"I'd like to be there when you find out. You know, if that's something you'd want."

He meets my steady gaze. "That was going to be my next question."

My heart swells as I realize what this means. Rydan and I had first connected in Trendalath as Cruex assassins, but our unspoken bond had always gone deeper than that. In more ways than one, we'd both been abandoned—orphaned. Left in the hands of a careless tyrant. We'd been the only bright spot in each other's dark, dismal history.

That had changed, of course, when I'd learned about my brother, my father, and my mother. Two of the three living. And, whether I'm ready for it to or not, it's about to change again, regardless of whether Rydan's family is alive or deceased.

"Hey," I say, scooting closer to him on the bed. "No matter what you find out, you'll always have me."

His gaze softens. "I know," he whispers. "Likewise."

I grab his arms, pulling him into a tight hug. "This is only good news, Rydan. I don't know what could possibly be bad about this."

He pulls away from me then, his expression turning serious. "That isn't the only news."

I search his face for his meaning but come up short.

"You won't believe who paid me a visit."

I can tell by the way his body tenses that he's recalling an unpleasant memory. "Who?" I press.

"Xerin." He pauses. "Shaped as Darius."

XERIN GREY

XERIN GLANCES OVER his shoulder, knowing that if he stops now, he's as good as dead. Traveling by foot is more exhausting than he remembers, but perhaps that's because his abilities are rapidly declining with each form he takes. It was bound to happen sooner or later, but no amount of preparation could have prepared him for the utter weakness that would overtake his body.

Mind? Foggy.

Bones? Frail.

The will to live? Present, but fading.

His teeth chatter as he continues along the stone-lined path, desperate for a place to stop. Preferably somewhere warm, indoors, *away* from the elements. It's appalling to think that anyone would willingly choose to live in snowy, frigid Sardoria compared to the seaside warmth of Trendalath. Darius had certainly chosen right in that regard.

He's no stranger to the Roviel Woods, however, even though he's more accustomed to flying over the treetops than walking through the actual woods themselves. The journey alone is proving to be a challenge. Throw in the unforgiving weather, the weakened state of his body, and his inability to shape at present and he may as well be a walking corpse.

A flickering of lights up ahead provides a brief dash of hope that he'll be able to escape the cold, but it's squandered when he realizes that the lights are drifting *away* from him— on a moving carriage, one that's traveling rather fast, in fact. If memory serves, the next town isn't for at least a few miles.

But at this rate, he'll never make it.

Gritting his teeth, he trudges onward, the aches in his joints bordering on unbearable. Somewhere along this damn path, there must be an abandoned house, inn, outpost . . .

But the outlook only grows bleaker.

The wind picks up, turning the once gentle snow flurries into small but deadly pellets of hail. Xerin lifts his arm to shield his face, but it doesn't do much in the way of protection. Squinting, he spots a weeping willow nearby and, while it may not be the shelter he was looking for, at least it'll provide cover and temporary relief from this raging storm.

Fortunately, the low-hanging branches aren't frozen just yet, allowing him to easily slip in between them. He moves further inward to the base of the tree, immediately warming from the inside out now that he's no longer being whipped around by the storm. He draws his cloak tighter, wishing he could shed it for a dry one, but layering isn't exactly an option right now. Sleep shouldn't be on the table either but with all the energy he's expended that he didn't even have to begin with, he's completely and utterly exhausted. Drifting off for a few minutes may not be the wisest choice, but it sounds infinitely more appealing than taking one more step in that relentless blizzard. Without even trying, his eyes close and he finds himself drifting into sleep . . .

❧ ❧ ❧

A blade pressed against his neck is the last way he'd expect to be woken up. Even more surprising is the person holding it there. His own flesh and blood.

"Give me one good reason why I shouldn't end your life right now," Vira seethes, eyes flaring with rage. "What the fuck are you thinking, Xerin?"

He cautiously raises his hands in surrender, hoping she won't do anything rash. He doesn't have an answer for her—not one that's satisfying, anyway—and, even if he did, it isn't like he's in the proper mindset to deliver it. But if there's one thing about Vira, it's that she pities the victim, having been one herself in Trendalath; so that's how he needs to present himself.

"You have every right to be upset."

"Upset?" A bewildered laugh follows. "I'm *livid*." A slight press of the knife against his throat draws a streak of crimson. "To think that all this time, you'd sided with Tymond, the very man who, for *years*, kept us apart, kept us separated from our family—"

"I know," he whispers. "But I need you to understand that he didn't leave me much choice. Not after he threatened to kill you if I didn't cooperate."

"Don't you dare act like what you did was noble." Tears line her eyes, her lower lip trembling. "The worst thing we could have done was leave the other to fend for themselves— and that's exactly what ended up happening."

"To no fault of our own," he pleads, wishing she would lower the blade. "It was the only way at the time."

"Oh, save it, Xerin. That's bullshit and you know it."

She's right. It is. But he doesn't dare admit it. Not when she's one thread away from unraveling entirely.

"Separation can be a thing of the past," he says. "We're being given a chance to make up for lost time."

"By siding with our sworn enemy?" Vira scoffs. "Some logic. Riddle me that, *brother*."

Xerin bares his teeth at the sarcasm dripping from her tone. "We all had a part to play, Vira, if we wanted to see this through. Seems you've forgotten."

She holds firm. "Perhaps I had a change of heart."

"Why? Because of Helstrom?"

Color blooms on her cheeks in response.

Her resolve is cracking, and it might just be enough for him to salvage at least one fragment of this misguided attempt. "I'm trying to *save* us. Our name. Our legacy. Our authority in Aeridon."

She lowers the blade. "We lost that a long time ago. In fact, I'm not sure we ever had it to begin with."

"We did," Xerin persuades, "you were just too young to remember. I need you to trust me when I say that Darius is merely a pawn in all of this. Someone to pin things on if things go awry. Why do you think I was shaped as him?"

Her silent calm is unnerving, but he can see the wheels turning in her mind and that's enough for him to keep spinning the story into something she wants to hear. "The Mallum is our ticket to freedom. We are on the precipice of having the option to wield *any* illusié ability for the rest of time."

"Which is why you went looking for the crescent fire," Vira whispers, finally understanding. "It's the one thing that can destroy the Mallum."

Xerin nods. She's got half the story, but that's all he needs her to have. "So, what'll it be, Vir?" He waits patiently for her to finish processing, to make her decision.

Them. Or him.

She squeezes her eyes shut before raising the blade once more. "I'm sorry," she says, her hand trembling as she tightens her grip, "but that crest doesn't belong to us. It isn't ours to take."

"Don't be blinded by love," Xerin warns. As soon as he says it, he realizes he's been approaching this all wrong. *Of course, why hadn't he seen it before?*

While she may refuse to side with him, he can find a different use for her. A trade. Her for the crest.

His gaze settles on the blade. He'll have to move quick to disarm her. He grabs the hilt and, using her own weight against her, bunts her with it right in the temple. She collapses almost instantly.

"I'm sorry, too," he whispers. How he wishes he meant it.

CERYLIA JARETH

THIS EVENING'S VISIT to the infirmary yields a surprise guest, someone she isn't quite ready to speak with just yet.

Her niece.

Nervous energy hangs in the air as Cerylia closes the door behind her. Slowly, she approaches where Arden is sitting, her nose in a book. It's an avoidance tactic—one that might be rather effective had Cerylia not already caught her eyeing the door when she'd first walked in.

"Good evening," she says as she drags the adjacent chair a bit closer. "I wasn't expecting company."

Arden keeps her eyes trained on the page. "Funny, I wasn't either."

Cerylia places her hands in her lap, the soul gem burning a hole in her pocket. It's a touchy subject, soul gems, especially after what'd happened in Midvale with Felix. Arden's made it clear that she blames herself for how things transpired, no matter her intentions or the fact that she'd been deceived in the harshest of ways. Broaching the topic won't exactly be easy.

Unbeknownst to the queen, Arden's sitting on news of her own.

"Minimal progress?" she asks, needing to break the uncomfortable silence.

Arden flips to the next page of her book. "I suppose that's one way of putting it."

The abruptness in her tone indicates that she's not too keen on talking. Cerylia clears her throat, debating on whether or not to attempt this conversation another time, perhaps when her niece isn't so preoccupied. But Arden surprises her by saying, "I need your help."

"Of course," Cerylia says with a nod. "With what?"

"Extracting." Arden sighs as if she's about to deliver bad news, then pulls a small sphere from her pocket. "From this."

Cerylia leans closer to get a better look at the speculor, hardly believing her eyes. "It's ancient," she breathes. "Where did you get it?"

"It was Queen Tymond's."

The admission feels like a slap to the face. "And what, pray tell, is it doing in your possession?"

"Braxton entrusted me—entrusted *us*—with it. He thinks there might be vital information within it; memories that, once unlocked, could change the course of everything. For illusié, for Aeridon." She hesitates before adding, "We originally planned on traveling to Midvale to use the cheval glass in the Archmage's office, but we have no idea how to use it . . . or if it's even intact. The risk seemed too great."

At the admission, anger begins to swell in the queen's chest, but it's quickly replaced with gratitude. She should be thankful that her niece trusts her enough to confess such things. Perhaps the rift she'd felt growing between them is finally on the mend. Instead of scolding or reprimanding Arden for a choice she'd *almost* made, she decides to bypass it entirely.

"The Tymonds are nothing if not secretive," Cerylia muses. Although obvious, she doesn't admit out loud that any memory involving her husband's murderer is one she'd rather not see. Forced to shove her feelings aside, Cerylia extends her arm and flattens her palm. "Let's see it."

Arden's eyes widen in surprise. "Really?" She digs in the pockets of her cloak to produce a speculor that looks vastly different from the ones she's seen in the past.

Cerylia closes her palm around the small object, suddenly feeling uncertain.

Arden takes notice. "What is it?" she asks, her voice full of concern. "What's wrong?"

"You said that this speculor belonged to Aldreda Tymond?"

"That's right," Arden answers, watching as her aunt sets the speculor on the table between them. "She left it for Braxton to find—she even hid it from Darius."

"Hmm," Cerylia ponders, studying it from her seat. "I've seen many speculors in my day and none of them have looked like . . . well, *that*."

Arden lowers her gaze to the small sphere as if she's just now seeing it for the first time. "The color *is* rather dull. Muted, even."

"Beyond that, if you look closely, you'll see layers of fog drifting within." Cerylia shakes her head. "Every speculor I've ever seen or extracted from has been bright and crystal clear—same with the memories."

"Do you think it's been tampered with?"

"It's certainly possible. However, in my humble opinion, if someone *has* attempted to erase the memories within this speculor, they've done a poor job."

"Who would want to erase Queen Tymond's memories?"

The question hangs in the air, unanswered.

Cerylia reaches for the speculor, hoping that a closer look will reveal *something* about why this one in particular appears different. She can feel Arden watching her, waiting for answers she won't be able to give. As much as she doesn't want to disappoint her niece, that's ultimately where they're headed.

A gasp pulls her from her thoughts as Arden brings a hand to her mouth, clearly remembering something.

"What is it?" Cerylia asks.

Arden tears her gaze from the speculor, eyes brimming with clarity. "This is going to sound absurd, but I just remembered something Braxton said when he was trapped in the Void and it has me wondering . . . what if this speculor contains a *veiled* memory?" She rises from her seat and begins to pace. "If Aldreda so desperately wanted to keep whatever's hidden in that speculor from Darius, wouldn't she take it to the one place he can't access? Especially knowing that her son *can*?"

To anyone else, the theory would sound outlandish, but given Cerylia's last stay at Midvale, she's been sitting on information that hadn't made sense until now. "I can confirm that Aldreda was, in fact, illusié. She occupied the very room I resided in during our last stay."

Arden's eyes grow wide. "Given how he treated Braxton, it's a good thing Darius never found out."

"Who's to say he didn't?" Cerylia counters. "Her death may have appeared straightforward at the time, having used you as the scapegoat and all, but something tells me there's significantly more to it."

Arden winces at the mention of the late queen's death, clearly reliving a memory she'd rather forget. "So," she starts, keen to change the subject, "this theory isn't only possible, it's highly plausible."

"Furthermore," Cerylia adds, "even if the Veil went down, as Darius surely counted on, the speculor would remain safe, its contents still entirely out of his reach."

Arden stops pacing. "It's the ultimate failsafe. I never took Aldreda Tymond for a mastermind but damn, color me impressed."

As much as it pains her, Cerylia is inclined to agree. Her arch-nemesis knew the importance of thinking ahead—a skill any effective queen ought to have.

Arden's excitement falters as she begins to work through the myriad details. "Correct me if I'm wrong, but in order to extract a veiled memory, wouldn't we have to be *inside* the Veil?"

Cerylia sighs, finally setting the speculor back on the table. "I wish it weren't so, but yes."

The Veil going down is an obvious issue, made even more problematic by the fact that they *need* its very existence in order to reveal whatever's contained in that speculor.

"How can we reinstate it?"

Cerylia doesn't have the heart to extinguish the dash of hope flickering in her niece's eyes. "My knowledge is limited on the topic, but I'm sure I can find someone who knows something."

Her response does little in the way of satisfaction. She glances at her father in his catatonic state. "How was the Veil being powered?"

Cerylia actually knows the answer to such a complicated question because the Archmage wouldn't shut up about it. *Cyfrin, lords rest her soul.* She shakes away the heavy thought, its presence looming like a storm cloud. "The Veil is powered by a crystalline grid."

Arden chews on her bottom lip. "Okay, well we already know the Savant played a part in the Veil's destruction," Arden deduces, a shadow passing across her face. "And that they needed Felix." Her voice drops to a whisper when she says his name, like she doesn't deserve to speak it.

"Why would they need an Amplifier?"

"I'm wondering the same thing. The Savant's Caster wouldn't make sense in this scenario, nor would their Multiplier," Arden says, ticking off each position in the Savant using her fingers. "It could have been the Conjurer."

Cerylia shakes her head. "The crystalline grid is unaffected by natural elements. Wind, water, fire—"

"—Lightning," Arden finishes with a shudder. "That would leave us with . . . the Savant's Curser."

Cerylia shakes her head. "A curse alone wouldn't be strong enough to take down the entire crystalline grid." She clicks her tongue against the roof of her mouth. "But pair that with a skilled Amplifier and you've got a recipe for destruction."

"That has to be it, then," Arden says. "So, now the question is: how do we remove the curse?"

Cerylia's surprised she knows the answer to this as well. "Only a Rescinder can remove a curse without being afflicted by said curse in the process."

"Do we know a Rescinder?"

A male voice sounds from the back of the infirmary. "I do."

Cerylia whirls around at the same time her niece does to find Gabriel, the assistant Healer, poking his head out from behind a curtain.

"And I'd assumed we were alone," she says to Arden who flashes her a grin. "Come on out, then," Cerylia says, angling her head at him. "Tell us what you know."

BRAXTON HORNSBY

RETRIEVING THE KEY had certainly been easier than sneaking it back in. If Arden catches wind that he *still* hasn't returned the key—a crucial part of their plan— she'd go ballistic. For some reason or another, Cyrus seems to have locked himself in his chambers, only leaving for a split second to seize the meals being left at his doorstep.

Braxton sighs, watching as the door opens from the shadowed alcove he's hiding in. It's not like he can keep skulking in the halls because, at this rate, someone's bound to notice such odd behavior. He just hadn't expected it would be Cyrus.

"Are you finally going to return the key you stole, or should we just keep pretending that I don't see you lurking, watching my every move morning, afternoon, and evening?"

Braxton freezes. Cyrus may be old, but he's still sharp.

"Must be tiresome, although I do admire your tenacity. The truth of the matter is, staying in my room day after day is beginning to bore me, so let's just get this over with, shall we?"

Defeated, Braxton hangs his head before retreating from the shadows. He pulls the key from his pocket as he approaches the door and places it in Cyrus's outstretched hand. His fingers curl around it. Hoping they won't have to discuss his transgressions further, he turns to leave, but the old man stops him.

"Not so fast," he says. "Have you eaten?"

It's such an unexpected segue that it causes Braxton to jerk his head up in surprise. "No, I haven't. I've been *lurking*, as you so adequately put it."

"Come inside. Stay for a bite."

"That's okay, I really ought to get back—"

"I wasn't asking," Cyrus interrupts.

Braxton drops his gaze to the wooden tray in Cyrus's hands. "Only if I can have the dinner rolls."

"Consider it done," he says, handing them over before ushering him inside. "Now, tell me what you've been up to and with whom."

Fat chance. He's already royally screwed up what should have been the easiest part of their well-devised plan, so there's no way he's going to just confess the details; which means he'll need to think on his feet. *Why else would he have needed that key? What else could he have been looking for?*

"For the record," he starts. "I acted alone." An idea comes to him then, a way to thwart revealing his real reason for stealing the key. "How I wish my father had, too."

Cyrus tears into one of the turkey drumsticks, his mouth near full as he says, "Please, be more cryptic. I beg of you."

Braxton doesn't smile. "In the tunnels. You were there. With my father. With all those bodies."

The half-eaten drumstick clatters to the plate. "I suppose I should have taken my meal *beforehand*—"

"An impossibility. You couldn't have known."

Cyrus leans back in his chair, lifting a napkin to dab at the corners of his mouth. "You ventured all the way back to Trendalath, *alone*, to visit the tunnels? What were you hoping to find?"

"Correspondence," Braxton answers. "Between you and the Savant, you and the king . . . something to indicate *why* the decision was made to keep a rotting pile of flesh beneath the castle grounds."

"Rotting? Who said anything about rotting?"

"Don't tell me you're nose-blind." Braxton stares at him in disbelief. "It smells absolutely atrocious down there."

"Ah, yes, well that would mean the ward is working, then," he says with a smirk.

"Ward? What ward?"

Cyrus sighs, running a hand through his thinning hair. "I placed a ward on the bodies to keep them from decomposing. The stench disguises it."

"Why not just make it smell pleasant?"

Cyrus gives him a knowing look. "Because anyone who happened upon it would have suspected that something was amiss."

"More amiss than disrespecting the dead?" Braxton heaves an exasperated sigh. "Regardless of whether they're rotting or not, the real question remains. *Why* is my father stockpiling bodies underneath the castle?"

"To eventually create a larger army, of course."

"Of the dead?"

"Well, they wouldn't be dead."

Braxton nearly spits out his dinner roll. "My father is considering *necromancy?*"

Cyrus nods. "It's an ideal scenario for him. After seeking control of the Savant, the Cruex, the King's Guard—and failing miserably—he's grown tired of free will. Hence the reason he outlawed illusié in the first place."

"It was something he couldn't control," Braxton murmurs, deep in thought. "With a legion of the undead, he'd be near impossible to defeat. You can't kill what's already dead."

"Precisely." Cyrus lifts his goblet to his mouth, taking a long drink. "Necromancy requires a soulless body that has limited deterioration and decay. The ward I cast ensures that the bodies remain structurally sound."

Having lost his appetite, Braxton sets the rest of his meal to the side. "I have to ask . . . does my father even *know* a Necromancer?"

"No, but your mother did."

Braxton can't help but lower his gaze at the mention of her. "And where would they be now? This Necromancer?"

"Lords if I know," Cyrus says. "They could be anywhere, really. My best guess is the Crostan Islands, seeing as so many illusié were exiled there once your father took the throne."

Braxton fidgets with the frayed edges of his napkin, the burden of this new knowledge already weighing on him. "So, with every illusié ability the Mallum absorbs and every subsequent soul it takes, my father is singlehandedly increasing his power, his numbers."

A shadow falls over the old man's face. "I'm afraid there's more."

Braxton doesn't know how much *more* he can handle right now.

"Your father has kept Arden close all these years for a reason. Although we all presumed Stanton dead long ago, your father knew that he was a Channeler—an incredibly powerful one at that. It was only logical to assume that Arden would eventually be the same once her healing ability morphed. However, when the time was right, Darius knew he could use her channeling abilities to redistribute the entirety of the Mallum's illusié abilities . . . to himself." Cyrus lowers his gaze. "But channeling at that magnitude? It would kill anyone, especially a novice like Arden."

Braxton looks at him in horror. "My father would then be able to wield every single illusié ability ever known to Aeridon?"

"As long as the Mallum had absorbed it, yes. Which explains his tireless efforts with the Cruex to locate and eliminate as many illusié households as possible."

Braxton runs a hand along his jaw, not sure what to make of the information—or what to do with it. "Will the crescent fire be enough to stop him?"

"In theory, yes. It can destroy illusié-made objects: the Mallum, the staff, and the ring are all at its mercy. Your cousin, however, is not."

Braxton shakes his head. "Arden hates my father even more than I do. She would never willingly yield and channel all that power to him—"

"That may be true, but there's one major factor you aren't considering."

"Which is?"

"Human emotion. If the trade at stake is in any way tied to that, well . . ." Cyrus pauses, brows furrowing in concern. "Then we all may as well dig our graves right now."

DARIUS TYMOND

LACK OF FOOD, WATER, and sleep is starting to wear on him. Time is as elusive as it gets down here. It could have been days, weeks, *months* since he's seen the surface, but he couldn't possibly know. His mind playing tricks on him isn't helping either.

Darius awakens to rumbling overhead. Another storm. There's plentiful rain in Trendalath but nothing like the Crostan Islands. Here, it rains almost daily and not just for an hour or two, but entire mornings and evenings. He's thankful for the water, however sparse, because it's the only thing keeping him somewhat lucid.

Every time he opens his eyes, either from sleep or a bout of unconsciousness, he can't help but wonder what Xerin is doing. If he's looking for him. If he even knows he's missing. He certainly should—they'd only traveled together, roomed together, drank together . . . The events at the tavern are still fuzzy, to say the least. It's entirely possible that Xerin's suffered a far worse fate and perhaps isn't looking for him at all because he's . . . well, dead.

Lightning strikes overhead, providing just a flash of light in the dank pit but it's enough for Darius to see that he isn't alone.

"My, you've certainly seen better days."

He'd know that voice anywhere. How he wishes he felt even a semblance of relief, but the level of disgust he has for Sir Ridley is far too strong.

"Let me guess," Darius croaks due to not having spoken in days, "you're casting an illusion. Of yourself. How original."

The Caster scoffs as he steps out of the shadows with a sneer on his face. "A good thing, too. Otherwise, we'd both end up stuck down here."

Darius pushes himself to a sitting position, dusting off the bottom half of his robe as if it'll somehow make it any less filthy. He leans back, resting his head against the damp stone wall as another flash of lightning illuminates his surroundings. "I take it you're here to gloat about your survival at Midvale."

"On the contrary," Clive answers, "I'm here to help you."

Darius scoffs, not believing a word. "You came here with good intentions?"

Clive sighs, his tone turning serious. "Whether I like it or not, there aren't many of us left. The events at Midvale wiped out the majority of Trendalath's forces. The Cruex, the King's Guard, the Savant—"

"I need not be reminded of what I've lost," Darius says.

Discomfort fills the space between them at the admission. Clive clears his throat. "The way I see it, we'd be fools for not sticking together."

"Like we ever had a choice."

Clive crosses his arms, impatience edging his tone. "If you prefer, I can certainly retract my offer; but, from the looks of it, it seems it's the only one on the table." His eyes rove over the king. "One more day down here and you'll be on your death bed."

Darius hates that he's right, but he *loathes* the idea of having to spend one more second down here with no viable way out. He pushes himself to his feet, brushing his hands together. "I'll accept your offer on one condition," he relents.

"Name it."

The words come easy. "We flee this lords-forsaken place and return home. To Trendalath."

"I take it you didn't receive the welcome you were hoping for?" Clive says as he lugs open the grate.

"Far from it."

"Pity. Then again, the Crostan Islands would still be uninhabited if you hadn't—"

Darius waves a hand in the air. "No need to remind me of my past decrees. I'm fully aware of my actions and their subsequent recourse."

Clive huffs a laugh, then vanishes from sight. When he returns, he tosses a rickety wooden ladder—held together by tied linens, of all things—over the edge of the oubliette.

Darius stares at it, slack-jawed.

"Courtesy of your trade embargoes," Clive says with a flourish of his hand. "You don't leave the people much to work with."

"You expect me to *climb* that?" He approaches the ladder despondently, tugging on one of the fraying linens. "The craftsmanship is questionable at best."

"Do you want out of there or not?"

Darius grits his teeth as he places both hands on the wooden bar. It barely reaches the height of his shoulders. As soon as he steps onto the lower panel with all of his weight, the ladder begins to creak and sway, doing little for his already waning confidence in this escape plan.

"Climb," Clive urges. "Now. Who knows how long this thing is going to hold?"

"Not . . . helping," Darius grunts as he climbs one rung after the other. By the time he reaches the top, his arms and legs burn and his sanity is hanging on by a thread. He straightens his robes, surveying the street for their means of escape, but there are no horses, no carriage . . .

"Don't tell me you came all the way out here only to have our escape plan be by foot."

Clive shrugs as he grabs hold of the grate and drags it over the opening of the pit. "Given our past, I wasn't sure if you'd be agreeable or not."

Darius could strangle him. "To be clear, you *didn't* have a plan after you'd located my whereabouts?"

Clive takes to the road, heading in the direction of the docks. "Stay, go, I didn't know what you'd choose. I figured if you wanted to leave, we could always catch a ship. And if you wanted to stay, well, no plan necessary."

He says it so nonchalantly, as if their livelihood isn't at stake, which Darius finds all the more infuriating. "Before we leave, there is a stop we need to make."

Clive sighs, halting his steps as he waits for the king to catch up. "I suppose I should be following you, then."

As it should have been to begin with.

Darius takes the lead, banking left to head toward the Wilmott residence. If Alyna's men haven't retrieved the staff by now, they'll need instruction on where to deliver it once they do. With a blood oath, he isn't willing to take any chances. But the further he gets into town, the more people seem to appear out of nowhere . . . until herds of them are swarming the streets, all heading in the same direction.

Toward the docks.

Instead of stopping by Alyna's house like he'd originally planned, Darius follows the crowd, knowing that she's likely the one leading the charge. It seems Clive's timing was as impeccable as ever, otherwise he'd be in a hole in the ground in a soon-to-be-abandoned town. His last encounter with one of the residents is still fresh in his mind, so, to further secure his identity, he pulls the hood of his robes snug over his head.

The discreet endeavor appears to work in his favor because he makes it all the way to the docks without a double take or a second look his way. As he'd suspected, Alyna is here, standing at the helm of a ship that's seen better days. In fact, all ten ships in their fleet are in dire need of renovations. The prospect instills little hope of their mission to Sardoria going well.

"Bellmoor residents are to board the first five ships on the left!" Alyna calls out. "Kilshade residents, take to the ships on the right!"

She's organized, he has to give her that. Darius watches as people dash to and fro, loading their weaponry and armor onto their respective ships. Even though he's standing a good distance away at the entrance to the docks, Alyna manages to lock eyes with him. She frowns, then whistles so loud that the commotion around them stops instantly.

"Well, well, well, look who's decided to join us."

All eyes track to him.

Even with the mounting pressure, Darius stands firm. He scans the crowd, searching for Xerin, but he's nowhere in sight. "My sincere apologies," he says as he removes his hood. "I was . . . indisposed for a time."

A murmur passes through the crowd as recognition takes hold. *This ought to be fun.*

"How do we know you'll follow through on your word?" a townsperson shouts.

"He took the blood oath!" another replies.

"Isn't *he* the reason we were sent here in the first place?" shouts another.

Darius raises his hands in the air, hoping it'll signal a form of surrender to the very angry crowd that's scowling at him.

"If you're so powerful, then why do you need us?"

"Prove that the Mallum is under your control!"

He looks to Alyna, noticing the unmistakeable challenge in her eyes. "Very well," he mutters under his breath. "If that's what you really want."

The crowd doesn't quiet down as he brings his hands together, the amethyst ring humming. He closes his eyes, calling forth the entity like so many times before. A dark cloud sweeps over the docks, a black mist crawling across the pier. It surrounds them, envelopes them, as it pushes its way past the ships and over the water. A hush finally falls over the crowd as they track its movements, backing into one another in an attempt to find safety. Even Alyna, who had been perfectly stoic when he'd first arrived, appears shaken at the presence of such a formidable force.

"It will not harm you," Darius says as he makes slow, steady strides toward Alyna's ship. "As long as you are loyal to Trendalath, to our cause, no harm will come to you."

There's a slight tremor to Alyna's voice as she says, "The Mallum has only one target left until redistribution of all illusié abilities can occur, and that target is The Caldari."

"I ask that we sail to Sardoria," Darius adds, "for you to reclaim what is rightfully yours."

"As decreed by the blood oath," Alyna says, pulling the crimson-stained skull from its place above the wheel and raising it into the air. "It shall be done!"

ARDEN ELIRI

ACCORDING TO GABRIEL, the Rescinder's name is Nevaeh Dulot of Miraenia. Having grown up next door to her—his childhood crush, as he'd so aptly put it—he'd seen the extent of her abilities.

"She was one of the fortunate ones," he'd shared. "As a Rescinder, the reversal of illusié was difficult to track. In fact, I'm not sure King Tymond was even aware of such an ability among our illusié ranks."

It's certainly the first I've heard of such an ability. Then again, that seems to be happening often these days. I'd never heard of a Channeler either and, not only do I happen to be one, but my father is, too. It makes me wonder how much more there is to illusié that I don't know about. As soon as I feel like I've gained expertise on one topic, something else is brought to light that makes me question everything. Who am I kidding? My inquiring mind loves the complexity, the ever-changing nature and landscape of illusié.

Having volunteered to go to Miraenia with Gabriel, we trek through the Roviel Woods on horseback, teeth chattering against the crisp wind. I've never had an issue with cold weather and snow—I actually quite prefer it—but having to make the journey from Sardoria to Miraenia in said snow is an entirely different story. The blizzard only began to let up about five minutes ago, hardly enough time for my body to defrost and function as normal.

Gabriel hops off his mare, seemingly unaffected by the frigid temperatures we just rode through, and ties the reins around a pole in the town square. I follow his lead, enjoying every bit of warmth the sun is now graciously providing. He points to a small cottage a few rows back. The red door is hard to miss.

"She lives *here?*" I whisper, hating how judgmental I sound.

"Were you expecting something different?"

His question gives me pause. Honestly, I don't know what I was expecting, but the residence, with its poor upkeep, vines growing up the sides, chipped paint, and rusty hinges looks more abandoned than lived in. I follow Gabriel to the door, side-stepping some fallen debris along the way, and wait patiently behind him as he knocks three times.

Footsteps sound from inside, followed by a strange rattling I can't place, before the door creaks open. I try to keep my jaw from dropping as the most stunning woman I've ever seen comes into view. Vibrant red hair falls in loose waves over her shoulders, her hazel eyes wide as she studies the two unexpected guests standing on her doorstep.

"Gabriel?" she says, recognition lighting her face. "Gabriel Thomason?"

"You're looking well, Nevaeh," he says with a grin. "How are things?"

Well is an understatement, if you ask me.

"A bit more of a struggle than they used to be—" Her words cut off when her gaze lands on me. "And who, might I ask, are you?"

In an effort to not look intimidated, I step forward, bringing my shoulders back. "My name is Arden Eliri. It's a pleasure to make your acquaintance."

Nevaeh arches a brow. "Eliri, eh? I never knew your lot to be so . . . formal." She shifts her gaze to Gabriel. "What are you doing bringing an Eliri to my doorstep?"

I fight the urge to slink back into the shadows, to turn around and leave. I can't help but wonder if I missed something—why this woman, whom I've never met in my life, seems to take issue with me, my family, my *name*.

"Have we met before?" The question slips out before I can stop it.

Nevaeh levels a steely look at me. "No, but we may as well have, seeing as I know almost everything there is to know about your line of Channelers." She leans against the doorframe with her arms folded across her chest. "Your kind confounds me—and not in a good way."

"Why is that?"

"Your ability to channel is the only one that cannot be retracted," Gabriel answers.

"Which means we have little to no reason to be in the same vicinity as one another, let alone work together," Nevaeh finishes.

"Not even if it means reinstating the Veil?" I challenge.

She looks to Gabriel for confirmation. When he nods, she says, "I suppose that *could* be of interest . . ."

"How extensive is your work with crystals?"

She steps aside to reveal what must be dozens of gems, crystals, and rocks covering nearly every surface of her home. "Some might say I'm somewhat of an expert."

"What about curses?" I press. "Or, more specifically, reversing curses?"

A hint of a smile touches her lips. "Not to boast, but I'm also quite practiced in that area as well."

I study her for a long moment, her stare not breaking from mine. "Then reinstating the Veil should be a breeze for you."

"Forgive her brashness," Gabriel says by way of apology, as if I'm always like this. "The working theory is that the crystalline grid was destroyed by the Savant's Curser. Not only that, but the curses were amplified."

At the mention of Felix's ability, my breath hitches. A knot forms in my stomach as I desperately try to push down the memory of his death by my own hand.

Nevaeh's gaze softens. "You lost someone."

"We all have," I mutter. "Doesn't make me special."

She goes silent, pursing her lips as she mulls the proposal over. Finally, she says, "Consider it done."

Gabriel grins. "You'll help us?"

She nods. "Give me a day or so to get my affairs in order. I'll meet you in Orihia and we'll go from there."

"We'll be there," I say, grabbing hold of Gabriel's arm. We need to leave before I have the chance to say something that might make her change her mind. "Thank you, Nevaeh."

"Don't thank me just yet."

Before I can question what she means, she retreats into the small cottage and disappears from view.

RYDAN HELSTROM

RYDAN WAITS PATIENTLY by Arden's door, the scroll containing his very livelihood in hand. He taps his foot against the marble floor. *As if that'll help pass the time.* He's only been waiting for an hour but it may as well be days. At least, that's what it feels like.

He doesn't know if he should find it funny or odd that a complete stranger is the one helping them both with varying matters—both urgent in their own way. Regardless, he's thankful for Gabriel's willingness to help. Without him, he'd probably still be on an unfulfilling quest for information.

Arden, too.

A familiar pair of footsteps echoes from down the corridor. He perks up, smiling when Arden turns the corner. As soon as she sets eyes on him, she grins.

"I take it Miraenia was a success?"

She meets him at the door, unlocking it with a key. "In more ways than one. Not only did we find a Rescinder, but she agreed to help us reinstate the Veil."

"Really?" Rydan follows her inside, shutting the door behind him. "So, Gabriel's lead turned out to be worthwhile."

She sits on the edge of the bed, eyeing the scroll in his hand. "Seems like you've had some success, too."

Rydan taps the rolled piece of parchment against his palm, suddenly feeling nervous. "I haven't opened it, if that's what you're asking."

"I wasn't—" She doesn't finish her thought as what he's just said sinks in. "What do you mean you haven't opened it?"

He shrugs. "I was waiting for you. Like I said I would."

"Well, get over here," Arden says, jumping up from the bed and pulling him over. "Sit. Open it. You've waited long enough."

She's right but that doesn't make what he's about to do any easier. The moment he reads whatever's in this scroll, everything changes. He's no longer orphaned or abandoned, a renegade Cruex or a rogue Caldari—he's a Helstrom. With parents. Possibly even siblings. An entire family tree.

"Rydan," Arden whispers, eyes alight with concern. "Are you going to open it?"

He'd been so lost in thought he hadn't realized he'd just been sitting there next to her in complete silence. The situation is already unnerving enough. "Yes. I just—"

Arden nods without him having to finish his sentence. "I understand. I don't mean to pry, I'm just anxious. This is what you've been waiting for ever since I first met you."

He smiles at the sentiment, but it quickly fades as another, more disturbing, thought takes hold. "What if I don't like what's in here?"

Arden turns so that she's fully facing him on the bed, crossing her legs in the process. "It can't be any worse than finding out you're related to the *Tymonds*." It's meant to be a joke but there's no mistaking the edge to her tone.

"I suppose you're right," he says, trying to keep things light.

"Hey," she says, nudging him with her knee. And then, more seriously, "I'm right here."

He lays the scroll between them on the bed. "Here goes."

He pulls on the tail of the velvet ribbon, the scroll loosening in response. Slowly, he flattens the paper from top to bottom. Arden sets her hands on the top corners to hold them in place as he works his way down. The page is covered in ink—Gabriel certainly hadn't left anything out.

"It's so . . . detailed," Arden whispers.

"My thoughts exactly," Rydan echoes as he begins to scan the page. There are so many names he doesn't know, doesn't recognize in the slightest, but one thing is clear: he comes from a long line of very powerful Ignitors. His heart swells at the thought.

He continues to search the document, finally locating his name at the bottom right corner. He follows the delicately drawn line to the two names above his. "Nyle Helstrom and Palma . . . Soames."

Hardly believing what he's just read, he blinks once. Twice. But the name remains. Guilt coils in his stomach at the realization, a knot forming in his throat.

"Did you just say *Soames*?" Arden asks in disbelief. "As in . . ."

"Radelle and Erle Soames," Rydan finishes, his voice cracking. His index finger follows the line of his family tree further. "My aunt and uncle."

Arden jumps up from the bed to stand next to him so she can view the document upright. She heaves a long sigh, then places a hand on Rydan's shoulder.

No words are spoken.

No sentiments are exchanged.

No excuses are given.

He'd blindly followed the king's decree and, in doing so, had murdered his aunt and uncle. Had he known they were family—his only living relatives at the time—the choice he made would have been vastly different.

Rydan runs a hand through his hair, fighting the budding sadness and rage within. Whether he means to or not, the rage always wins. Maybe that's just what he needs.

Before he can fully process what this means, there's a frantic knock at the door.

"Rydan? Are you in there?" Avery calls.

Distracted, Rydan clears his throat before answering.

"Is Vira in there with you?"

He exchanges a glance with Arden. She rushes to the door. "What's going on?"

"It's Vira," Avery pants. "She's missing."

Rydan doesn't look at either of them as his hands curl into fists. It seems Arden was wrong. The bad news just keeps coming.

XERIN GREY

HE CAN FEEL Vira writhing against his scales midflight—as if she has anywhere to go if she were to somehow break free. He'd hoped the tonic he'd administered before strapping her to his back and shaping into a dragon would have lasted longer; then again, one hour should have been plenty of time.

From his vantage point in the clouds, the Crostan Islands begin to take shape along with . . . a fleet of ships. By the looks of it, about ten of them. The abstract skull stitched onto the sails is an exact replica of what the islands look like from above, which is how he knows it's Alyna and the legion she'd promised. Their direction indicates that they're headed to Sardoria.

A horn blares from below, startling both him and Vira. One of the perks of shaping into a dragon is being granted impeccable eyesight—but this is something he would have rather not seen.

Darius stands at the helm with Alyna, a smug look on his face, his robes billowing in the wind. The likelihood that any of the townspeople had helped him out of the oubliette is slim, so how had he managed to escape? His question is answered almost immediately as a mess of curly red hair climbs the steps that lead to the helm. Clive Ridley.

Damn Caster.

He hadn't expected any of the Savant to make it out of Midvale alive, so the sighting comes as a shock. Clive *should* be dead, like the rest of them. His survival certainly puts a minor dent in his plans, but nothing that can't be retooled.

He banks left, turning around to head back the way they'd just come. Vira tugs at the straps, hard enough so that the leather grinds into his scales.

What, he growls, unwillingly opening up their line of communication.

Where are you taking me? He can sense the confusion in her tone. *We just came from that way.*

We go where the ships go.

She pauses. *You know they'll come looking for me if they haven't already.*

Xerin scoffs. *I wish them luck searching the endless expanse that is the skies.*

She pulls on the straps again, even harder this time. *What kind of person would even consider kidnapping their own sister?*

The kind that's running out of options. Although he thinks it, he doesn't send it down the line.

You're of sound mind, yes?

Vira sighs. *Unfortunately.*

Then make yourself useful, he says, dipping underneath the cloud cover for a moment to check the trajectory of the fleet.

And how do you suggest I do that?

Put out the call. Summon dragonkind to Sardoria.

Vira laughs. *Over my dead body.*

It will be, Xerin retorts, *unless you do as I ask.*

You'd kill your own sister for disobeying?

Perhaps we should pay Rydan a visit first . . .

Leave him out of this, Vira growls.

Are you in really in a position to be bargaining?

Defeated, Vira sighs. *How many dragons are we talking?*

Xerin banks right. *However many answer.*

DARIUS TYMOND

SARDORIA IS WITHIN SIGHT. If the Queen's Guard hasn't spotted them by now, they will soon enough. Darius pushes off the railing and begins to pace the upper deck. Everything he's worked for is finally coming to a head. Sardoria is the last province in Aeridon to be visited by the Mallum. The entity had only made it through a quarter of the town when it'd entered the castle to take his son's deviating abilities. While it'd been unintentional, it'd ultimately worked out for the best. He returns to the railing, squeezing the metal as he recites a silent prayer to the lords above.

"I see you're not the only one who prefers solitude."

He jumps at the sudden interruption, turning to find Alyna standing at the top of the staircase. Her fringe that rests just above her eyebrows scatters in the wind, revealing a scar that draws from her temple to her hairline. Darius averts his eyes as he says, "Only because it helps to clear my head."

"That makes two of us." She joins him at the railing, tugging on her fur vest as the wind whips wildly around them. The rest of her attire is hardly appropriate for such severe weather—including a sheer dress with a deep plunge neckline and thick, cuffed necklaces adorning her neck and decolletage—but she doesn't so much as shiver. "You know, when I first saw you, I wanted to kill you."

The statement should come as a surprise, but it doesn't. Ever since he can remember, he's been someone's target. Even with nothing at his disposal, it seems the target remains.

"If it weren't for Xerin, I probably would have."

"It's a good thing he softened the blow, then." Darius keeps his eyes trained on the sea. "But, seeing as Xerin isn't here, what's stopping you?"

She chuckles, her slender, pointed nails digging into the railing as she says, "Unlike in Trendalath, we honor our oaths. Especially when they're made in blood."

"I can appreciate that," he says, meaning every word.

"I wasn't able to catch Xerin before we departed. Is he meeting us in Sardoria?"

"Yes," Darius lies, knowing that if he reveals he has no idea where Xerin is or where he's been, she might very well kill him on the spot.

"It's a shame he's missing our voyage across the seas. In my experience, it's where camaraderie is formed."

Darius is about to respond when the wind picks up even more. A shadow is suddenly cast over the ship. He lifts his gaze to the skies, unable to stop the grin spanning his face. "I have a feeling he's not missing anything."

Alyna tracks his gaze, mouth agape as she witnesses a rare sight: a dozen or so dragons circling just above their fleet. "How—?"

"One thing you'll learn about Xerin, if you haven't already, is that he's full of surprises."

And what a welcome surprise this is.

"I'll say." Alyna pushes off the railing and makes for the stairs, no doubt wanting to see the reaction on the rest of the crews' faces.

He doesn't blame her. It's just the finishing touch they needed. Between their fleet, the Mallum, and now a host of dragons, Sardoria better get their defenses ready. Darius brings his hands to his mouth, warming them in the crisp wind. It seems he's finally gotten the upper hand.

About damn time.

CERYLIA JARETH

SHE'S RELIEVED TO hear that Gabriel and Arden's trip to Miraenia had gone well. So much so, in fact, that she's invited the entire castle to a celebratory feast. With little to rejoice over these days, it's the least she can do.

Even though she's the esteemed host, she's the last to enter the Great Hall, nodding as she passes by those rising from their seats, bowing to show their respect. Delwynn pulls out her chair from the main table, motioning for her to sit. Instead, Cerylia lifts her glass of verdot in the air. "Hear, hear," she cheers.

"Hear, hear!" the hall echoes.

She nods at the Caldari who are already seated at her table before taking a drink of her verdot. They follow suit. One look at the exchange between Arden and Rydan tells her she must have missed something important because soon after the food is served, her niece pushes back from the table, eyes trained on the queen. Fork poised in the air, Cerylia sighs, bringing it back to her napkin.

Arden kneels beside her, her voice barely above a whisper. "Vira is missing."

Cerylia looks around the table, wondering how she hadn't noticed the empty seat earlier. "For how long?"

Arden shrugs. "I'm just relaying what Avery told me; but Rydan and I have covered every inch of the castle and she's nowhere to be found."

"I'll send Delwynn to do his rounds."

"The Queen's Guard, too?"

Cerylia arches a brow at the suggestion. "If Delwynn returns suspecting foul play, then yes, I'll get the guards involved."

Rydan clears his throat from the other side of her seat, startling her. When he'd gotten up and made his way over, she doesn't know. "Pardon the intrusion, but I've been led to believe that we *should* suspect foul play."

"And why is that?"

Rydan doesn't so much as hesitate. "Xerin was here."

Cerylia motions for them to duck even lower so that their heads are beneath the table, away from prying eyes. "When?" She directs the next question at her niece. "Was this before or after our conversation in the infirmary?"

"Before," Arden says glumly.

"And you didn't think to mention it?"

She shakes her head. "I was just so focused on the speculor—"

"He wasn't here long enough to have done any real damage anyway," Rydan interrupts. "Plus, it seems Vira scared him off . . ."

"Perhaps she went with him, then," Cerylia says sharply. "He is her brother after all. Now, can I return to my meal before it gets cold?"

"We just thought you should know," Arden says icily as she pushes herself to her feet. "He might try it again."

"I'll send word." She straightens in her seat, then picks up her fork to resume eating. She's interrupted, yet again, however, as four guards come rushing into the Great Hall.

"Your Greatness, the watchtower has spotted ships heading in our direction. An entire fleet of them."

One of the smaller guards, about Delwynn's height, steps forward and hands her a piece of parchment. "The crest on the flags resembles this."

Cerylia doesn't have to look twice to know that the crest belongs to the Crostan Islands. They may have seethed in silence for years after the Tymonds took the throne, but their stance has always been clear. So why are they coming to Sardoria? And why now?

The parchment crinkles in her hands as they involuntarily tighten into fists. Darius, with no numbers, no army, no leg to even stand on, somehow got to them. Or Xerin did. They must have been promised something otherworldly in return for their cooperation. Something to make them forget the past and the hardships they've endured. It's enough to make her blood boil.

"We don't have much time," she says, using her rage as fuel. She hands the wrinkled parchment back to the guard, then scans the table, formulating a plan as she goes. She can send Avery and Estelle to their respective hometowns of Chialka and Miraenia to rally whatever troops remain. Haskell can transport them, stopping in Declorath on their way back. Arden can accompany the Rescinder to Orihia to get the Veil reinstated, as they'd originally planned. Braxton will undoubtedly want to stay behind knowing his father is on that ship, which means Lane will also want to stay. As for Rydan, with what he's just discovered about his family, he'll be out for Darius's blood, too.

"Caldari," she says as she stands and drops her napkin across her untouched plate. "I require your assistance in the war room."

They look to one another but don't ask questions as they rise from their seats and make haste toward the doors.

Cerylia's about to follow them when one of the guards takes her gently by the arm. "There's something else, Your Greatness." The look in his eyes says it all.

"Dragons," she finishes for him. "They've summoned dragons to their fleet."

BRAXTON HORNSBY

THE DECISION TO leave the staff with him had come easy. Of everyone in Sardoria, Darius will have the hardest time taking his own son's life—his only heir to the throne. Not that Braxton would ever take it. Once the Tymond's midnight reign is over, it's *over*, seeing as it'd never been theirs to begin with.

Braxton leans forward as he tries to fasten the staff to his back, failing miserably with each attempt. The scurrying in the halls isn't helping his patience—if anything, it's only increasing his anxiety that he isn't moving fast enough.

Another pair of footsteps rushes by his partially cracked door, stops, then backtracks. A jet-black head of hair appears in the doorway, golden-flecked eyes assessing the situation at hand. "Need some help?" Rydan asks.

Braxton grunts, tossing him the useless contraption he'd made from various leather straps. "I just don't want to have to carry the damn thing."

"I hear that, loud and clear." Rydan grins as he removes his cloak and turns, showcasing the crescent fire strapped to his back. "Great minds think alike."

"Seems yours is greater than mine," he retorts. "No matter which way I fasten it, it hits the ground."

"Because it needs to be diagonal," Rydan says, his hands deftly working the leather. "If we just cross this strap right here . . ."

In the amount of time it'd taken Braxton to get just half of the sling functional, Rydan's managed to fully fashion one—and with less material. "It'll be lighter this way."

Braxton appreciates his modesty as he turns and extends his arms behind him, wriggling on the straps. The fit is near perfect, better than his many futile attempts, and he turns sheepishly to thank the ex-Cruex.

"Ah, can't forget the final touch," Rydan says, grabbing the staff from where it's leaning against the armoire. "This damn thing will be the death of us."

"Not if I have anything to do with it," Braxton says as he tests his mobility. "My father will have to pry that staff from my cold, dead hands."

"Well, in this case, your cold, dead back." Rydan gives the staff a sharp tug. "It's not going anywhere, though."

Braxton nods in appreciation, then turns to the open drawer containing blades and daggers of various sizes. He begins sheathing them as he'd been taught during his minimal time in the Cruex, wondering if Lane is already out there with the rest of them.

Rydan retreats toward the door, pulling his cloak on as he goes. "I'll see you out there."

"Hey, Helstrom," Braxton calls out before he leaves, "do not let that crest leave your person for any reason."

"I expect the same of you with that staff."

Braxton nods. "Cold, dead back?"

Rydan gives an affirming grin as he echoes, "Cold, dead back."

ARDEN ELIRI

SADLY, ORIHIA IS less spectacular than I recall. The vibrant colors are dull and muted; the animals are quiet and in hiding; and the overall atmosphere has an air of desertion to it. Perhaps abandonment is a more appropriate term. Whatever the case, it's less than welcoming.

"What a shithole," Nevaeh says, startling me from my thoughts as she walks up from behind me. "It's been some time since I've been here, but damn, I don't remember it looking this bad."

"It wasn't always like this," I say, surprised at how quickly I'm jumping to its defense. "It was actually quite astounding before . . ."

"Before those idiots took down the grid," she finishes, her strides short and hurried. "We'll get it back up in no time, don't you worry."

The sentiment does little to console me, seeing as I wasn't worried before, but now I'm wondering if I should be.

"If memory serves, what we're looking for is a waterfall, correct?"

I reply in the affirmative, keeping a close eye on the Rescinder as she continues to lead us down the trail, as if she's walked this very path hundreds of times before. I want to take advantage of this small stretch of time to learn more about her, but question-wise, I'm coming up short.

"Has Sardoria always been the place you call home?"

The question throws me, causing me to fumble my answer. "I don't live there full-time. At least, I didn't before. I grew up in Trendalath—against my will," I add quickly. "But yeah, I guess you can say Sardoria is my home now."

"It's beautiful up there, though I'm not one for the cold," she says, veering left at the fork in the road.

"What about you? Can the same be said for Miraenia?"

"Born and raised, happily occupying my little corner of Aeridon." She turns over her shoulder with a smile on her face, as if to emphasize her point. "Well, unless you take Midvale into account, but they weren't too keen on having my kind around."

The shift in her tone is subtle, but noticeable. "You were a student at Midvale?"

She nods, stepping over a fallen tree trunk. "Let's just say they didn't take too kindly to me or my abilities. When your only purpose is to retract the effects of illusié, it kind of defeats the purpose of *being* illusié."

Her answer makes me wonder if my aunt feels the same way, what with being an Extractor and all. I'd never considered the other side of the coin until now. I also can't help but wonder that if she'd been there the night of the attack, perhaps she could have removed the Caster's illusion in time for me to see the truth.

"If you ask me, that's Midvale's loss. I could have used someone like you by my side countless times," I tell her, meaning every word. "In a surprising way, your ability gives second chances. There aren't many that do."

"Doesn't yours? As a Healer?"

Not when it morphs into something else is how I should answer, but instead I just say, "I suppose so."

We continue along the trail in silence, the soles of our boots crunching across the frost-tipped grass. Something I've said seems to stick with the Rescinder because the next question out of her mouth is, "You're big on second chances, I take it?"

At first, I don't know how to respond. Having been raised in the Cruex as an assassin, second chances were few and far between. It just wasn't in the code. But ever since finding the Caldari and my brother, my aunt, my cousin, my father . . . it seems my life is the posterchild for second chances.

"I guess I am," I reply. "I find solace knowing that if things don't work out the first time around, there's always another opportunity waiting in the wings, even if it looks vastly different from the first."

Nevaeh turns her head and smiles. "Certainly keeps life interesting."

"I'll say." We reach the part of the cliff that'll take us to Midvale, the waterfall rushing into the spring below. I'm in the middle of reliving the memory of jumping off the edge with Rydan when the most unexpected question leaves the Rescinder's mouth.

"If you could have a second chance, what would you use it on?"

I don't even have to think about it. *Felix.* My throat constricts as I try to form an adequate answer—one that won't reveal too much about my past and what I've done.

"I hurt the person I love," I say quietly. "So, I suppose I'd want a second chance at that. At us."

Nevaeh's gaze tracks to the waterfall. "Love will do that."

Before I can respond, she takes off in a sprint and disappears over the cliff's edge. I grip my pocket watch and dive in after her.

❧ ❧ ❧

"Tell me about him."

I follow closely behind Nevaeh as we walk along the desecrated bridge, trying to keep the images of fallen bodies from flashing across my mind—which is difficult to do with what she's now asking of me.

"Him who?" I ask, side-stepping some debris, even though I know full well to whom she's referring.

"The lover you want a second chance with."

She says it as if it's completely feasible and in the realm of possibility—and I suppose, in her line of work, it is.

"Well," I say, not knowing where to start, "we most definitely didn't start off on the best foot. Quite the opposite in fact."

"Is that so?" Nevaeh pushes on the half of the door that's still intact, ducking underneath crooked beams and fallen pillars as she makes her way inside what used to be a fortress. "You weren't kidding when you said you all did a number on this place."

"Well, since we were attacked rather unexpectedly, we weren't given much of a choice." I don't know why I sound so defensive, but the harshness in her tone rubs me the wrong way.

"Let's just hope we can get where we need to go." She pushes past torn drapes hanging haphazardly from nearly disassembled rods. Nothing is where it was before. Nothing is where it should be. The order and structure to Midvale is no more.

"Please, continue. You were saying that your lover was once your enemy?"

"I wouldn't go that far, but we certainly weren't fond of each other in the beginning."

Nevaeh points to a stairwell for direction. I nod.

"But he always kept a close eye on me, was always there. Even when I wasn't looking or paying attention, there he was."

Nevaeh lets out a small laugh. "Sounds to me like he knew exactly what he wanted right from the beginning."

I shake my head adamantly even though she can't see me. "No, he made it pretty clear that I'm someone he wouldn't tangle with, believe me."

Nevaeh turns over her shoulder, throwing me a sly smile as she says, "Being protective automatically implies that he cares, no matter what he chooses to say or keep to himself."

She's got a point. If there's one thing Felix had always been, it's protective. Sometimes annoyingly so. But, just like him, that protectiveness had grown on me. Now that I don't have it, I miss it.

And him.

"What happened to him?"

A knot forms in my throat at the question, at the simplicity of it, when the answer is so complex. "I . . . killed him."

To my surprise, Nevaeh chuckles. "By accident, I assume."

"Yes, of course by accident. I'm not a monster."

She shrugs. "Your words, not mine."

Before I can let myself ruminate any longer, I say, "I thought I was killing someone else. King Tymond, to be exact."

"How'd you manage that? Getting them confused and all?" She makes a ghastly noise. "Don't tell me they look alike."

"Not in the slightest," I say, grimacing. "It was the Savant's Caster. He made me see Darius when it really wasn't." My voice cracks. "I never would have brought my blade down had I known—"

"I'm going to stop you right there. Given the situation, I would have done the same thing, Arden."

Finally, a response of solidarity.

"And this happened in Midvale?" she asks.

"In one of these very halls."

She goes silent for a moment. "What happened to his body?"

"It was never retrieved. After the queen used a soul gem—"

"A soul gem?" she repeats. "Damn, you really should have led with that." Nevaeh hops over a collapsed column, then turns to help me jump over it, but I don't take her hand. I launch myself in the air, expertly landing on two stable feet. "Impressive," she murmurs.

"We don't have the soul gem, though," I continue glumly. "It was taken."

"What does that matter?"

I counter with my own question. "Why are you speaking as if he's still here? As if I haven't lost someone?"

"As long as the soul remains in the gem, there's hope."

That's certainly news to me. "Okay, but there's no telling what's been done with it." My hands ball into fists at the thought, at what Xerin could have planned for the Amplifier. If he so much as lays a finger on Felix . . .

"That would require an Extractor—an incredibly skilled one at that. To my knowledge, there's only one of such caliber that exists in all of Aeridon."

"Queen Jareth," I affirm, wondering why she's telling me what I already know.

Nevaeh stops suddenly, nearly causing me to run into her. "This must be it." She pulls two plum-colored leather gloves from her pockets and puts them on, then walks around the grid, pausing every so often to move one crystal after another back into its original position. I stand idly by, quietly watching as she works, until the entire grid is back in formation.

"Rule number one," she says as she walks back to where I'm standing. "Never touch anything that's been cursed with your bare hands." She raises her gloved hands for emphasis. "Unless you want to die an unnecessarily brutal death."

"I'll pass," I say, pulling my own gloves from my pockets. "Though I didn't plan on touching anything while we're here."

"Smart girl," Nevaeh commends. "Rule number two. I require absolute silence while I work so I can determine exactly which curse was used." From her pockets, she produces an instrument I've never seen before. It's dome-shaped and appears to be crafted with its own crystalline structure, but what's most surprising is how it works.

She approaches the crystal nearest us, then whispers something in a language I don't recognize. The instrument floats out of her hand and down to the crystal in question until it's hovering just above it. Areas of the dome begin to illuminate in all sorts of colors with red being the most prominent.

Nevaeh grunts in frustration. "I should have guessed."

"What?" I ask, feeling completely in the dark. "Is it reversible?"

"It is. But with the amplification that was used to curse them to begin with, this could take a significant amount of time and energy to reverse."

The mention of Felix's ability feels like a punch to the gut, but I manage to ask, "I hadn't accounted for that. How can we speed things up?"

Nevaeh chews on her lower lip, the first sign of nerves I've seen from her since we've met. "We'd have to do what they did, but in reverse."

I instantly catch her meaning. "With an Amplifier?"

She nods. "I don't suppose you know of one?"

"If you count one being trapped in a soul gem, then yes," I joke.

She levels an intense stare at me. "Your lover was an Amplifier?"

"That's right."

"And you're an Eliri . . . which means you're a—"

"Healer turned Channeler," I finish. "Although not a very experienced one."

Nevaeh claps her hands together in what can only be described as childish glee. "Have you ever channeled his amplification abilities before?"

"Yes," I answer slowly, wondering what she's getting at.

"Then it looks like we have everything we need."

I angle my head in confusion. "How so?"

"I'm going to remove the curse while you, in turn, amplify said removal by channeling your lover's abilities from the soul gem."

I stare at her, eyes wide. "I can *do* that?"

"It's just like I said," Nevaeh says as she kneels by the first crystal, motioning for me to join her, "as long as the soul remains in the gem, there's hope. Subsequently, if this is where it happened, then his presence still lingers."

I feel frozen in place, unable to respond.

"You need to *feel* it. *Use* it," Nevaeh continues, as if those aren't the most abstract instructions she's ever given.

"I'll try," I say somewhat reluctantly as I close my eyes, searching for that tether that binds us, the otherworldly connection I haven't felt since the day I'd ended his life.

Felix . . . Felix . . .

I wait. As expected, only silence and darkness greet me, an infinite void that threatens to swallow me whole. I push past my doubts and continue to search.

Felix . . . Felix . . .

More emptiness.

More darkness.

Deafening silence.

Still, I search.

Felix . . .

I wait.

And wait,

And then I sense it. A pulse. It's faint, but it's there.

I need you.

A flicker.

Please.

A glimmer.

And then, by some miracle, I can *hear* him.

I promised I wouldn't amplify, a voice—*his* voice—says.

It's really you? I choke on a sob. *Felix, I'm so, so sorry.*

We're not here to rehash the past. There's a lightness to his tone. *Do I have your permission to amplify?*

Yes. I suck in a breath, wishing we could talk longer, but like he said, that's not why we're in contact. If I had known I even *could* communicate with him, I would have reached out weeks ago.

An invisible wave with the might of a thousand oceans suddenly washes over me. It all comes rushing in.

Do your worst, Eliri.

I smile, despite the weight in my chest and tear-streaked cheeks. I let the amplification build and build and build—and when I finally open my eyes, a roar rips through me as I direct every ounce of energy I have to give at the crystalline grid.

I can sense Nevaeh working next to me as she retracts the cursed crystals, one by one. I track her movements, directing the channeled energy exactly where it needs to go. We work fast, faster than I ever have before.

"Last one!" she shouts, her eyes glowing with pride.

I wait for her to finish, then direct the final flow of amplification at the crystal she's just backed away from. The ground beneath us hums as the crystals begin to glow, the ley lines that connect them illuminating from underneath the grid. The energy around me might be thrumming, but the energy within me is diminishing, depleting with each passing second. My heart sinks.

You're leaving.

A wink in the growing darkness. *I'm never really gone.*

I blink back a tear. *It sure feels like you are.*

Another glimmer, this one fainter. *We'll meet again, and sooner than you might think.*

"Promise me," I say aloud without realizing it.

There's a light squeeze on my forearm. "Let him go," Nevaeh says. "He needs to recharge. As do you."

Now that she mentions it, I do feel rather dizzy.

"Come now, the kitchens are likely still stocked—"

I shake my head, taking the hand she offers as I stumble to my feet. "No time. I need to see what's in this speculor."

"Let's hope the Archmage's cheval glass is still intact."

"You've used one before?"

Nevaeh looks at me incredulously. "All your time here and you weren't trained in the art of cheval?"

"I know *of* the cheval glass, but as far as how to use it? You may as well be speaking a foreign language," I admit, clutching onto the railing of the staircase for support as we climb back to the main floor.

"When Cerylia, Midvale's only Extractor, left, combined with the location of the springs being *outside* of the Veil, the Archmage needed a way to view speculors on her own terms, so she had a cheval glass constructed," Nevaeh explains, even though I hadn't asked. "I'm shocked it wasn't a part of your training regimen as a student here."

"Perhaps I wasn't here long enough," I muse. "I'd like to think that, given the chance, the Archmage would have shared in the knowledge."

"Hard to say. Cyfrin was more guarded than she let on," Nevaeh says, her pace slowing. "Now, let's see if this works." With the grid powered back on, she's easily able to conjure a portal, which both my weakened body and mind are thankful for. From the lobby, we enter the shimmering gateway that'll take us to the floor the Archmage's office is located. I try to suppress the memory of fallen bodies, of both friend and foe, as we enter the room. Nevaeh leads me to the very back, all the way behind the desk, to an alcove I faintly remember from my first visit with Cyfrin.

There isn't enough room for both of us to fit in the cramped space, so I wait patiently by the late Archmage's desk as the Rescinder wheels out what looks to be a very ordinary mirror with one minor distinction: part of it seems to be missing.

"See that hole in the top of the frame?" she asks, pointing it out.

"It's hard to miss," I answer. "It almost makes the piece look unfinished."

"In a lot of ways, it is. A cheval glass is only complete when it's revealing what cannot be revealed otherwise." She eyes the pockets of my cloak. "Do you have the speculor?"

I nod, reaching for one of my interior pockets. "It's right here."

Nevaeh nods in approval as I bring the speculor into her line of sight. "I'll let you do the honors."

"I just . . . pop it in?"

"No force necessary. The cheval glass will do all of the work."

And it does. The minute I raise up on my tiptoes and bring the speculor near the metallic frame, it seems to draw it in, like a magnet. I release my already loose grip on the speculor, watching as it clicks into place, the glass on the mirror fogging before growing crystal clear. Nothing—and I mean *nothing*—could have possibly prepared me for what I'm about to see.

I watch in both horror and shock as the memory Aldreda so desperately tried to conceal is revealed right before my very eyes. I take a step back, bringing my hands to my mouth as it leaves me completely and utterly speechless.

RYDAN HELSTROM

RYDAN PUSHES PAST the Queen's Guard with only one thing in mind: vengeance. The courtyard is full of guards and mages from Midvale, huddling amongst themselves to fight against the biting cold. Rydan takes the liberty of igniting some nearby pyres, to which the groups scurry to, nodding in appreciation.

A crisp, unforgiving wind nips at the back of his neck. It's the only area of his body that isn't covered by clothing, save for his face. It'd be wise to wear a helmet, but the last thing he wants is his view obstructed as he takes the life of the man who'd forced him to do the unthinkable.

Assassinate his own blood.

A fury lit within, Rydan storms out of the courtyard to the clearing that leads to the Sardorian shoreline. Just as the guards had declared, there is indeed a fleet of ships sailing directly for the coast. He continues to cross the snow-blanketed field, kicking up fresh powder with each step taken. When he finally reaches the banks, he takes a stance reminiscent of his Cruex days: knees locked, legs shoulder-width apart, hands clasped behind his back. He digs his boots even further into the snow, determined to stay put until the ships approach land. It's the only way he can ensure that he'll get to Darius before anyone else does.

Another wintery blast slams into the side of his face, the waves crashing into the rocks with so much force, he swears the ground beneath him quakes. Even so, he holds his ground. The sound is near deafening between the howling of the wind and thrashing of the waves, but, even still, he can sense that he's not alone. A brief glance over his shoulder is the only confirmation he needs.

Braxton flanks him on his right, his white-blonde head of hair nearly identical to the surrounding landscape. Lane is hot on his heels, her long ebony braid whipping in the wind, and behind her, two dozen or so guards follow. To his left are some of the Midvale mages he'd lit a fire for in the courtyard. Donning navy-blue robes with gold stitching, he instantly recognizes their purpose: Shielders.

Good. They'll need a lot of them by the looks of things.

Rydan turns back toward the sea, toward the fleet that's drawing closer and closer. A shift in the clouds above draws his attention as they fade into the shape of giant spike-tipped wings. Dragons, a whole host of them, soar through the air, circling over the ships below.

It'd been foolish to hope that the guards were mistaken about the dragons. They were right on target. Rydan steadies himself as another blast of wind, this time coming from above, threatens to knock him from his feet. All things considered, the mages are the ones who'll need to take on the dragons if they hope to come out of this alive. It seems they know it, too. In the background, he can hear the Shielders calling for their Elemental counterparts. It's a clever maneuver, to say the least. Using the forces of Mother Nature Herself is the quickest and surest way to take down one of Her most enduring creations.

Rydan continues to scan the skies, sucking in a sharp breath when he spots one particular dragon with a distinguishing feature: blood-red eyes. There's no mistaking who it is. He watches as Xerin breaks away from the group, soaring sideways as if to boast a victory he hasn't yet won.

Or perhaps he's drawing attention to something else . . .

Rydan narrows his eyes, his heart nearly stopping, as a petite, blonde figure comes into view atop the dragon's back.

Vira.

His breath hitches as he follows the flight path of the dragons, who all, coincidentally, seem to be following her.

Because *she* summoned them.

Disappointment throttles him to the core. First Xerin, now Vira. Siding with the enemy. If only Vira knew what the king had forced upon him, what he'd been ordered to do . . .

She of all people should understand. Tymond had kept her, against her will, as a servant in Trendalath. It's how they'd met. At the time, she'd been meek and fragile and distressed.

Unless that's exactly what she'd wanted him to see.

No. He tightens his grip on the hilt of his sword. He refuses to believe that Vira would turn on them like this, after everything they've been through. It's preposterous and entirely out of character.

So why the dragons?

Unless her life had been threatened . . . but Xerin's her brother, her blood. He wouldn't possibly consider such a thing. Would he? Perhaps Rydan's underestimated just how far the Shaper will go to get what he wants—and what he wants, Rydan currently has in his possession.

The crescent fire.

"If it's a trade you want, it's a trade you'll get," Rydan murmurs, hoping that for the first time in a long time he's wrong; but something tells him an unfair trade with unbearably high stakes is exactly what the Shaper has in store.

XERIN GREY

FROM HIS VANTAGE point, which is quite clear being in the skies, the Sardorian defense appears bleak at best. They're outnumbered and outmatched—two things that will certainly work in their fleet's favor.

Vira had summoned more dragons than expected. He hadn't realized her training at Midvale would yield such promising results. With dragons at their command, Sardoria may as well just surrender now.

Mages line the outer perimeter of the castle, as do some of the Caldari. Rydan stands at the front, his expression contorted into a scowl. Even at a distance, Xerin can see the fury blazing in his eyes, but it isn't directed at him or the familiar rider strapped unwillingly to his back.

It's focused on the head ship where Darius stands at the helm. Which brings him to one logical conclusion: the Ignitor's finally learned about his relation to the Soames bloodline. An assassination he'd been there for, shaped as a young boy—Rydan's cousin, rather—to ensure it was actually carried out. And it had been—although his partner had almost seen to it that it wasn't.

Arden's been a real pain in his ass.

Speaking of Arden . . .

Xerin scans the sparse battlefield, his gaze traveling over Lane, Braxton, the mages, and more than a dozen guards, but her absence sticks out like a sore thumb. She's missing. Oddly enough, so is her brother.

It doesn't come as a surprise that Cerylia's calling in reinforcements—which should be rather easy given the fact that all of Aeridon despises Trendalath. The provinces rallying together is something he should have expected, but didn't count on.

Xerin banks left, his flight path interrupted as a sudden sensation creeps along his spine. The trickling of energy, the hum of power, the overflow of a thousand tiny connections all roaring to life. Suddenly, Arden's precise location couldn't be any clearer. He should have known the grid wouldn't stay dormant for long.

The Veil has its power back.

CERYLIA JARETH

CERYLIA RUSHES TO the infirmary, guilt eating at her with each empty corridor she passes. She should be out there with the rest of them, leading them, but not before checking on her brother-in-law. With Arden in Orihia and the unexpected news of dragons joining the enemy's fleet, she's going to need all the help she can get.

"Give me his status and make it a good one," Cerylia says to Edith as she weaves through the line of beds.

"It was never guaranteed," the Healer replies, "though he did exhibit tremendous promise."

"What's changed between now and then?" She glances at Stanton who looks no worse or better than every other day she's visited. "Where did this *tremendous promise* go?"

"Everyone reacts differently to the salves," Edith explains. "At first, the patient exhibited rapid signs of improvement, but it slowly began to taper off—"

"His name is Stanton," Cerylia interrupts through clenched teeth. "Do not speak of him or to me as if we are complete strangers. You act as though you've completely removed yourself of any hope there once was for him to make a full recovery."

Edith falls silent. Sometimes no response is the loudest one of all.

"So, we leave him to die, is that it?"

"Of course not," the Healer snaps. "We can arrange for a carriage, send him to a neighboring town—"

"Everyone is coming *here*," Cerylia emphasizes. "To fight. As allies. There's nowhere for him to go."

"We'll lock the doors."

Cerylia throws her hands up. "It won't be enough."

"Then fortify the damn doors."

Cerylia gapes at her tone but, oddly enough, respects the hell out of her for it.

"If he's that important, then see to it that no one even makes it to this floor."

"I can't make any guarantees," Cerylia says, echoing her words back to her, "but I'll reposition some of the mages and the guards as an extra precaution." She turns to leave when the Healer stops her.

"We must come out of this victorious. The survival of Aeridon, of illusié as we know it, depends on it."

"Then let's hope our allies arrive in time." She heads for the exit in a swift stride, only stopping to say, "Lock this door and do not open it for a single soul."

"Understood."

"Not. A. Soul." Cerylia repeats.

Edith gives a firm nod.

Hardly satisfied, Cerylia closes the door behind her and bolts it shut before heading to the one place she should have paid a visit to after word of the impending attack: the armory.

DARIUS TYMOND

IT DOESN'T COME as a surprise that Sardoria's forces are armed and waiting, but what *is* shocking is just how minimal their presence is. With his fleet alone, he has four times the manpower—add dragons into the mix and Queen Jareth would be wise to surrender now.

Then again, perhaps he's spoken too soon.

One of the ships signals to the coastline, drawing attention to the occupied streets that lead into Sardoria. Visible from the sea are hundreds of flags emblazoned with the crests of Miraenia, Declorath, and Chialka. Considering the size of each of the towns, even combined, their numbers are nowhere near what he has. Still, the provinces *do* have one thing going for them: their hatred of Trendalath and, subsequently, its king. That kind of common ground could be enough to change the tide.

Darius marches over to where Alyna is currently steering the ship. "We need to move faster."

She gives him a dubious look before saying, "I thought it was perfectly clear that we're already going as fast as we can."

"There must be something we can do—adjust the sails, shift direction—"

"I assure you, this is the quickest route. Considering the weather, we're making good time."

Darius looks to the shore, at the roads brimming with townspeople, all armed to the teeth and ready to fight. With such dismal numbers, he shouldn't be concerned . . . but when *he's* the main target, it changes things. He'll be dead before he even steps foot on land.

"Two things need to happen," he says, scanning the vessel for Clive and motioning for him to hurry over. "We need the dragons to attack the roads leading into Sardoria to deplete their numbers."

"Let me guess," Clive starts, joining them at the helm, "you want me to cast an illusion so elaborate that Sardoria will have no choice but to question the position of our fleet."

"Yes. Preferably at the same time."

Clive sighs. "I suppose I've got the second part covered, so I'll leave it in your very capable hands to direct the beasts where they need to go."

Darius nods, looking to the sky, wondering how he's possibly going to get Xerin's attention when he's met with a disturbing sight—or lack thereof. The dragons seem to have disappeared altogether. He tries to quell the rising panic as he focuses on the dense cloud cover, searching far and wide for flapping wings, the flash of a tail or talons, but the skies are empty.

All he has to do, however, is look ahead as the dragons race toward the roads filled with people, one red-eyed beast leading the charge. It seems, as per usual, that Xerin is one step ahead.

BRAXTON HORNSBY

BRAXTON WATCHES IN horror as the dragons change course away from Sardoria, away from the castle, toward the innocent people coming to their aid. It would be a swift death being charred by dragonfire, but unjust in every sense of the word.

He looks at his hands, feeling helpless and useless at his inability to deviate. If he were still illusié, he could deviate the attacks—he could turn the fire right back around on the beasts. Seeing as there's only one of him and twelve dragons, it wouldn't be enough, but at least he'd be able to contribute in some way. Instead, he's equipped with a sword and two daggers. *A lot of good those will do him.* He's considering his next move when it suddenly occurs to him he'd left something behind in his room.

A crossbow.

That's it.

Feeling a rush of adrenaline, he darts back toward the castle, arms pumping at his sides. If he can get to the armory and equip every guard with a crossbow, they might just have a chance.

Lane seems to notice his abrupt departure because within moments, she's jogging next to him, eyes blazing with curiosity. "Are you headed where I think you're headed?"

"If it's the armory you're referring to, then yes, you're right on target." He banks left, nearly colliding into one of the servants. "We need crossbows."

"And selphinium. It's the only known poison to take a dragon down within seconds."

Selphinium. Where had he heard that word before?

Braxton lifts a brow. "You weren't kidding when you said you knew everything there is to know about the animals that inhabit Aeridon."

"It comes with the territory, I suppose. Reading their minds and all."

"And they willingly gave up this information?"

She falls silent for a moment, hesitation lining her eyes before admitting, "Not exactly. I may or may not have been eavesdropping during one of my excursions to Drakken Isle."

He doesn't know why, but the news comes as a surprise to him. "When did you go to Drakken Isle? And why?"

"Your father sent me on a couple Cruex missions, no doubt looking for the very thing you happened to find in the Void."

"The crescent fire."

Lane nods. "Exactly."

When they reach the doors to the armory, which happen to be wide open, they're dismayed to find that the majority of the weapons, including the crossbows, are so picked over that only a few remain: two longswords and a single crossbow.

"Seems someone had a similar idea," Lane comments, reaching for the bow. She hands it to Braxton, but he shakes his head, shoving it back in her direction.

"You take it. I have one in my room."

Lane doesn't argue as she secures the bow across her back and follows him out of the armory, quickening her stride to match his as they climb the staircase. They're about to pass by Avery's room when a memory resurfaces. He'd heard of selphinium because Hanslow had mentioned it before his departure from Sardoria; that it was being brewed by none other than their very own herbal alchemist right here in the castle.

Braxton stops in his tracks. "How much do you want to bet Avery's got a stash of unlawful tonics hidden in his room?"

Lane grins. "I'd take that bet any day."

As expected, the door is locked, but between Lane's metal hair pin and Braxton's substantial experience picking locks in Athia, the door opens with ease.

Plumes of white smoke over the apothecary station indicate that it'd only been in use mere hours ago, likely moments before Avery had been assigned to leave with Haskell and Estelle. Lane opens one of the cabinets, rifling through its contents. The bottles clink together as she checks each label.

Braxton follows her lead, opening another one of the cabinets, but quickly realizes he has no idea what he should be looking for. "How will I know when I find it?"

"Oh, you'll know," Lane says, popping a cork from one of the bottles and taking a whiff. "It'll smell like burnt hair, but worse."

Braxton nearly gags at the thought of the overly distinguished smell. "Worse? How can it possibly be worse?"

"Like I said," Lane says, replacing the bottle and picking up a new one, "You'll know when you smell it."

Braxton grimaces, suddenly wishing he'd had the foresight to have an empty stomach, but just as he's about to uncork one of the bottles, a label in the back catches his eye. He sets the other bottle down, reaching for it with both hands. It's larger and rounder than the others, and the topper isn't made of cork but of metal. Braxton can't help but smile at the scrawled writing on the label.

"What are you grinning about over there?"

Braxton turns the bottle toward her so she can see.

DO NOT INGEST—DRAGONSBANE.

Lane rolls her eyes. "How original." She takes the bottle from him, studying the metal stopper. "Selphinium is so potent, it would eat through cork within seconds. But, just to be sure . . ." She lifts the stopper ever so slightly, makes a face, then immediately closes it. "Yep, there's no doubt about it," she says, coughing as she hands it back to him. "That's selphinium."

Braxton grins, but it quickly fades as another problem presents itself. "There's only one bottle," he says as he digs around in the back of the cabinet. "How can we possibly distribute this one bottle to all of the guards' arrows?"

"You're absolutely sure it's the only one?"

Again, Braxton checks the remaining bottles. "Yes."

Lane flings open a few of the other cabinet doors, rifling through them just as she'd done before. "Nothing here." Her shoulders slump. "Well, shit."

"Think," Braxton says, more to himself than to her.

"I am," Lane retorts as she slams the doors to the cabinet shut. "Braxton, my cousin is on those roads. So is yours. And so is our only hope of getting more of this stuff made."

She's right. Braxton searches the room, hoping an idea will strike, when his eyes land on the window.

"How good is your aim?"

Lane raises a brow. "Decent."

"From a distance?"

She shrugs. "Better than most."

That settles it.

"Take this." He hands her the bottle of selphinium as he rushes past her and out the door toward his room. "I'll meet you at the watchtower!"

"Braxton!" she shouts after him. "Where are you going?"

"Get to the watchtower!" he shouts back. "Now!"

He doesn't wait for her response as he rounds the corner that leads to his room.

ARDEN ELIRI

I CAN'T GET back to Sardoria quickly enough. Everyone in that castle is in even more danger than I'd realized and I'm the only one who knows. Lords, the weight of that is crushing.

Nevaeh had stood alongside me, watching in confusion as the memory unfolded in the cheval glass. I'd been just as confused, but for different reasons. She'd recognized the man in the memory—honestly, anyone would—but trying to explain the complexity of what we'd witnessed is something I just don't have the capacity for. Especially when I'm still trying to sort through exactly what it all means myself.

Our return to the mainland is anything but swift. Seeing as the Crostan Islands' fleet had taken the direct channel to the Sardorian coast, we're forced to go the roundabout way, which includes sailing *past* the Crostan Islands to return to the docks. Much to my surprise, Nevaeh's kindly offered to come back to Sardoria with me. I'd initially suggested we part ways upon returning to Miraenia—until we arrived there, to a literal ghost town. Well, almost. If I had to guess, it hasn't been long since it'd been vacated, given the few stragglers clunking around in their makeshift armor toward the winding path that leads to Sardoria.

"Seems Cerylia's finally called in her favor," Nevaeh says, mouth quirking to the side. "It's about time she used it. She's done so much for the people of Aeridon."

Pride swells in my chest at the remark. "Is your home nearby?" I ask.

She points down a tree-lined road, one that looks awfully familiar, although I can't quite place it. "It's at the end of the footpath. Speaking of," she says as she brushes past me, "I need to grab a few things before we head north. Feel free to tag along."

I wave a hand in the air. "I'll wait for you here."

"Suit yourself," she says with a shrug before waltzing down the street.

I wait until she disappears from view before examining the road further. *Have I been here before?* Curiosity gets the better of me as I follow in Nevaeh's footsteps, looking side to side and up and down for anything recognizable. It's only as

I'm nearing the end that I see it. A weathered two-story dwelling with navy shutters. An oversized bronze knocker in the shape of a lion's head on an emerald green door.

The Langley residence.

My breath hitches as the events of Rydan's fourth Cruex mission come rushing in. The same mission I'd followed him on, unbeknownst to him. The same mission that had resulted in his unsightly scar. Who knows if that had been another unjustified assignment, just like the one Radelle and Erle Soames had faced, at our hands?

I carefully approach the door, lifting my hand to the knocker but before I can even make contact with it, the door creaks open. I clear my throat, gently pushing it the rest of the way open. "Hello?" I call out. "Is anyone home?"

How could anyone be home when you're the one who killed them? my mind retorts. Perhaps Graham Langley had kids. Siblings. A wife . . .

The residence isn't much—it's quaint with its one washroom, a bedroom upstairs, a bedroom downstairs, and a kitchen. Although there isn't a sitting area in the home, there *is* an entryway. I take my time walking across the uneven floors, my gaze landing on some framed portraits decorating the walls. From the looks of it, the Langley family was rather small. The guilt sitting heavy in my chest eases a bit, until I see a ceremonial portrait of Graham and a woman that must have been his wife. It seems they'd wed young because I hardly recognize the man in the rendering. The woman, however, looks oddly familiar. Had she been there the day of the mission? I furrow my brows. I don't remember another female being present other than myself.

I stare at the woman's face. Whatever happened to her?

Within the glass, I can't help but notice the piece of parchment that's curled up at the bottom right edge of the portrait. I don't think twice before gingerly removing the frame from the hook on the wall, then detach the back siding and slip the piece of parchment out. As I'd suspected, it's a marriage record from the province of Miraenia. Graham Langley's name is written first. As for who he'd wed . . . my eyes drift farther down the document, my heart pounding as I come across the other name.

Edith Caldwell.

It can't be.

The paper flutters to the ground as both hands fly to my mouth. The Healer in Sardoria . . . she hadn't spoken her last name when we'd first met. She'd only introduced herself as Edith. Perhaps that had been for a reason, one I never even considered because there wasn't a need to.

I study the wedding portrait with fervor, trying to match the features of this younger woman to the one in Sardoria, but the effort is futile since I've only seen Edith a handful of times. However, there *was* one thing that had stood out about her: the gold pendant she'd worn around her neck with its intricately woven strands.

A wedding gift. From my husband, she'd said.

It has to be the same woman. It just has to. What are the chances a Healer from Miraenia would end up working in the infirmary in Sardoria at the same time my incapacitated father arrived in desperate need of help? Who *also* just so happens to be the father of the assassin who'd murdered her husband?

While the mission had been assigned to Rydan, I'd ultimately been the one to do the king's bidding. I'd been the one to take Graham Langley's life. And if Edith, his *wife*, had somehow figured that out, what better way to exact her revenge than to kill someone I love?

I inhale a sharp breath as I roll both the portrait and the marriage record into a scroll and stick them in the waistband of my trousers. I need to find Nevaeh and get back to Sardoria before it's too late.

⚘ ⚘ ⚘

The Rescinder and I find ourselves on horseback, racing through the wilderness—and against a ticking clock. The blizzard doesn't let up in the slightest as we venture deeper into the woods, making it difficult to tell just how much farther we have to travel. The distinct sound of a dragon roaring in the near distance, however, is an obvious sign that we're close . . . closer than I thought.

"What's the plan once we get there?" Nevaeh shouts from atop her black steed, her voice muffled by the dense snowfall.

"It depends on what's happening when we arrive—"

"Allow me to rephrase," she interrupts. "Who do we need to find?"

I steal a glance at her riding next to me, our horses perfectly in sync. I take a breath, the frigid wind burning my throat as I say, "Queen Jareth."

"What about your father?"

"He'll be next in line." Knowing what I now know about channeling abilities from soul gems, I've realized that I can wake my father from his comatose state, hopefully before Edith can do any more damage. Because, fuck, are we going to need him if what I saw in that cheval glass is true.

"How exactly are we going to manage this amidst a full-fledged battle?"

I shoot her a glaring look to let her know she isn't helping.

She puts a hand up, backing off. "I'm just saying, there's only one of you. I can help."

"I thought your help was implied," I retort, applying more pressure to the sides of my horse to get us moving even faster. I've only briefly thought it over. Since my presence is required to release my father of his current condition, that leaves sending Nevaeh, a complete stranger, to deliver news to my aunt that will absolutely devastate her. Not ideal.

Cerylia needs to know what we're up against, but, as much as I hate to admit it, without my father, we're destined for failure. I make my decision right then and there.

"As soon as we arrive, I need you to find Queen Jareth," I instruct Nevaeh. "Tell her that we were successful in reinstating the grid and that I've found a way to wake my father. I need her to meet me in the infirmary."

"Understood," Nevaeh affirms.

I turn my focus to the path ahead. It's growing harder to make out the more snow that falls. *Please let us make it in time. Please grant us the strength needed before it's too late.*

We'll make it in time. It isn't too late.

But I find the more I tell myself that, the less inclined I am to believe it.

RYDAN HELSTROM

THE DRAGONS CHANGE course. Where they were once headed straight for the castle, they're banking west toward . . . their reinforcements.

"Shit," Rydan mutters under his breath, glancing around frantically to see who's currently equipped with the proper gear. "Draw your bows!" He points to the sky. "Strike them down! All but the one with the rider!"

If Xerin goes down, Vira does, too.

It's a risk he isn't willing to take.

Less than half the guards on the lower battlement have bows strapped to their backs and, even though there are only twelve dragons, their chances of taking them down are dismal. Arrows alone won't be enough.

Rydan turns to the mages, hoping that there are at least a few skilled in long-range magick. Not that he knows what sort of illusié can even take down a dragon—and by the stunned looks on their faces, they don't either.

He looks over his shoulder in the other direction, noticing that two of his own are missing. He turns in a circle, scanning the field for both Braxton and Lane, but they're nowhere to be found.

Arrows fly haphazardly through the air. The effort is rushed and uncoordinated and it shows. Seeing no other choice, Rydan leaves his post and sprints over to where the guards are fumbling to load their next round of arrows.

"Lords above," he grunts, holding his hand up to tell the guards to wait. Surprisingly enough, they listen. "On my command," he orders.

The wind dies down, slowing the dragons' speed just enough to provide a window of opportunity that likely won't come again.

"Draw!" Rydan commands.

The guards nock their arrows.

"Aim!" He points to the sky.

The sound of bowstrings creak as they're pulled taut.

"Release!" he shouts.

The arrows sail toward the dragons in unison, hitting true. Four of the beasts falter in their flight path, turning back to tend to their wounds.

A cheer erupts from the guards as they ready their bows for the next attack. Rydan's preparing to give another set of commands when he notices that the four dragons they've just injured aren't retreating at all. In fact, they're heading back in his direction.

Straight toward the field.

Their intentions are made perfectly clear as they unhinge their jaws, roaring before blasting fire through the heavy snowfall.

"Shields!" Rydan yells, ushering the guards toward the mages. "Enact the shields!"

The arctic wind is replaced by a scorching heat, one he's all too familiar with as an Ignitor. The heat only intensifies as he drops to his knees and covers his head. It's a useless position in this case, but the shimmering blue shield above him isn't. In fact, it's rather effective at staving off the fire altogether.

"Hold!" the mages shout to one another as another fiery blast travels toward the shield before dissipating upon impact. Rydan can't help but stare through the protective layer above him as dragon after dragon attempts to penetrate the shield.

"There aren't enough of us," one of the mages cries. "We can only hold them off for so long!"

As if his plea had been answered, one of the dragons suddenly thuds to the ground, the snow blanketing its body as if it were an open grave.

"What in lords' name . . .?" Rydan starts until he hears the sound of cheering coming from the watchtower. He narrows his eyes to get a better look and, sure enough, there they are: the missing Caldari. Braxton and Lane are on the offensive, firing fluorescent, green-tipped arrows into the sky. Arrows that are somehow managing to take down dragons weighing ten tons with a single hit.

Relief rushes through him as one dragon after another collapses into the snow. His confidence begins to soar, but it's short-lived the moment he turns his attention to the sea. To the fleet of ships, or lack thereof, that have somehow vanished without a trace.

DARIUS TYMOND

THEY'RE HEADED STRAIGHT for the shore but, thanks to Clive's inconspicuous casting, no one's the wiser. Clive's assured them that, from the field's vantage point, the sea will appear empty, giving their ships a major advantage: the element of surprise.

"I'll have to drop the illusion once we storm the field," Clive says, arms raised as he weaves the invisible fabric around them. "I can't fend off the guards and cast an illusion of this magnitude simultaneously."

"Fair enough," Alyna says as she steers the ship into port. "I'll signal to the others that it's to be a discreet attack."

Darius is only half-listening as he scans the field, spotting only one familiar face: that of an ex-Cruex.

Rydan Helstrom seems to be leading the attacks on the dragons, although, by the looks of it, it's a wasted effort on his part. Their arrows will have little to no impact on such scaled armor.

Darius narrows his eyes, hoping it'll grant him a better view as to who exactly is firing the arrows, but there isn't anyone noteworthy as far as he can tell. He must admit, he's surprised to see that his son isn't among their ranks . . .

But then he spots him. Atop the watchtower. Braxton fires a single arrow, aiming at one of the dragons that's headed straight for him. Darius can only watch in sheer and utter amazement as that single arrow strikes true and manages to take the dragon down in one fell swoop.

"They have selphinium?" Alyna shouts in disbelief.

Darius tightens his grip on the railing. Perhaps he should have placed an embargo on that particular herb when he'd had the chance. But that's the least of his concerns as Braxton turns, revealing the obvious misshapen shadow at his back. *He has the staff.*

With his eyes fixed on his target and not a word to the others, Darius disembarks the ship.

"Tymond!" Clive calls from behind him. "Where do you think you're going? The other ships haven't even—"

But Darius doesn't care to hear the rest as he breaks into a frenzied sprint toward the watchtower.

CERYLIA JARETH

THE MADNESS IN the king's stare is something she hasn't seen since the days Trendalath was seized from her. She emerges from the formation that's keeping her hidden from view, guards flanking her on all sides, and dashes toward him, estimating exactly when she'll need to unsheathe her sword.

It takes a moment for the guards to realize what's just happened right underneath their noses. They circle around themselves in distress, searching for their queen, before breaking formation to charge after her. But Darius is alone and so Cerylia ought to be as well—unlike him, she fights with dignity and honor. She sheds her robes, knowing that they're only weighing her down, the snow piercing her eyelids as it falls on her freshly exposed skin. She can hear the guards yelling in protest from behind her, but she doesn't break her stride. She won't stop running until she forces Darius to stop in his tracks.

She's more than halfway across the field, rapidly closing the distance between her and the Trendalath king, when he glances in her direction, finally laying eyes on her. The smirk on his face only makes her run faster, the fool be damned.

Even through her obstructed view, the amethyst ring glints in the snowfall, beckoning for her to retrieve it. And take it she shall. A glance at the watchtower makes it painstakingly clear as to why Darius is in such a rush, why he's stormed the field alone. *She'd* been the one who'd given Braxton the staff. And Darius had acted exactly as she'd expected—impulsive and desperate.

What she *hadn't* expected is for the king to stay the course, even with an armed woman charging at him. The realization that he doesn't see her as a threat weighs heavy on her heart, but it also fuels her rage as she catapults forward, unsheathing her sword in midair.

Sensing the impending attack, Darius turns his head, eyes widening as he dodges the blow with a hasty forward roll. The snow cushions Cerylia's landing, giving her ample time to change direction to attempt another strike. But as Darius climbs to his feet, so does a stormy black mist. It casts a deep gray shadow on the snow beneath her.

"Coward!" Cerylia shouts, knowing better than to stick around and face the Mallum. She may be a part of the Sacred Trinity of abilities that cannot be touched by the Mallum, but what good is her ability if she isn't alive to wield it?

"I'm not the one running," Darius retorts.

"You will be soon enough," she mutters under her breath, making a beeline for the mages. "Shield!" she commands, but the color leeching from their faces tells her everything she needs to know. Just like her, and everyone else on this damn field, the mages are defenseless against the Mallum—and at risk of losing the only thing that's giving them a fighting chance of coming out of this mess victorious.

XERIN GREY

XERIN CIRCLES THE area where the dragons have fallen, doing a quick count in his head. They're at less than half the numbers they'd started with—a grim outlook at best. He scours the field for the weaponry responsible for such demise but finds himself distracted by the commotion near the lower entrance of the watchtower. Why Darius hasn't summoned the Mallum up until this precise moment is beyond his comprehension until a helmet comes off, showcasing a white-blonde head of hair. Xerin huffs. *And this is why the king should have remained in the oubliette.*

Momentarily forgetting the rider on his back, Xerin takes a sharp dip to the left, soaring in the direction of the tower.

"Watch it!" Vira calls out. "Lest your plan is to fling me off into the clouds!"

It isn't his plan, per se, but it *does* give him an idea.

I need you to summon more dragons, he orders.

Why, so you can get them killed, too? Vira chides.

Do it, he snarls, *or you won't like the second option I have in store.*

Oh, so there are options now, are there?

Between the Trendalath King's incompetence and Vira's unwillingness to cooperate, the single thread holding his patience finally snaps. *Fine. Have it your way.*

Midflight, he arcs his back with such force it bucks Vira right off. She shrieks as she goes flying through the air, cursing his name as she begins to freefall. Xerin swoops just above her, catching her outstretched arm in one of his talons. A gash runs the entire length of her arm, blood spurting from the wound as he grips her tighter. She howls in pain, kicking and swinging her legs in the air as if that's somehow going to help her escape.

"If your plan is to use me as collateral, you'll need me alive!" she cries, wincing at each word she throws at him.

Injured is still alive, isn't it?

He can't see her face but he's certain her eyes have widened in shock. "Xerin, you can't be serious—"

But he's no longer listening as he spots Rydan Helstrom huddling with the mages in the northeastern corner of the field. He's done with the façade, done pretending like he gives a shit about his so-called "sister". The truth's bound to come out one way or another. It's about time he gets what he came here for, regardless of what it takes to get it.

BRAXTON HORNSBY

BRAXTON AIMS HIS arrow left, right, left again, sighing in exasperation as his view of his father and Queen Jareth diminishes in a thick black haze. "Damn it," he swears under his breath. He should have taken that ring when he'd had the chance. They'd be way better off than they are right now—who knows, they may have been able to avoid these attacks all together.

"Whatever you're thinking, stop," Lane says from beside him as she lowers her bow. "If we focus on anything other than what's happening right now, we'll fail and Aeridon as we know it will crumble."

She's right, but it doesn't keep the roiling shame from eating him alive. He tracks Cerylia's movements as she takes off in the opposite direction, breathing a bit easier knowing she's gotten away in time. His gaze lands on his father whose stare is now pointed directly at him, the look on his face one of pure malice and determination. Using the Mallum as cover, he continues his trajectory toward the watchtower's entrance.

"You need to go," Braxton says, ushering Lane to the exit. "We'll have a better chance if we split up."

"I'll strike true," Lane says, drawing her bow and squinting her eyes. "If I can take down a dragon, I can certainly do this."

Braxton presses a hand on the end of the arrow, giving her no choice but to lower her weapon. "You need to *go,*" he repeats, more firmly this time, "while you're still illusié. We don't need you losing your ability, too."

She opens her mouth to counter but seems to decide against it. Instead, she closes the distance between them and places a hand on his shoulder. She leans in, her mouth brushing his ear as she whispers, "Take. Him. Down."

It isn't a request. It's a command.

"Go," he says again. "And take this." He hands her the bottle of selphinium. "Gather the guards and coat as many arrows as you can. There are only a few dragons left."

Four if you count Xerin.

Lane nods as she takes the bottle and makes for the stairs. Braxton rushes to the edge of the tower. He looks across the field for a sign of his father, but it seems he's underestimated the king's speed. Which means . . .

A shriek echoes from the staircase, chilling him to the bone. *Lane.*

He runs for the exit but backtracks as soon as he reaches the wooden door. The Mallum emerges, followed by his father who currently has Lane in a chokehold, a blade pressed to her neck.

He steps in front of the Mallum. "My son," he says, a sinister grin creeping across his face. "I believe you have something that belongs to me."

ARDEN ELIRI

THE FRONT OF the castle is eerily quiet as Nevaeh and I tie our horses off. An uneasy feeling settles in my stomach as I look to the drawbridge and the lack of guards at the entrance. *Something isn't right.*

"Where is everyone?" Nevaeh questions, echoing my thoughts.

"They've been called to duty," I say, rushing by her to climb the steps. "We need to get to the infirmary before the walls are breached."

Nevaeh motions to the lack of human presence around us. "I think we're safe in that regard."

"Listen," I say as I point to my ear, then to the opposite end of the castle, hoping she can hear what I hear, however faint. "The rear of the castle is under attack. That's where they've infiltrated. Which means there might still be a chance the infirmary hasn't been besieged."

"And if it has?"

I don't want to entertain the thought—not with my father in there, completely defenseless. "Stay close," I tell her as I carefully open the door and peek inside. I refuse to fall for another one of the Caster's illusions. I refuse to be the reason someone else loses their life.

My assumption of the attack taking place at the rear of the castle seems to be correct because the halls are as empty as I've ever seen them. Step after marble step we climb to the infirmary, only stopping to check behind us to ensure we aren't being followed. Nevaeh's so close, I can feel her breath on the back of my neck and, if I didn't know her any better, I'd say she's nervous. Which she should be. I'm on edge, too.

I find I can breathe a bit easier as we pass a familiar statue, indicating we're only a short distance away. But as I make the final turn down the hall, I'm stopped by what must be half a dozen guards. The one in front aims her spear at me, eyes growing wide once she realizes who I am.

"Lady Eliri," she says respectfully, immediately lowering her weapon. "My apologies. You're the last person I expected to see."

"I'm here for my father." I advance, but she doesn't budge. None of the guards do.

Remorse clouds the guard's pallid face. "I'm afraid I'm under stringent orders to ensure no one leaves or enters the infirmary at this time."

Her tone is polite enough, but after traveling miles from Orihia in what can only be described as frigid, death-defying temperatures, my patience is wearing thin. "I will enter the infirmary now. Unless you all want to die a gruesome death by the hands of my good friend here."

At mention of the threat, Nevaeh's head pops up from behind me. "Trained with the Savant, I have. Which, might I add, are some of the best—"

I resist the urge to smack my hand over her mouth.

The guard's eyes narrow. "You're fraternizing with the enemy."

"*Trained*," I say, emphasizing the word in past tense. "It doesn't mean she's currently siding with them. Need I remind you of my past with the Cruex?"

Her eyes widen as they track to my sides where my chakrams are sheathed. "That won't be necessary." She takes one more look at Nevaeh before sighing, her decision made. "Clear a path for Lady Eliri and her . . . friend."

A quiet murmur passes amongst the guards as they look to one another for direction.

"Move!" the guard snaps. "Now!"

The guards obey, bowing their heads as they step out of the way.

"Thank you," I say, placing a hand on her shoulder.

Nevaeh nudges me forward. "Enough with the niceties, we need to get going," she whispers.

We stride through the doors and make our way across the room to where my father is stationed. Unless my eyes deceive me, I'm both pleased and dismayed to find that he looks the same as the last time I visited. Nevertheless, he's still breathing.

"Sit," Nevaeh orders, pulling a stool over to the bed. "Do exactly as you did in the Vaults—"

"What are you doing in here?"

I glance up to see Edith emerging from behind the curtained workstation. She's carrying a small wooden bowl, her eyes rimmed with dark circles as she scurries to Stanton's bedside. The proper, poised woman Haskell had foolishly appointed to look after our father's health is long gone.

"You shouldn't be here," she snaps. "Your father will soon wake. I have everything under control."

"Take one step closer," I say as I unsheathe my chakrams, "and you won't live to see another day."

Edith's eye twitches as she looks from me to Nevaeh, her brows furrowing in confusion. "I don't understand. If you don't allow me to administer the salve—"

"Then my father will live?" I challenge, raising my blades at her. "Let's get one thing straight, Edith Caldwell *Langley.*"

She pales at the use of her maiden and married name.

"The assassination of your husband by the decree of King Tymond may not have been fair or deserved, but it doesn't give you the right to target an innocent man nor forego your oath of healing."

She's still for a moment before breaking into hysterical laughter. "Innocent? Is *that* what the Eliris are?"

"That's quite enough, Edith," a male voice says as the curtains are drawn back. "An oath is an oath." Gabriel's expression falters when he spots Nevaeh beside me. "Well, this is unexpected."

"Perhaps you mean unwelcome," the Rescinder corrects, stepping toward the two Healers before snatching the bowl straight from Edith's hands. She empties it onto the surface of a white marble table to reveal a silky blue powder.

"Aconite?" she accuses, nostrils flaring. She knocks the bowl to the floor. "So, you really *are* making him worse, not better."

Caught red-handed, Edith just stands there in silence.

"And you," Nevaeh continues, leveling a steely gaze at Gabriel. "You've been helping her! I was right to suspect the tinge of blue underneath your fingernails when I last saw you."

I steal a glance at Gabriel, noticing that he looks just as caught off guard as I feel. There's a sharpness to his tone as he turns to face Edith. "You told me that, in some recorded instances, trace levels of aconite can actually have a positive effect on patients who suffer from a similar condition."

"Did she happen to mention that, in those recorded instances, only a quarter of the patients survived?" Nevaeh interjects.

"It's the perfect cover," I murmur, my hands tightening around the hilt of my blades. "Until you get caught."

Color blooms on Edith's cheeks as she searches for a way to defend her actions.

"I think we're done here," I say, trying to quell my budding anger. "If I were you, I'd pack my things. When Queen Jareth learns of your transgressions . . ."

At the mention of stripping her of her status, Edith falls to her knees in a grand display of dramatics. "It was all in the name of research," she implores, completely changing her tune. "Against all odds, I truly believed my formulation would be the one to work."

"Even if that *were* true," Nevaeh points out, "it's still problematic because you're willing to risk the lives of your patients if it means making a discovery in your name."

"How else am I to leave my mark on this wretched world?"

I stare at her in disbelief. "Perhaps by upholding your oath and healing the very people who have been placed in your care, regardless of the events of the past or who your patient happens to be related to."

"For starters," Nevaeh scoffs.

"We'll have the guards escort you out momentarily," I continue before looking to Nevaeh. "Can you reverse whatever it is she's done?"

The Rescinder pushes past both of the Healers until she's standing within arm's reach of the bed. She closes her eyes and presses her palms together, then, after a few seconds, places them just above my father's head. She keeps her eyes closed as they hover there, her forehead creasing as she makes her assessment. From her expression alone, I'm not expecting good news.

Nevaeh sighs, bringing her hands back to her sides. "I'm unable to detect even the slightest trace of illusié for me to reverse."

"And you won't," Edith has the nerve to say. "The herb works entirely on its own. It does not require illusié to enhance its properties—"

"Of poison," Nevaeh interrupts. "We've heard enough from you." Her head whips toward the window as a rumble tears through the skies. "Better do it now."

"Do what?" Gabriel asks, looking between the two of us.

"What you two should have been doing all along," I reply simply as I focus my energy the same way I did in the Vaults. "Except I'll be using the capabilities you already possess to do so." I almost add, *And if I take every damn ounce of your wasted abilities to heal my father, then so be it,* but decide it's best to carry on with as little resistance as possible.

"You don't mean—"

But Edith doesn't get to finish her thought as I begin to withdraw any semblance of healing from her, amplifying with all my strength as I channel it directly to my father.

RYDAN HELSTROM

R Y D A N   H E A R S   T H E   shriek before any of the others. He breaks away from the mages, lifting his gaze to the sky. The cloud cover seems to be growing denser while simultaneously shifting lower, making it difficult to see exactly what's going on above him. That all changes, though, as two dangling legs appear amidst the endless expanse of white. The shriek suddenly makes sense.

The bastard's holding Vira with his damn *talons*.

Rydan watches in horror as Xerin jerks his sister around, carelessly dipping and dodging the pellets of hail flying at them, her body swaying violently with each maneuver. Beady red eyes lock on his own and, as if he can read the Caldari's mind, Rydan takes off in a sprint toward the courtyard. He's well-aware that Xerin's after the crescent fire, but would he really sacrifice his own sister to get it? With the way he has her dangling as if she's something to be discarded, he wouldn't put it past him.

His trek is cut short, however, as those bearing the emblem of the Crostan Islands charge in his direction, seemingly out of nowhere. As if an invisible curtain is being lifted right before his very eyes, the fleet that had disappeared from sight begins to reappear—and they've all managed to make landfall in record time.

It was an illusion.

And a damn good one at that.

The shield the mages had enacted is rendered useless as hundreds of Crostan warriors storm the field. Their weaponry is impressive, considering their exiled status, and there's no shortage of knowledge when it comes to how to wield them. Spears sail through the air, striking down Sardorian guards with shocking ease. Metal blades clang as they cross with their opponents'. Daggers are used in close-range combat, piercing through shoulders, necks, and any exposed skin not fully covered by armor.

Knowing he needs to clear a path for himself and fast, Rydan sheathes his sword and removes his leather gloves before tightening his hands into fists. He squeezes his eyes shut, if only for a moment, to bring to mind the infuriating image of Vira in harm's way. Heat courses through his body and, just as he'd orchestrated in his mind, his hands burst into flames. His eyes shoot open just as a Crostan warrior is about to bring a sword down on his left shoulder, but he deftly spins away in the opposite direction and aims a fiery blast right at the poorly-armored man. The warrior screams as his clothes instantly catch fire, his sword glowing bright orange as it falls from his grip, hissing the moment it hits the snow.

Rydan turns in a circle, igniting the area surrounding him so that the snow has no choice but to melt, leaving the Crostan warrior no relief from the flames engulfing his entire body. The spectacle draws unwanted attention as many of the warriors change tactics and begin to head his way, no doubt wanting his head on a pike for using illusié against one of their own.

An indigo flame shoots across his eyesight before icing over at his feet. Startled, Rydan turns toward where it'd originated from. A blonde male about ten or eleven years his junior stands just far enough away to be out of reach. His features strike Rydan as familiar, although from *where* exactly eludes him. The male is completely unfazed as he steps into the ring of flames surrounding them both.

"Rydan Helstrom," the male says, eyes gleaming with predatory intent. "I wasn't sure I'd live to see the day."

Rydan tracks the male's movements, every one of his senses heightened. "Who are you?"

The male raises his hand to his chest in mock offense before sending another spear of ice directly at him. "Consider me the nightmare from your Lonia mission. The boy you failed to kill."

Rydan's mouth goes dry.

"I was supposed to visit my nana and pops that day, you know. Maybe if I had, they'd still be alive." His gaze hardens. "Maybe if I had, you'd be dead instead of them."

The Soames boy. He can see it now. The blonde hair, the golden eyes . . . but the boy hiding under the table had had red eyes. He turns his gaze to the sky. Yet another instance of Xerin pulling the strings. He'd wanted to ensure the Soames mission was carried out . . . but why? Even more disconcerting, were all the Cruex missions tainted by Xerin as well?

The shriek that tears through the sky indicates he doesn't have much time if he hopes to save Vira. He clears his throat, pulling at his mind for a way to placate the seething male before him. "I know you have no reason to trust me, but I need you to hear me when I say that your nana and pops were actually my aunt and uncle, although I wasn't aware of our relation at the time." He sucks in a sharp breath at the admission. "I will forever hold shame around that day and its outcome. But no more Draconian blood need be spilled. Please, cousin. I implore you."

The boy's expression softens, but his stance remains on the defensive. "We're . . . cousins?"

"Yes," Rydan says. "I carry our family's crest on my back as we speak."

The male's eyes well with tears. "I thought I was the only one left," he says as he wipes his cheek with the back of his hand. "I'm Andri Soames."

"I'm glad to meet you, Andri, although I wish it were under better circumstances." Rydan looks to the sky in search of Xerin, hoping Vira's managed to hang on long enough. Another shriek draws his attention northwest, where he spots them flying for the courtyard. There's no way he'll make it in time having to trudge through the rapidly accumulating snow. It'll be too deep.

"Quick," Rydan says as he pulls an extra tunic stitched with the Sardorian emblem from the satchel at his side. "Remove any article of clothing that might indicate you're allied with the Crostan Islands."

Andri takes the tunic, then rids himself of his current armor. "You always carry spare clothes on you?"

Rydan forces a smile, not the least bit inclined to share that it'd become a habit over his years in the Cruex. Being covered in strangers' blood will do that to a person.

With each piece of armor that's discarded, Rydan takes it upon himself to bury it in the snow. "So, you're an Ignitor who wields ice?"

Andri chuckles as he removes the last piece of Crostan gear. "I'm what's called an Inhibitor. Like an Ignitor, yes, except I wield ice instead of fire."

That's why he'd felt frozen in the boy's presence the day of the mission. Even though it hadn't been Andri and instead Xerin *shaped* as Andri, the boy's power could be wielded.

"Listen, the reason I was able to recognize you is because that dragon, there"—he points to where Xerin's currently soaring—"is actually a Shaper in disguise. One who was shaped as you during the mission I was sent on."

A shadow falls over Andri's face. "For what purpose?"

"It's hard to say," Rydan admits. "But he's been working with King Tymond since the very beginning. I was only carrying out orders." He takes a shaky breath. "How I wish I hadn't."

"Why are you telling me this?" Andri whispers. "What do you expect me to do?"

"Nothing," Rydan replies. "I don't expect you to do anything . . . but, while it may sound selfish, I do *hope* you'll fight alongside me . . . alongside Sardoria."

Andri points to the sky. 'They're fire dragons, are they not?"

Rydan nods. "To my knowledge, yes."

Andri rubs his hands together. "Then I can do more than just fight." Before Rydan can ask what he means, his cousin says, "Fire and ice never did mix well," then takes off in the direction of the courtyard.

Rydan blindly follows, knowing neither of them will make it very far with the current depth of the snow. When he's finally beside Andri, he raises his palms so that they're facing out, then releases a deep bellow, blasting the area directly in front of them with a wall of flame. Andri whoops as the path clears, the heat nearly burning their legs as they sprint along the blazing trail. If he didn't know any better, he'd think he were made of fire himself. A battle cry sounds from behind them as armed civilians from Sardoria's neighboring towns begin to pour in from all sides. Relief washes over him when he sees Haskell leading the charge from the east, Estelle from the west, and Avery up the center.

Finally. Their reinforcements have arrived.

Both he and Andri arrive at the marble archway that leads to the courtyard without any interference. The area is completely empty, save for the countless statues that Xerin could undoubtedly use to his advantage. Rydan tries to keep his imagination at bay, but, aimed over the right one, a drop from that height would kill Vira on impact. Rydan shudders, shaking away the image as he weaves through the hedges, searching for an opening large enough for a dragon to land.

"All clear," Andri says, even though Rydan never asked.

The wind picks up around them, as if urging him to hurry and make his decision. He eventually settles on the gardens since there are less statues to be impaled on and more greenery and shrubbery to pad a potential landing. The only exception is the four-tier marble water fountain that's surrounded by a frozen-over pond in the center of the gardens, but, by his logic, one statue is better than ten.

"Give me a boost, would you?" he asks Andri. His cousin obliges, hoisting Rydan onto the smoothest edge of the water feature. His original plan was to somehow draw Xerin's attention, but his effort is hardly necessary as the dragon comes swooping into view with Vira still very much alive—and still cursing her brother's name to hell and back.

XERIN GREY

VIRA IS ABSOLUTELY relentless as she continues to shout profanities at him midflight. If it weren't for her life being his only bargaining chip, he would have dropped her to her death long ago—but seeing as Rydan's played right into his hand, it's worth the headache.

At least, it will be soon enough.

"Xerin, I swear to the lords above—"

Enough, he snaps. *You will do exactly as I say or I will fling you onto one of those spires before another profanity can leave your mouth.*

Her shouting ceases.

Order Rydan to toss the crescent fire to the highest point on the fountain, he snarls. *And do it quick.*

"If you think there's even the slightest chance that I would allow such a powerful object to ever come into your possession, you're more delusional than I thought," she seethes.

Do it. Now.

"It doesn't belong to you!"

Do it. Or I'll drop you.

She has the audacity to laugh. "You wouldn't dare—"

He roars, releasing his grip just enough to have her scrambling for purchase, his talon nearly slicing her other arm along the side.

"What the fuck, Xerin?" she screams. "I'm the only sister you've got!"

Do not test me. Tell him. Now.

He tightens his grip as he swoops lower, waiting for her to follow his orders. Smart girl that she is, she does; but not before a second figure emerges from behind Rydan. One Xerin is all too familiar with.

Andri Soames.

How did he get here? And why is he with Rydan?

Vira's yelling pulls him from his thoughts. "Throw the crescent fire to the top of the fountain! And hurry!"

If it weren't for the wind masking the shakiness in her voice, Rydan would easily surmise that this wasn't her idea.

From the sky, Xerin catches Andri placing a hand on Rydan's shoulder, as if giving his cousin advice on how to proceed.

"Why would I do that?" Rydan finally shouts back.

Xerin roars again, if only to remind Vira that the clock is ticking.

"Just do it!" she screams, a sob breaking free. "Please!"

"Vira—"

"He'll kill me!" she shrieks. "Do it! Now!"

A wordless exchange passes between Rydan and Andri.

"The only way he's getting this lords-damned crest is if he guarantees your safety!"

"Damn it, Rydan, this is so not the time to be negotiating—"

He has a deal.

"What?" she asks, looking up at her brother through tear-stained eyes.

Tell him he has a deal.

"You'll let me live?"

If it'll get me what I want, then yes. I'll drop you in the hedges, but only after the crescent fire is in my possession.

Vira nods, her voice trembling as she relays the information to Rydan. He nods before both he and Andri scramble to get the crest off his back. Much to Xerin's surprise and delight, the Ignitor tosses the crest up to the fourth and highest tier of the fountain without the slightest hesitation.

It was almost too easy.

Xerin banks left, making a semicircle in the air before gliding low enough to snatch the crest with the talons on his free foot.

Vira screams as she's nearly taken out by the side of the fountain, pounding on his foot to release her. He *could* keep his word, but a sharp turn toward the spires looks awfully intriguing. Instead of soaring lower, he begins to make his ascent when, suddenly, he feels a raging heat burn his leg. If it were an Ignitor, he wouldn't feel a thing, but it isn't fire he's being attacked with. It's the opposite. Spikes of ice blast right through the scales on his leg, causing him to release his grip on Vira. Xerin swears under his breath, regretting his past decision to not kill the Inihibitor when he'd had the chance. It takes all his strength to keep the crest in his grasp as Vira goes flying, rather ironically, aimed straight for the hedges, just as he'd originally promised.

CERYLIA JARETH

SHE MAY NOT be willing to face the Mallum today, but there *is* one person on this field she'd be more than happy to encounter. A deafening battle cry has Cerylia whirling around, swinging her sword to parry an oncoming attack. She renders the sad excuse for an opponent weaponless in seconds.

"Yield," she demands. "Or a gruesome death awaits."

The middle-aged man spits at her feet. "Yield to illusié? To a false queen? Ha! I'd choose death any day—"

Her already fading tolerance diminishes with that last statement as she drives her sword straight into his jugular, slicing the blade sideways to decapitate him. "Have it your way," she says with no remorse as the headless body drops to the ground. If there's one thing she absolutely will not allow, it's disrespect—especially when it occurs on her grounds, in her queendom.

Speaking of disrespect, she searches the field left and right for the one man she's determined to thrust her blade into . . . and it isn't Darius Tymond. She's well-aware that most of the Savant hadn't survived the events at Midvale—rightfully so—but she'd selfishly hoped the Caster hadn't been among them. Dane's blood is on his hands; it's only right for his blood to be on hers.

Her gaze sweeps across the field once more, her frustration climbing until . . . *there.* Atop the very ship he'd sailed in on. She'd recognize that unruly copper head of hair anywhere. Given the frantic expression on his face, he knows he's vulnerable. An illusion of that size and magnitude can only be cast for so long before it withers away.

Time's up.

A quick estimate of the distance between them puts her at a disadvantage, however, seeing as she's opposite the side his ship is docked. Surely, she could plow her way through the lines of defense with startling ease, but, with such a massive target on her back, there's no guarantee he'd still be there by the time she arrived.

Options. She needs options . . .

A flash of green light to the east draws her attention. Haskell appears with a slew of others, preoccupied with transporting more of their allies to the field. A noble cause, one she'd be remiss to interrupt. As for the center of the field, it's alight with a ring of fire, Avery standing proudly within his creation, shooting a devastating wall of flame at anyone who dares to get too close. Which leaves the west, where Estelle should be . . .

An invisible force grasps her forearm, yanking her to the ground. The shimmering curtain around her obscures her view just enough to indicate that she's currently cloaked and out of sight.

"What the hell are you doing out here?" Estelle hisses, sounding an awful lot like a mother figure instead of a subordinate.

"What does it look like I'm doing?" Cerylia retorts. "I'm defending Sardoria."

"Like hell you are." Estelle pulls on her arm so forcefully that Cerylia has no choice but to walk alongside her. The Cloaker expertly weaves the two of them through the chaos, completely undetected. When they arrive at the castle's rear doors, Estelle wastes no time getting them inside.

"I understand that you want to be out there, fighting alongside your people, but what I *don't* understand is risking your life to the likes of the Mallum." Estelle releases the queen's arm in a huff, bringing down the invisible curtain around them. "In case you've forgotten, we *need* you, Cerylia. You're the only practicing Extractor in Aeridon."

"Which is exactly why I need to be out there," she counters. "If any other Savant survived, only I can take from them the one thing that's giving them any power."

"You know as well as I do that they didn't survive Midvale. We saw that with our very own eyes." She wavers as an obvious realization sinks in. "But this isn't about the Savant as a whole, is it? This is about the *one*. The Caster."

No use denying it. "Of course it's about him! He's the reason my husband isn't here today or any other day to come." It takes all her strength to keep her voice from breaking. "I need to do this."

Much to her surprise, Estelle doesn't challenge her. She doesn't reprimand her. Instead, the Cloaker's expression softens. "Then I will help you. Under one condition, though."

Cerylia nods. "Name it."

"I go with you. And we remain cloaked until we're within striking distance. Clive will never see us coming."

Cerylia nods again. "I can agree to those terms."

"Good." Estelle takes a sharp inhale. "But we need to move quickly before he attempts to cast another illusion."

"If he does, it won't be very realistic or for very long," Cerylia remarks. "He's used up the majority of his ability hiding the fleet."

"Where was he last seen?" Estelle asks, peering out of the castle windows.

"At the helm of one of the ships, docked to the west."

Estelle nods as she takes Cerylia by the forearm, pulling the invisible shield over them once more. "Then it's west we'll go."

DARIUS TYMOND

THE TERROR IN his son's eyes is well-deserved. Lane whimpers as he presses the blade against her neck, forcing her to walk back through the watchtower's door. The two of them may have escaped him that day in the tunnels but, with Lane at his mercy, there's nowhere for them to run.

"If it's the staff you want, it's yours," Braxton says as he sets his crossbow aside and raises his hands in the air. "Lower your weapon, father."

The use of the word causes him to waver in his resolve, however briefly. "First, the staff."

Braxton narrows his eyes. "Lower your weapon," he repeats. "There's been enough bloodshed today."

Darius flicks his gaze between his son and the staff strapped to his back, debating his next move. "You seem to forget the power I hold." He angles his head toward the Mallum. "You've already lost your ability to deviate. Are you really willing to let your fellow Caldari experience the same fate?"

Before he can respond, the Mallum glides right by him and descends onto the field below. Panic swells in his chest as he spots Haskell, Avery, Rydan, and Vira . . . all swiftly brought to their knees, one after the other, as the entity sweeps the field, drawing their abilities from them. The Mallum scours the docks next, seemingly to no avail, when Estelle suddenly appears on the battlement, doing everything in her power to draw the Mallum away from the ships. Her plan works for whoever it is she's trying to save, but the same can't be said for her. She's forced to her knees within seconds as the Mallum absorbs her ability to cloak. At this rate, there won't be any illusié left . . . which is exactly what his father's wanted all along.

Braxton searches the field far and wide for both Cerylia and Arden, feeling relieved—and somewhat distressed—when he can't find either of them. The Mallum takes another jaunt around the field, no doubt looking for its next victim, but, coming up short, ultimately returns to the watchtower.

"Finally," Darius whispers as the entity floats back toward him. "The power I seek is mine."

Braxton levels a steely gaze at him. "At what cost?"

"Everything comes with a price." Darius smirks. "You of all people should know that . . . Braxton *Hornsby.*"

Enraged, Braxton spits at his father's feet. "You are a disgrace to the Tymond name."

"You forget your place, boy," he snarls. "I am the sole reason the Tymond name has any meaning to begin with."

Braxton takes a step closer. "And yet the crown you wear, the throne you sit on, the land you rule . . . it's all tainted, isn't it, *father?* The Tymond name is marred with secrets and shadows, thanks to you." He shakes his head in what can only be described as pure disgust. "It's a wonder I stayed in that lords-forsaken kingdom for as long as I did."

"You did your mother and me a favor when you fled," he seethes, refusing to loosen his grip on the blade. "If only—"

"—if only she could see you now," Braxton interrupts.

Braxton," Lane whispers, her eyes wide with warning.

"If it's the staff you want, father, it's yours," he says, removing it from his back before tossing it on the ground between them. "But I surmise there aren't enough words in the world to undo the damage you've inflicted on your beloved, now are there?"

Darius's breath hitches.

He knows the truth.

Blinded by rage, Darius flings Lane away from him, the blade slicing through the fabric on her upper sleeve as she slams into the side of one of the turrets. He's reaching for his sword when he notices that Braxton isn't doing the same. Unarmed, his son raises his balled fists to the sides of his jaw, his stance shifting so that his dominant leg is behind him.

Darius laughs. "Did your time in the Cruex teach you nothing?"

"On the contrary," Braxton says, remaining in his defensive position. "It taught me everything I need to know." He kicks the staff out of the way. "Go on, father. Send *her* to do your dirty work for you, yet again." He angles his head at the Mallum.

Darius growls, lunging for his son with outstretched arms. Braxton doesn't even bother dodging the attack as they tumble to the ground. His father's hands grab and tighten around his throat.

"Give your wretched mother my best," he hisses, his grip growing tighter.

Ice-blue eyes stare up at him. It's unnerving how calm, how *unalarmed* his son is, seeing as he's on the brink of death. But Braxton doesn't fight back, doesn't so much as lift his hands to try and release the pressure. His eyes begin to roll to the back of his head as his airway is cut off, his body shuddering at the lack of oxygen.

His adrenaline having taken over, Darius hardly notices the frantic shuffling behind him, the sharp metal blade that pierces his skin. His grip loosens as pain shoots down his right arm at the point of impact.

He doesn't have to look to know that Lane delivered the blow and is currently wrenching the very blade he'd cornered her with from the underside of his arm. Darius jolts upright, howling in pain as the dagger is ripped from his skin. Lane expertly drops the blade into Braxton's open palm as she loops her other arm around the king's neck, placing him in a similar chokehold to the one he'd had her in earlier.

Darius sputters at her uncanny strength, realizing he'd underestimated the pair yet again and that, by kneeling, he'd placed himself in a vulnerable position. His back arches the more Lane pulls against him, leaving him utterly defenseless. From underneath his robes, a steady stream of blood travels down his right arm. There's a brief moment of relief as Braxton lifts it in the air, staunching the flow of blood, but it's quickly replaced by a new surge of agony as one of his fingers is sliced clean off. He doesn't have to guess which finger it is. The clink of metal as the dismembered flesh hits the ground tells all.

He struggles against Lane, fighting for purchase, but her stance gives him no choice but to remain kneeling. She loosens her grip around his neck just enough to where Darius can see his son place the amethyst ring on his finger, the staff gleaming in his other hand.

"Bow before your king," Lane murmurs in his ear as she forces his head forward and down.

Given the unnatural position, Darius coughs, struggling to breathe. He knows he's only got one shot at breaking free, and it happens to be at this very moment. He takes as deep a breath as he can muster, using the slight forward angle he's positioned in to rear backward, headbutting Lane in the nose. There's a shriek as bone cracks, her hold on him loosening just enough for him to slip through.

With the Mallum no longer at his disposal, Darius should be far more concerned that his very livelihood is at stake, but the need for vengeance clouds any and all logic. The injury to his dominant arm is rather unfortunate as he attempts to fling a blade at his son's chest, missing his target by a long shot. The Mallum advances, although, given the bewildered expression on his son's face, it doesn't appear to be on his behalf. With Darius in its path, Lane is next in line—an outcome Braxton would never risk.

"I'll do it myself," Braxton says aloud, but it isn't enough to stop the Mallum in its tracks.

Darius stumbles backward as a chilling gust of wind sweeps around him, a knot forming in his throat. He never thought he'd know what it's like to be on the other side of such an entity, but here he is, staring into a faceless void—and it's downright horrifying.

His gaze shifts to Braxton as he realizes that his son will be the last thing he sees. Strangely enough, he can find solace in that. But Braxton isn't focused on him or the Mallum, but on something *behind* him—the only other person on the watchtower.

Mortified, Braxton yells, "Lane, no!"

Everything around Darius slows as a hand grips his forearm. He becomes overtly aware of the sound of a ticking clock, although he can't place exactly where it's coming from. One minute, his feet are planted firmly on the ground; the next, he feels as though he's floating, as if he's taken the form of the Mallum itself.

"I'll find my way back!" he hears Lane shout, but her voice sounds far away, muffled.

He blinks and the watchtower is gone. Braxton and the Mallum vanish. The chill of the northern winds diminishes. The echo of clanging metal and soldiers shouting fades into nothing. Even the grip on his forearm lessens until it disappears entirely. But it's the lack of feeling that pulls him under and he realizes . . .

Lane's banished the both of them to the Void.

BRAXTON HORNSBY

TIME STANDS STILL.

Lane is gone.

His father . . . gone.

Only he and the Mallum remain on the watchtower.

The shapeless form approaches him, the black specks in stark contrast to the blinding snowfall. There's a single thought running through his mind.

This is how I meet my end.

Not valiantly in battle.

Nor passionately for the people he loves.

There's no dignity in dying by the hands of the Mallum.

And yet, here he is. Just another insignificant soul to add to its death toll.

If given the opportunity, he'd fight until the very end; but that choice, like so many others, has been taken from him.

With the Mallum mere steps away, Braxton mentally braces himself for whatever's to come. Black mist swirls around him, enveloping him until his view of the watchtower is completely obstructed. A bright flash of light follows, transporting him to a world much like the Void except it isn't gray and absent of color. . . it's the most magnificent shade of blue he's ever seen. Much like the Great Ocean, waves roll all around him, but he isn't in the watery depths surrounding Aeridon. Instead, he's floating along what would be the horizon, if there happened to be one.

Much to his surprise, the Mallum is nowhere to be found. Which has him questioning . . . Is this the liminal space between life and death? If so, it isn't at all what he'd expected. It's peaceful, almost unnervingly so, but it's also chilling in a preternatural way.

He glances at his hands, the amethyst in his newly acquired ring gleaming a shade of violet he's only seen in paintings. The metal encasing the stone begins to hum as more and more energy is drawn to it—although he can't be sure from where the energy is coming from. He can't help but extend his arm outward as something invisible tugs at the ring.

Involuntarily, he's thrust forward, falling to his knees as the ring continues to pull. Braxton bites back a howl as he attempts to make a fist, his knuckles turning white in the process. It crosses his mind that, for the past decade, only his father has worn this ring—is this what he'd had to endure? Or is what he's currently experiencing the result of the ring finally changing hands? Whatever the case, it's relentless.

And painful.

Just when he feels as though the ring is going to be wrenched from his finger, the tugging stops. The pressure ceases. The forcefulness he'd felt earlier dissipates entirely. His hand near numb, he lifts his head to look at the stone. The once bright and sparkling amethyst is now dull and lifeless in comparison—but the form now standing before him is anything but.

It's a woman who looks to be around his father's age. Half of her shoulder-length brown hair is fashioned into a series of braids which are delicately pulled back at the sides, further accentuating her defined cheekbones and jawline. A deep burgundy satin dress billows around her, bringing out the magnificent jade hue of her eyes. She looks like . . .

"My, how you've grown," she says with a soft smile. "I always hoped your features would favor your mother's."

Braxton blinks, hardly believing his eyes. "You're . . . It's you? You've been trapped inside the Mallum this entire time?"

"Soul magick," she says with a sigh. "It's been years since I've been able to take my true form." She flips her hands over, back and forth, as if it's her first time seeing them. "I suppose all it took was for the ring to change hands to my nephew—my blood. Tell me, how is my daughter?"

The note his mother had left suddenly makes sense. Some of the letters had been printed differently, scrawled even. It'd been noticeable but he'd hardly thought anything of it.

Until now.

My dear son,
The time h*a*s come to retur*n* to Trenda*l*ath. There is *m*uch to be said for th*e* past, and even more to be gaine*d* for the future. I hope you both can fo*r*give me one d*a*y.

Your *loving mother,*
Aldreda

He can see it now, clear as day. Rearranging the scrawled letters leaves him with three words.

Arden.

Mallum.

Mother.

The woman his father had truly loved wasn't Aldreda, but her *sister*.

It's why Arden has encountered the Mallum numerous times with little to no repercussions.

It's why it speaks to her and no one else.

It's why she hasn't lost her abilities—or her life.

"You can call me Aunt Lavinia, if you'd like." She smiles, but it doesn't reach her eyes.

Braxton can barely speak the words as the realization settles in. "You're Arden's mother."

RYDAN HELSTROM

RYDAN DOESN'T HAVE time to mull over the fact that the Mallum's finally managed to take his abilities. Or question Vira's loyalties—not with a gash that size running down her arm. "We need to get her to the infirmary," Rydan urges as he and Andri carry her to an alcove in the gardens, "or to see a Healer, at the very least."

"If the Mallum hasn't already gotten to them," Andri says glumly. "All these years I've been able to avoid losing my abilities."

"It seems being tucked away in the Crostan Islands had its advantages."

"More than I realized."

Vira winces as they set her down. Her words come out forced. "I don't mean to sound rude, but who are you?"

Andri's mouth quirks up at the sides. "I'm his cousin," he says, motioning to Rydan. Vira gives them both an incredulous look, but before she can ask additional questions, Andri says, "Let's save the introductions for later. Getting this wound cleaned up needs to be our main focus."

"How bad is it?" Vira braves a glance at the rip in her sleeve, the crimson staining it.

Rydan schools his expression into one of neutrality, but the break in his voice gives him away. "It could be worse."

"Really?" she challenges. "So, the bleeding's stopped?"

Rydan gives a half nod as more spurts from the wound.

"You always were a terrible liar," she says with a roll of her eyes. "What do we do?"

"The infirmary is out of the question," Rydan thinks aloud. "As extreme as it sounds, I could have cauterized it with my abilities—"

"Except you don't have them anymore," Andri points out.

Rydan presses his mouth into a firm line. "Yes, thank you, cousin. I'm well aware."

"Is Avery out on the field?" Vira asks.

Rydan surveys the wreckage in the fallen snow, spotting the fellow Ignitor in the center. "He is."

"What are the chances he still has his abilities?"

Rydan grimaces as Avery straightens his palms, clearly trying to ignite without so much as a flicker. "I'd say slim to none."

"Well, shit." Vira chews on her lower lip. "Do we just . . . amputate it?"

Andri shakes his head. "Nothing like that. We'll think of something."

As their conversation carries on, Rydan continues to watch Avery, an idea striking as the Ignitor uncorks a small vial from a belt loop in his trousers. The Mallum may have taken away his ability to ignite, but not his knowledge of herbal alchemy.

"Avery may not be able to cauterize it, but there is another way he can help." Rydan doesn't offer further explanation as he pushes himself to his feet, ordering Andri to stay with Vira.

Before either of them can utter another word, Rydan dashes onto the field, praying that Avery has the good sense to be carrying at least one tonic that can heal Vira's ailment.

ARDEN ELIRI

WITH NEVAEH ON one side of my father and me on the other, we descend the steps of Sardoria castle.

"This doesn't look like Midvale," Stanton mumbles, still only partly coherent.

"That's because it isn't," I reply gently, even though a war is waging inside my mind. I'm beginning to lose faith that we'll come out of this on the other side . . . that we'll live to see tomorrow.

"Listen to me, Stanton," Nevaeh says as we round the corner that'll take us to the final staircase. "We're in Sardoria and it's under attack. King Tymond, the Mallum, the citizens of the Crostan Islands—"

Stanton stops walking, pulling us back with him. "The Crostan Islands? But they're sovereign and have been for as long as I can remember . . ."

"Well, it looks like Darius got to them," I explain, urging him to keep walking.

We stride through the massive doors where a grim reality awaits. Bodies lay slain, scattered left and right, all dignity lost. Dragon corpses begin to disintegrate, their once fiery insides turning to ash. Blood-soaked weapons lay discarded, staining the ground a dreadful shade of crimson.

I look to my father, his expression mirroring my own.

"Lords have mercy," he breathes.

"There," Nevaeh points. "Queen Jareth."

I look to where she's pointing to find my aunt, cloaked in her blue and silver robes, approaching the docks. Alone. All around her, hordes of people scramble to board the ships. Above her, what few dragons remain fly overhead. It doesn't take long to figure out why my aunt is over there. A copper head of tight spiral ringlets gleams against the snowfall.

The Caster.

So he *is* alive.

Likely not for long with Cerylia on the move. If she kills Clive, the man she *thinks* murdered Dane, then, at least in her mind, justice will be served. She'll have avenged her husband's untimely death. But therein lies the issue.

Clive didn't kill Dane.

And neither did Aldreda.

I'm the only one, besides Nevaeh, who knows the truth.

"We have to intercept her," I say, dread curling in my stomach. "She cannot make it to that ship."

I look up, hoping that the few remaining dragons circling overhead won't pursue their relentless string of attacks on the rest of the field, but their focus seems to be on something else entirely. I survey the grounds until I find what's distracting them: Rydan and Avery, sprinting from the center of the field to the arched entrance of the gardens. I look ahead, to their destination, and see Vira alongside a man I don't recognize; but, even from this distance, I can tell she's sustained some serious injuries.

What happened over there?

I squeeze my eyes shut, wishing I could wake up from this nightmare. Rydan and Cerylia are on opposite ends of the grounds, which means I can't help them both. Trusting that three Caldari are better than one, I make my decision.

"It's okay, Arden," my father says, as if reading my mind. "Tell us what you're thinking."

"If we're going to stop her in time, we'll have to run." I can't help but glance at his current disposition as I say it.

"You're right." Stanton gives a weary nod. "I'll only slow you down. You go. I'll follow as best I can."

As much as I don't want to leave him *again,* I know he's right. Lords, if anything happens to him . . .

Nevaeh seems to sense my distress. "Go, Arden. I'll stay with him." She takes a step back before placing my father's arm over her shoulders.

I relinquish the weight, shifting it over to her. "Thank you," I whisper.

"Don't mention it," she says with a warm smile. "You best get moving before your aunt does something she'll regret."

I give her an appreciative nod before breaking into a sprint. At this juncture of the attack on Sardoria, a clear, direct path is near impossible to find. As an assassin, dodging blow after blow is something I'm used to *and* happen to excel at, but hurdling over hundreds of lifeless bodies? And in the snow, no less? It isn't something I'm even remotely skilled at.

After more near misses than I care to admit, I'm finally climbing the steps to the docks. Thankfully, the hordes of Crostan warriors fleeing to their ships seems to have slowed my aunt down just enough for me to catch up.

"Queen Jareth!" I shout through labored breaths. "Aunt Cerylia!" When she doesn't turn my way, I begin to push my way through the crowd, elbowing people left and right. As much as I want to glance over my shoulder to see where my father and Nevaeh are, I know to keep my focus on that beacon of silver and blue.

I finally reach a small clearing in the crowd, my arms pumping at my sides, thighs burning and legs aching as I push myself to go faster. What was once labored breathing shifts into uncontrollable panting. My body feels like it's simultaneously freezing and burning as beads of sweat form along my hairline, refusing to roll down my face, courtesy of the dropping temperatures. By some miracle, I manage to close the distance between us, so I yell again, hoping she'll actually hear me this time. Instead of calling her name, I try a different tactic. "Stanton Eliri is awake!"

Cerylia's head whips toward me, her eyes wide.

Finally.

Her gaze tracks far, far behind me, to where Nevaeh and Stanton are. The look of relief on her face is more than justified. As I'd hoped, she changes course, going against the tide of people clambering to the ships. Fortunately, they all seem preoccupied with fleeing, making it swift and easy for her to reach me. I grab her hand and guide her the rest of the way off the docks. We don't speak to one another once we've stepped foot on the field; we just run, side by side, to where Nevaeh and Stanton are waiting for us.

As we approach, Cerylia flings herself at her brother-in-law and pulls him into a rather long embrace. I let them have their moment, knowing that my father has a lot to fill her in on, but it doesn't ease the guilt around the news I'm about to deliver. I already know it won't be received well.

When my aunt finally releases Stanton, I catch her pocketing not one, but *two* soul gems within her robes as she turns to face me. Questions line her eyes, no doubt about what my father's just revealed to her . . . What we'll be forced to do in the very near future. She blinks a few times before wiping her eyes, but it doesn't hide the glassiness. While it comes out as hardly a croak, she manages to ask, "I take it you were successful on more than one account. The Veil?"

I nod as I find my voice. "Yes. I'm pleased to report that the Veil has been reinstated, thanks to the work of Nevaeh." I bow my head in her direction to show my gratitude. "We also had some help from . . ." I gulp. "From Felix."

"Felix?" Her expression brightens. "Is he here? How did you—?"

"No," I interrupt, wishing I could say the opposite. "He isn't here. But I was somehow able to channel his abilities *through* the soul gem." I motion to the Rescinder. "With Nevaeh's knowledge and experience on the matter, I felt confident enough to channel healing to my father."

"You channeled healing?" Cerylia looks at me in disbelief. "From whom?"

"Does it matter?" I intentionally sidestep the question. The last thing I want to talk about is Edith Langley. "Clearly, it worked."

"If you must know, Arden channeled healing from one of your Healers in the infirmary," Nevaeh whispers, answering for me even though I didn't ask her to.

Cerylia's face pales.

I give Nevaeh a warning glance, then look to my aunt to explain. "Before you reprimand me, I'll have you know Edith's husband was the victim of a Cruex mission—one that Rydan was originally assigned to, but I ended up carrying out. Of course, I wasn't aware of this when I first met Edith. I only found out upon our return from Orihia while we were passing through Miraenia." I suppress a shudder as the wedding portrait flashes across my mind. "I suppose since I took someone from her, it'd only be fair to take someone from me, at least in her mind." I exhale a shaky breath. "The salve she was administering to my father contained aconite and it was killing him, albeit slowly."

"I suppose I should have listened to Delwynn when he warned me of the dangers of bringing in outside aid." Cerylia purses her lips. "So, where is she now?"

"She's still alive, if that's what you're getting at," Nevaeh answers. "But her illusié ability will be exhausted for some time since Arden channeled an exorbitant amount of said healing properties."

"An *exorbitant* amount? How much exactly?" My father regards me with a withering glare. "Arden, this is exactly what got us into this situation—at Midvale—in the first place. You can't handle that much power on your own—"

"Actually, it seems I can," I counter. "You're awake, aren't you?"

"Yes, but—"

"And I wasn't alone. I had help." I nod at Nevaeh, hoping I won't have to mention Felix's name again. "All of this is beside the point, though, because we have a way bigger issue on our hands."

"No, it's *exactly* the point—" Stanton starts, only to be cut off by the sound of wings flapping overhead.

"Look out!" I yell, pulling Estelle and Cerylia out of harm's way. We roll forward onto the ground, not bothering to dust the snow from our hair and clothes as two giant clawed feet touch down where we'd just stood. I glance to the left, relieved to see that Nevaeh's grabbed my father just in time.

I shield my eyes at the blinding flash of gold light that follows, heart pounding as Xerin's familiar shape takes form. I look to my aunt, desperate to shield her from the pain of what I've only just found out. I need to tell her what I know, but something tells me I won't get the chance.

I look past those blood-red eyes to see Haskell and Estelle rushing in our direction, Rydan, Vira, and their unfamiliar companion not far behind. I notice that Braxton doesn't appear to be on the grounds. Nor does Lane. The field has mostly cleared out, save for the remaining mages who continue to reinforce the shield that's protecting Sardoria from the dragons' fiery wrath.

"Quite the fight you've put up," Xerin says with a fiendish grin. "But how much more can your forces endure?"

Cerylia steps forward, bristling with rage. "As Queen of these lands, I demand you surrender at once."

"Do you now?" I can feel the Caldari brace themselves for whatever's to come, myself included, when Xerin surprises us all. His eyes soften. "I'm glad to see that you're still as headstrong as ever."

Cerylia unsheathes her sword before pointing it directly at him. "Surrender," she demands again through gritted teeth. "Or you'll leave me no choice."

He chuckles. "That would be a shame, seeing as you've been longing to see me."

"Longing? To see *you*?" Cerylia scoffs. "There's only one person who fits that description—" Suddenly, as if she's had the wind knocked from her lungs, she takes a step back, her sword lowering involuntarily. "No." She stares at him in disbelief. "You wouldn't."

"But I did," he says, his features morphing right before our eyes. Blonde hair turns black as night. Matching facial hair appears over once smooth skin. Previously crimson, wrinkles now line bright cerulean eyes.

Cerylia drops her sword as she stumbles backward, the blade sinking into the snow. Recognition takes hold, causing her to raise both hands to cover her mouth. "This can't be—it isn't possible—"

"But it is," I whisper, hating that she's finding out this way. "It's what was contained in Aldreda's veiled speculor." I brace myself for her reaction. "It wasn't Dane who died at the hands of Aldreda and Clive. In fact, Dane never died at all. It was *Xerin* who was shaped as Dane. Xerin's the one who was murdered . . ."

"I have returned, My Queen," Dane says as he opens his arms in a grand sweeping gesture. "In truth, I never really left."

RYDAN HELSTROM

THE GATHERING IN the center of the field should be the thing that grabs Rydan's attention, but it isn't. It's the man standing where Xerin once stood; the man who looks vaguely familiar, even though he can't seem to place where he's seen him before.

"Who is that?" Vira asks from beside him. "And where is my brother?"

Fortunately, Avery had saved the day with one of his exceptionally brewed tonics, but only for a short time. He'd made it quite clear that Vira still isn't out of the woods just yet. She'll need to see a Healer within the hour or face dire consequences.

"I'm not sure where your brother is, but this man . . . I've seen him before," Rydan says as he squints to get a better look. "I just can't place exactly where—"

"Why would he pretend to be my brother?" There's no denying the panic in her tone or the alarmed look on her face. "*Where* is Xerin?"

"He was right there, just moments ago," Avery says from behind them. "I saw it myself."

"Wait, the dragon who just tried to kill her is her *brother*?" Andri whispers a little too loudly.

Rydan's tempted to turn around and smack them both on the head. He needs to keep Vira calm, especially in her current condition, and this certainly isn't helping. Too much adrenaline will send all her blood rushing to the weakest spot—to the wound that's currently on the mend.

"I'm sure there's a logical explanation for what we just saw," Rydan says firmly, not believing the words himself.

She whips her head toward him. "Then what is it, Rydan?" There's a fury in her gaze he's never seen before and hopes to never bear witness to again. "Please, enlighten me. What possible explanation is there?"

Although he doesn't mean to, he snaps. "Lords, Vira, listen to yourself! Do you really think your own brother, your own *flesh and blood*, would kidnap you and use you as collateral for his own gain?" So much for keeping her calm. "Do you really think he'd threaten to kill you? To injure you badly enough to be on the verge of bleeding out? Is *that* the brother you remember?"

Vira's eyes bulge at the outburst. She shakes her head as tears begin to fall down her cheeks. "He would never do that. Xerin wouldn't—"

"Then that *wasn't* your brother," Rydan interrupts, "and hasn't been for a very long time."

"Then who—?"

"I already said I don't know!"

Vira pushes away from him, even though he's the only thing keeping her balanced and upright.

He takes a breath, cursing his damn temper. "I only said he looks familiar, that I can't remember where I've seen him before—"

"Then think harder!" she shouts. "This is my brother we're talking about!"

"Like I just said, I don't know where—"

All it takes to change that is a flash of the crescent fire.

Rydan pauses mid-sentence as recognition begins to seep in. "It's him," he whispers. "The man from Opal's memory."

"What?" Vira presses. "What are you talking about?"

"Don't you remember? The night Xerin showed up unannounced in Orihia and nearly bled out on our floor?"

"Of course I remember." She nods fervently, desperate for answers. "How could I forget?"

"In Opal's memory, it wasn't Xerin. It was that man," he says, pointing across the field.

Vira gives him a dubious look. "Are you sure?"

"Positive."

Vira squeezes the bridge of her nose, clearly trying to recall something important. "What was it Opal said she was doing? Traversing veiled memories?"

Rydan swallows the knot that's forming in his throat. Cerylia's warning had been loud and clear and yet Opal had taken the risk anyway. She'd known before any of them, had kept it to herself until she could be absolutely sure—and yet, he and Arden had made *her* out to be the monster.

"We have to get over there," Vira urges, clutching her injured arm as she picks up the pace. "I need to know who that is."

Rydan doesn't need to voice his agreement—he's just as curious as she is. He matches her stride, only coming to a stop when she does. It's sudden and unexpected. But so is the transformation that happens before them.

Silver and blue robes, the same as Cerylia's, appear out of thin air, before winding themselves around the man. In the same instant, a bejeweled crown appears, floating down from the sky before landing atop his head. The resemblance is uncanny.

"Holy shit." Vira's mouth drops open. "Is that—?"

There's only one person it can be, someone they'd presumed dead for nearly ten years. "It seems the King of Sardoria," Rydan answers, "is very much alive and well."

CERYLIA JARETH

SHE CAN'T MOVE, can't think, can't breathe. Her husband is . . . *alive.*

Impossible. She'd laid him to rest, had seen his corpse with her own two eyes. And yet, Dane had been a Shifter—and a rather skilled one at that. Always changing his appearance, no matter how small or insignificant, seems to have paid off. It'd seemed inconsequential at first—the sudden appearance of facial hair, the shifting hue of his irises, the slight alteration in his stature and build. But it'd all been for a larger purpose, one far more sinister than she possibly could have imagined.

A purpose so great, he'd chosen *it* over a life with her.

To think of the countless nights she'd pored over his burial site with tears streaming down her face . . . and for what? The man standing before her may as well be a complete stranger.

Cerulean eyes lock on hers—one original trait of his he'd seemed keen to return to—and if it weren't for the ruthless stare he has her pinned with, she might just break all together. She straightens, knowing she must keep her composure, if not for her own sake, then for the Caldari. And yet, sentiments from years past claw at her, desperate to be heard. But they'd be wasted on him, this imposter parading around as her husband.

She searches for something to say—something that'll capture the magnitude of what she's feeling at this very moment, but words elude her. Perhaps it's because there are none. Perhaps it's because her grief and rage and disbelief are all-consuming.

She feels her niece at her side, tugging at her arm, but Cerylia is shell-shocked. She continues to stare blankly at the man who'd promised her a lifetime together.

Under any other conditions, she'd be thrilled to see him—irrevocably ecstatic. But this level of deception isn't something she can ever recover from. No matter what he says, no matter the pleas he makes, no matter the explanations he's inclined to give . . . the betrayal is far too great.

If what Arden said is true, then it's Xerin she'd buried that day. Xerin she'd mourned over. Xerin she'd cried countless tears over. Which means Dane hadn't cared in the slightest what his loss would do to her. He hadn't cared that she'd suffer for years and years and *years*. And that can only leave her wondering . . . had it all been a ploy from the beginning to arrive at this very moment?

Suddenly feeling unsteady on her feet, Cerylia starts to sway, her hand brushing against the pocket of her robes as she tries to regain her balance. *The soul gem.* It'd been in Dane's study, a place where only *he* would think to hide it. She hadn't considered such a possibility because, in her mind, Dane was dead. It hadn't existed up until now.

Had he really dabbled in soul magick and captured Xerin's very essence all those years ago? Only to be used, over and over again, at his beck and call? It would certainly explain why he'd been able to shift himself countless times into a form that wasn't his own without growing weary and powerless. Xerin had been the perfect disguise. And he'd paid the ultimate price: his soul for Dane's new life.

A life that didn't include her.

"I thought you'd be pleased to see me," Dane challenges, attempting to mask the hurt in his voice.

Cerylia glowers at him. After a long stretch of silence, she finally says, "Under any other circumstances, I suppose I would be."

It isn't the answer he'd hoped for.

"I'm sorry to disappoint."

Cerylia nearly laughs aloud at the absurdity of his choice of words. "Oh, Dane," she scowls, her hands curling into fists. "Disappointment doesn't even *begin* to cover it."

277

DANE ELIRI

After years of hiding, he'd nearly forgotten just how good it feels to take his true form. No more masking, no more lying, no more pretending to be someone he's not . . . Although, he must admit, Xerin had been the perfect scapegoat. One of the oldest illusié families, imitating a Grey had been rather simple. With missing parents and an estranged sister, playing the part of the lonesome, elder Caldari couldn't have been a more perfect fit.

As expected, he'd executed the imitation flawlessly.

What he *hadn't* expected in the slightest, however, was the overwhelming grief that would come along with seeing his wife again—and the cost associated with playing such a role for so many years. Cerylia is just as stunning as the day he'd met her. The fine lines that now grace her face only point to the wisdom she's accumulated over the years . . .

Years *without* him.

Years spent alone.

For not having spoken for nearly a decade, he'd hoped for a warmer greeting. "I wish it hadn't come to this," he says, determined not to wither under her stare. He palms the crescent fire at his side. "But, surprisingly enough, being presumed dead ended up having more benefits than staying alive."

Her sword buried under the mounting snow, Cerylia's hand moves to the dagger sheathed at her belt, her grip resting on the hilt. "You had more to gain by leaving your queen, kingdom, and people to ruin under the tyrannical reign of the Tymonds?" Any hint of grief or longing in her eyes vanishes. "Lords, Dane. Do you hear yourself? What *happened* to you?"

Her words cut deep, but Dane doesn't so much as falter as he says, "Knowing Tymond's plan was to rid Aeridon of illusié, I made a choice. One I knew you'd ultimately never approve of."

Her face pales at his meaning. "Well, you chose wrong."

Having just proved his point, he claps his hands together. "I'm afraid that's where we don't meet eye to eye— and never have. Which was precisely my concern when I agreed to marry you and assume responsibility as the King of Aeridon under the Jareth name."

"Is that what this is about?" She whispers, her head shaking in disbelief. 'The *Eliri* name?"

"A bloodline as superior as ours deserves more credit, wouldn't you agree?" He directs the question at his brother, only to be greeted with contempt.

"Perhaps you and Darius Tymond are more alike than you realize," Arden says, answering for her father.

Dane tilts his head at his niece. "And how do you figure that?"

She narrows her eyes. "Well, for starters, you're both power-hungry assholes."

Dane chuckles. "Don't tell me you've already forgotten the power you felt at Midvale—the overwhelming urge to keep it for yourself? If memory serves, you did just that, however brief. But, with nowhere to go, you unleashed a culmination of such power that it wiped out nearly everyone and everything in its vicinity."

"If only you'd been included in the rubble," she growls.

"Come now, you know I'm far too clever to end up like that," Dane derides. "Especially when you've all played so seamlessly into what I've so carefully orchestrated."

A visible swallow is his only reply.

"Or didn't your father tell you?" he prods. "We Eliris cannot resist what is our birthright nor should we have to. Why do you think he locked himself away in the Veil?"

"That's quite enough, *brother*," Stanton barks, ushering Arden back with one arm. "I was right not to trust you."

"I never needed your trust. Only your compliance."

Stanton snarls. "You don't have that either."

"Oh, but I will," he replies with a knowing smile.

"I wouldn't count on it," Arden says as her gaze shifts over his shoulder, a smirk tugging at the corner of her mouth.

"And why is that?" Dane scowls.

"Because," Braxton responds from behind him, "there's one remaining Tymond you've severely underestimated."

BRAXTON HORNSBY

HE'D EXPECTED THE expression on Dane's face to be anything but pleasant, given the Mallum's looming presence, but the ex-king hardly seems rattled.

"It seems you've bested your father, unless he's lurking in the shadows somewhere." Dane narrows his eyes as he briefly surveys the field. "I must admit, I'm shocked to see *you* as the victor. A welcome surprise, I assure you. I was beginning to grow weary of your father."

Of all the things Braxton had expected him to say, that was certainly at the bottom of the list. Hell, it hadn't even been *on* the list. To speak of a victor as if it'd been planned, preconceived somehow . . . He clears his throat before saying, "Perhaps you've forgotten the power the Mallum holds. I'd be glad to give you a refresher."

Dane regards him with pure disinterest. "I can assure you I haven't forgotten. It should go without saying that I'm quite familiar with the Mallum." He glances at the ring glinting on Braxton's finger, finally putting two and two together, but his expression doesn't waver. What he says next is even more confusing. "If the ring fits, I suppose."

"What are you waiting for?" Stanton shouts. "End it!"

Dane chuckles derisively. "You really believe the Mallum would bite the hand that's been feeding it all these years? The very hands that created it to begin with?" Shadows darken his eyes. "Sent on a fool's errand to retrieve the ring, the staff . . . distractions, all of it. Even your father couldn't read between the lines," he scoffs. "The only potentiality to thwart my plans is now in my possession." He grips the crescent fire tighter. "Thanks to an ill-fated decision by one of your own."

The group turns to look as the Ignitor and Summoner approach. Having heard every word, Rydan growls, "You nearly killed her, you bastard."

"Ah, yes—my 'sister', as it were," Dane comments. "That's neither here nor there. In the end, she served her purpose. Although, sparing her life *did* come as a surprise, even to me."

"Fuck you," Vira seethes.

Dane has the nerve to laugh. "How spirited you are. Reminds me of your mother. She, too, fought to the very end."

Vira pales at the admission.

"A foolish endeavor, I might add," Dane continues. "Once she'd served her ultimate purpose in uniting me with dragonkind, my bond eventually strengthened enough to where I no longer required her services."

Vira scoffs. "She'd never agree to help someone like you. Especially if she knew her aid would be used for evil."

"That's neither here nor there, though, because with your father's life as collateral, she didn't have much choice, now did she?"

Vira goes silent, her expression bleak.

"I'm sure the beasts would agree that your parents made quite a satisfying meal—"

"Enough," Rydan snaps, not wanting to hear anymore.

"Perhaps she should sic the dragons on *you*," Braxton threatens.

"And how would she do that?" Dane clicks his tongue against the roof of his mouth. "Seeing as she's no longer able to speak to them, let alone summon them."

Braxton looks at the ring adorning his finger, trying not to feel utterly defeated.

"So, what, then?" Stanton asks. "You've gathered us all here to gloat?"

A muscle feathers in Dane's cheek. "Come now, brother. I thought you knew me better than that."

The words come out clipped. "Clearly, I don't know you at all. Nor do I want to."

The Shifter's eyes turn frank and cold. "The reason I've gathered you here is quite simple, really. Since the Mallum has absorbed your abilities, my dear brother will act as the initial conduit to channel those abilities to Arden, who will then channel them to me."

Cerylia levels a steely gaze at her husband. "Making you the only person who can wield the entirety of illusié in all of Aeridon."

"Precisely," Dane answers.

Arden's mouth tightens in disapproval. "And what makes you think my father—or I, for that matter—would be willing to go along with this?"

Dane smiles, but it doesn't reach his eyes. "We *are* family, are we not?"

Arden scoffs. "Not if I have anything to do with it."

"Well," Dane says with lethal calm, "if the family name means so little to you, then I suppose you'd forego the opportunity to meet your mother."

Arden stiffens, shoulders tensing. "My mother is long since dead. Killed by the Savant."

"Is that so?" Dane taunts. "Or could she perhaps be standing among us right now?"

This is it. It's now or never.

"It's true," Braxton says. "The note my mother left, the one I showed you . . . I finally decoded it. I've only just confirmed what I hoped wasn't true—"

Glassy-eyed, Arden turns to face her cousin. "Confirmed *what*, Braxton?"

"I didn't know how to tell you this. I still don't." He lowers his gaze, the words like acid on his tongue. "But the Mallum and your mother . . . are one in the same."

ARDEN ELIRI

I WAIT FOR Braxton to laugh, to crack a smile, to do *something* that'll soften the blow of the news he's just delivered, but he remains stoic. *He can't be serious.* I twist my head toward my father, who looks just as stunned as I feel.

"Think about it, Arden," Braxton goes on, knowing how difficult this must be for me to process. "Why is it that the Mallum yielded to you at every turn? Your abilities were never absorbed, your life was spared over and over again, you were even able to find a way to *communicate* with it—"

I inhale a sharp breath. It makes sense. All of it. Everything he's saying. But that doesn't make it any easier to digest.

"You mean to tell me that my mother is the reason you lost your ability to deviate?" I challenge. "That she's the reason countless illusié are either powerless or dead?"

Dane raises a finger in the air. "Close, but not quite," he interjects. "Similar to a soul gem, your mother is connected to the Mallum in that her soul is bound to it." He arches a brow. "Much like someone else you know."

I resist the urge to spit at his feet. "You have some fucking nerve." The fact that he's bringing Felix into this is enough to make my blood boil. "Where is he?" I demand through clenched teeth.

Dane waves a flippant hand in the air. "We'll worry about him later. For now, you have quite the decision to make."

"And if I refuse?"

"That would be unwise." Dane tilts his head, his face a mask of cold indifference. "Especially since your mother's soul would remain trapped, as would Felix's. It's quite simple, really: illusié will either perish or it will live on through me."

"As the sole wielder of all magick," I bite out.

Dane's smile turns lupine. "Better an Eliri than someone less deserving, wouldn't you agree?"

The statement gives me pause, and for good reason. This is it. My opening. The ideal segue to save us from the downward trajectory we're on; but it'll mean breaking the trust of everyone around me . . .

Everyone I've come to hold dear.

I meet my uncle's stare. "Actually, I suppose I would. Agree, that is."

A collective murmur passes amongst the group.

"Surely you don't mean that." My aunt's voice borders on hysterical. "Arden?"

But my mind is made up. "I'll do it."

"Excellent decision," Dane purrs.

"She will not," Stanton decrees. "I will not allow it."

I look at him, knowing we're about to put on the show of our lives. I nearly choke on a sob as our brief conversation in the infirmary replays in my mind—the same one he'd discreetly shared with Cerylia. He'd only just awoken but with no shortage of words. "At the risk of sounding paranoid, I can no longer keep this from you."

Nevaeh had looked between us, clearly sensing the need for privacy, but Stanton had urged her to stay and listen.

"After all these years, Arden, you deserve answers. You deserve to know *why* you were left in the care of the Tymonds. As heart wrenching as it was, I left you with family. I'd hoped Aldreda, being your mother's sister, would look out for you, but that was before I learned of Darius's affinity for Lavinia . . . for my wife. After what I'd assumed to be the murder of my brother, I knew I'd be the next target. As the sole channeler in Aeridon at the time, I couldn't risk my position."

"So, you disappeared," I'd finished for him.

"It was the only way. When Haskell didn't demonstrate a proclivity for channeling, I knew the ability would lie with you, although I wasn't sure what form it would take or when it would make its appearance."

"Why would that matter?"

He'd exhaled a heavy sigh. "In an effort to keep the scales of illusié balanced, many years ago, the Council decreed that only one Channeler could exist at a time. I attempted to plead my case, to poke holes in their logic by convincing them that a novice would eventually require a teacher, hence the need for *two* Channelers, but they didn't even deign to consider it. That's when I decided to leave, to feign death—or whatever they chose to believe happened to me—and entered the Medial instead."

The admission had felt like a dagger to the chest. "Then how are we both here right now, existing?"

"That's something I'm still trying to reconcile. I can only assume that being in the Medial for so many years acted as a barrier between the Council and me. But, if what occurred at Midvale is any indication, I'm much weaker than I'd anticipated."

The mention of Midvale had brought the memory spiraling back—how I'd nearly killed him during my failed attempt to channel all the Savants' abilities simultaneously.

And that's when I'd had the harshest realization of all.

"My life is costing you yours."

"It is," he'd said with a solemn nod. "And I need you to know it's a price I'd pay a million times over if it means getting to have you as my daughter . . ."

Much too soon, Dane's laugh throttles me back to the present.

"Oh, you won't *allow* it?" Dane chides, sneering at my father. "You mean to say that you'd willingly let your daughter die? Because you and I both know that channeling that much power is a death wish for one individual—but not for two."

Stanton's eyes flare with believable rage as he turns to me, his only daughter, to plead his case. "The cost is too great, Arden. If we yield everything to him—"

"Did she mean nothing to you?" My voice is barely above a whisper as I tug at every strand of despair I can find. "My mother? Because I would give anything to see the person I love again, to hear him speak my name just one more time."

He brings a hand to his chest. It may be a façade, but the emotions are real. "I loved your mother dearly, there's no doubt about that. But would I bring her back given the current landscape?" His eyes flick to Dane before giving a sad shake of his head. "Not at the expense of the greater good, I'm afraid."

"I suppose that's where we differ, then," I retort, doing everything in my power to keep my tone even. "This world has been cruel and unforgiving, thanks to a decision *you* made out of self-preservation." Even though I don't mean them, the words cut through me like glass. "You weren't there to defend my mother when she needed you most, just like you weren't there to raise me as your own. Instead, you left me to the wolves—to the *Tymonds*, of all people—to fend for myself."

Any trace of color drains from his face. "My past actions need not define the future."

"It seems they already have," I choke out, hating what I'm about to do. I close my eyes and turn away, unable to look at him as I allow the power within to build. Once I feel the heat coursing through my veins, my body humming as if it's been struck by lightning, I know there's no turning back. It takes every ounce of strength I have left to block out the outraged cries around me. I can only hope the Caldari won't be foolish enough to intervene.

Even though war wages within me, still, I persist. I open my eyes, reluctantly lifting one arm in the direction of the Mallum, the other at Dane. Never have I seen a look of such satisfaction. Guilt coils in my stomach, but, even so, I keep my focus trained on the energy swirling around me. Muffled shouts reach my ears, but it's the look on Rydan's face that nearly unravels me.

I'm sorry, I mouth as he watches in horror.

Cerylia dives for Braxton, moving him out of harm's way as a stream of illusié energy is ejected from the Mallum. I reach my arm toward it, waiting for the arrival of the sensation I've become all too familiar with, but something's blocking it. And I hate that I already know what it is.

My father.

A guttural sob wrenches from my throat as Stanton takes the brunt of the impact, his mouth opening in a silent scream as he acts as a conduit to channel the stream of energy to me. I want to tell him to stop, that I can do it, that even if it kills me, at least my mother will be free, but the words are lodged in my throat.

The initial torrent of energy runs its course as I direct it in a horizontal line, straight from one arm to the other. My outstretched hand trembles as the sheer force of it reaches my fingertips. I pause, steadying myself with a deep inhale, before finally releasing it. Out of the corner of my eye, I can see Dane's palms open at his sides, eyes bulging as the power of all illusié seeps into his veins.

I want to stop. To scream. To thrash and fight. But that isn't what we agreed on. That isn't how we're going to win this. And, above all else, we *have* to win this.

I'm on the verge of tears, but it's almost over. I look back toward the Mallum, waiting for the right moment—the one my father instructed me would eventually come. And it does, painstakingly so, my body on the verge of collapsing as the last of the energy is drained from the entity, the Mallum merely a shell of what it once was. But a shell that contains my mother's soul, nonetheless.

He may not realize it—and I'm counting on it—but Dane is simultaneously at his strongest and his weakest as his body adjusts to its newfound power. As I'd hoped, it's just the distraction I need. With all the strength I can muster, I shout, "Now!", watching as my aunt hurries to position herself at the appropriate distance from the Mallum. Soul gem in hand, she begins to unweave the tangled threads that are keeping my mother tied to the Mallum.

My father falls to his knees and, as much as I want to go to him, to be there while he takes his final breaths, I know we aren't finished yet. There *will* be one Eliri that walks away from this as illusié . . . and it sure as hell won't be Dane.

DANE ELIRI

The power he's sought after all these years is finally his. From within the pockets of his robes, the draconian crests glow in their respective colors, signaling that the transfer of energy is complete. Without the assembly of crests on his person, channeled power of that magnitude would have destroyed him from the inside out, until only ash remained.

Victorious, Dane lifts his arms overhead in triumph. Illusié surges through him, electrifying every muscle, every bone, every fiber of his being. Heady from the energy flow, he lowers his gaze just in time to see the Mallum shrink in size as Lavinia's soul is extracted by none other than his wife. She pockets the soul gem before rushing to Stanton, who's lying motionless on the ground. Arden has fallen to her knees, heaving jagged breaths as she attempts to heal herself from the onslaught of power she's just unleashed.

Only two things remain in the way of his reign—and they're standing before him, exposed and vulnerable.

Channeler.

Extractor.

If he hopes to keep his newfound power, which he has every intention of doing, his wife's existence poses a very real threat, as does his niece's. The extraction of his abilities would kill Cerylia, no doubt, but he wouldn't put it past her to attempt it if it meant restoring the balance of illusié. Along the same lines, all it would take for him to lose everything he's just gained is for Arden to channel it to someone else.

"As much as I hate for it to end this way," he says, the veiled tethers of death rising, "I'm afraid your purpose has reached its inevitable end. Since the Mallum couldn't do it for me, I'm left with no choice but to do it myself."

Cerylia bares her teeth. "You've already managed to kill your brother. Now you want to add your niece and your wife to that list?"

"If that's what it takes."

Much to his surprise, neither she nor Arden move out of the way, nor do they attempt to flee or hide, or even beg for mercy. Their indifference is somewhat disconcerting, but, truthfully, it's none of his concern. So be it. They're only making things that much easier for him.

To his right, Haskell shoulders his way forward, joining Cerylia at his father's side. "You're a pathetic excuse for a man, you know that?"

Dane laughs in amusement. "Is that so? Because, last time I checked, having the ability to wield any and all illusié abilities isn't even the least bit pathetic. In fact, I'd say it's quite the opposite."

A gravelly voice interjects, "Not *all* abilities."

Dane's gaze travels to Arden, who's managed to push herself to her feet, despite her painfully slow progress in healing herself.

She clears her throat. "Seeing as the Mallum was limited in its ability to absorb channeling and extraction, your *library*, as it were, will always be incomplete. You'll never truly know the full scale of illusié—"

Dane scoffs as he opens his mouth to counter, but he isn't quick enough.

"But I will," she finishes. Her face is pallid, lips cracked and mouth dry as she meets his stare and . . . smiles. As if that weren't unnerving enough, she proceeds to utter a word he wasn't expecting.

"Rescinder."

His heart misses a beat. *Impossible.* He'd made it his prerogative to ensure those with rescinding abilities were taken care of for precisely this reason. He'd even bypassed using the Mallum altogether, preferring to carry out the acts himself. Those he'd captured had endured little suffering and a swift death by his own hands—a kindness he never felt inclined to give the others. Furthermore, the Mallum had just absorbed every last ability of those remaining on this field, unless . . .

"Channeler, Extractor, *Rescinder*," Nevaeh says, coming into view.

"The Sacred Trinity of abilities unavailable to the Mallum," Arden adds, taking a bold step forward. "It seems your reign is about to be even shorter than your first."

Dane looks between the two women, refusing to believe he's been bested. His roster had been complete. He'd been sure of it. But missing *one* is all it would take to thwart his plans.

"Farewell, Dane Eliri," Cerylia glowers as she stands, nodding at Nevaeh. "You will not be missed, you spineless—"

But he doesn't hear the rest of the insult as the Rescinder blasts into him, reversing the very thing he's waited his entire existence for. He desperately reaches for the obscure tethers of energy as they leave his body, writhing as they revert to the last living thing they'd come into contact with *before* him. He can only watch, in utter agony and despair, as Arden receives every last strand of illusié.

CERYLIA JARETH

SHE CAN ONLY hope that the decision to revert the energy back to her niece is the right one, given the near catastrophic events of Midvale. She may have been oblivious to it, unlike Stanton, but Arden's hesitation had spoken volumes. Now, as Cerylia witnesses the exchange of power from her husband to her niece, it's hard not to be reminded of the many things that could go wrong.

Dane desperately reaches for the final thread of energy as it's taken from him. As if, somehow, he can pull it back through the motion alone. Gaining everything had somehow cost him everything, including his original ability to shift. He clutches his chest as the last illusié spark fades, leaving him void of any and all magick.

He glares at the Rescinder, his hands curling into fists before finding the audacity to lunge for her, but Cerylia intercepts the attack by flinging a dagger at his shoulder.

Dane cries out in pain, hand flying to the hilt of the dagger. His knees buckle in protest as he tries to remain upright, his gaze tracking the origin of the blade until it lands on her.

Cerylia strides forward, noticing the hint of betrayal that flashes across her husband's eyes. *Good.* Now he knows how she feels. She's been blinded by rage before where the outcome had been less than pleasant. Unwilling to repeat the mistakes of her past, she approaches him with lethal calm.

With Dane distracted by his wound, she steals a glance at Arden who's keeled over at the waist, panting. Truthfully, it's a miracle she's still standing. Whatever time she can afford her niece is crucial in order for her to heal and fully integrate all the magick she's just absorbed. She takes a breath, facing forward as she closes the distance between her and Dane.

The color has completely leeched from his face and there's an evident tremor in his voice as he says, "You have every right to be upset with me."

As if it's merely a quarrel, a spat they've had over dinner, to be forgiven before the night's end. Cerylia scoffs in disbelief. "Being upset would require you to be someone I have mutual respect for."

He flinches at the insult.

"If you don't hear anything else, hear this, Dane. You are, no more, no less, a stranger to me." She bites back the sting of her words, determined not to crack under their weight. "Tell me, how does it feel to have it all and lose it all in the same breath?"

Dane clutches the dagger, eyes narrowing. "Deny it all you want, but we're one in the same, you and I."

She's about to ask how he could have possibly come to such a preposterous conclusion when she realizes . . . she doesn't care. It doesn't matter that she'd fallen in love with him all those years ago. It doesn't matter that they'd ruled together, side by side, for a time. It doesn't matter that she'd mourned a death that had never even happened. *None* of it matters because nothing this man can say will change his fate.

A glint in the snowfall steals her attention. There, on the traitor's ring finger, is his wedding band. She lets out a low growl at the sight of it. She's been calm and of sound mind up until this point, but something about seeing that ring changes things. What a mockery of marriage, and a royal one at that. What a fool he's made her out to be.

Cerylia lunges for the dagger, pulling it from its deep position in Dane's shoulder. Wide-eyed, Dane howls as the blade slices back through its entry point. Blood drips onto the blanket of white at her feet as she positions it above his left wrist. Before he can even register what's happening, she's sliced clean through skin, tendon, and bone.

Dane shrieks, a sound she never thought she'd enjoy hearing, especially having been of her own doing. She slips off her own wedding ring before hurtling both it and the decapitated hand across the field.

Powerless and one-handed, Dane still has the nerve to snarl. "You foolish bitch. I hope you realize the mistake you've just made." Pure venom laces his tone. "We could have had it all. You've thrown away the only secure future available to you."

Cerylia laughs quietly. "If that's your definition of a secure future, I want no part of it." She turns a heartless stare on the man she once loved. "And the only mistake I ever made was offering the Jareth name to someone like you."

Dane dry heaves, from either the blood loss or the cruelty of her words, she can't be sure. "Why not just kill me, then?"

Cerylia turns over her shoulder, motioning to someone Dane can't see. "While you've stolen much of my life from me, there's *another* person you stole a life from."

A tangle of blonde hair appears beside her. Vira stares him dead in the eye as she says, "You degraded my brother's name, his reputation, his family . . ." She sucks in a breath before continuing. "Have you no remorse?"

Dane's eyes flick to the wound he'd given her mid-flight, his tone sharp as he replies, "I should have dropped you to your death when I had the chance."

"Fuck you," Vira growls.

"I'd watch how you speak to her," Cerylia warns, "since she'll be the one deciding your fate."

Dane's face falls.

"I yield to you, Lady Grey," Cerylia says. "I know it won't bring your brother back or ease your strife, but whatever punishment you deem appropriate shall be carried out without question."

A smile tugs at the corner of the girl's mouth as she tilts her head to the sky. There isn't the slightest hesitation as she voices her decision. "The dragons can have him."

RYDAN HELSTROM

RYDAN CAN ONLY watch in both horror and fascination as a dragon swoops down from the sky, its massive claws crunching bone as it lands over Dane's legs. A horrific shriek fills the air, but it's cut short as the dragon moves its other claw over Dane's chest, its mouth hovering just above the ex-king's head. Having seen enough blood for one day, Rydan turns away, the sound of snapping jaws echoing in his ears.

It's then he spots Arden, who's fallen on all fours, shaking as she retches violently across the snow. Lords, she must be freezing. He rushes over to her, removing his cloak in tandem, before wrapping the extra layer tightly around her shoulders. "We need to get you inside," he says, gently pulling her to her feet.

She lifts her gaze to where Dane had been just moments prior, less than half of a bloody carcass remaining. She heaves at the sight.

"It's over," Rydan assures her, turning them both away from the wreckage. "Dane is gone."

Legs trembling, Arden winces as she takes a step toward the castle. "It's far from over, Helstrom."

They pass by Haskell, who's draping a spare cloak over his father's body. Avery joins him, offering to help bring Stanton inside the castle. Haskell gives him a solemn nod before meeting Rydan's stare, then Arden's. His expression hardens.

"It was the only way," she chokes out. "He knew, Haskell. I promise. He was in on it, it was his idea—"

Haskell waves away her attempted justification. "Not now, Arden. It just . . . isn't the time."

Guilt-ridden, she lowers her head. Teardrops splatter against Rydan's arm. "I'm sorry," she whispers.

Haskell just shakes his head.

"Come on," Rydan says, ushering her forward. "Let's get you near a fire."

It only dawns on him right then that since he's no longer illusié, he can't offer his oldest friend the one thing she so desperately needs . . . but she, herself, can. Arden currently has the capability to wield any illusié ability she so desires, including that of an Ignitor.

The thought is jarring.

"I know what you're thinking," she says as she wipes her cheek with the back of her gloved hand. "And there's nothing to worry about. I'm going to give it all back. I have to."

He tries to hide his sigh of relief, but it's impossible to do so in such inclement weather.

She turns her wide eyes at him. "Did you really think I'd be selfish enough to keep it?" The blatant hurt in her tone causes him to flinch. "I may bear the Eliri name, but I'm nothing like that asshole."

"And thank the lords for that," he says, giving her a small smile. "But I have to ask . . . why not include me in your plans? Or Haskell? Or anyone else for that matter?"

"Time, for one. Moreoever, my father, Nevaeh, Cerylia, and I were the only ones left with illusié abilities, ones the Mallum couldn't take." She sighs. "It didn't feel right to include anyone else, to put any of the Caldari at risk when you've all already given so much."

Rydan forces a nod. It's a logical answer, but that doesn't mean he has to agree with it. "It was the only way," he says slowly, repeating her words back to her. "That's what you said to Haskell just now."

Her voice strains. "There's a reason we've never come across another Channeler until my father. It's because there can only be one. My father's decision to banish himself to the Medial afforded us time—time for my abilities to fully morph and develop into what they are now. He knew that, one day, I'd need a teacher, and that the only person who could fulfill that role was him. All these years, the Medial granted him protection from the Council, acting as a sort of barrier to keep him off their radar."

Feeling her grief, Rydan holds on to her a little tighter as they climb the castle steps. "So, in the end, there was no saving him."

"My being alive cost him his life," she admits despondently. "Talk about a twisted illusié ability to pass down."

He can feel the guilt emanating from her as if it were his own. "Your father knew, Arden. He made his choice long, long ago. You've only just found out." He shudders at the blast of warmth that greets them as they step inside the castle.

Her entire demeanor shifts suddenly, as if she's just remembered something. "Speaking of just finding out, there's something I need to show you. I would ask if you're up for a trip, but it'd be a moot point."

She's piqued his curiosity. "And why is that?"

She sighs, pulling her pocket watch from within her breastplate. "Because it'd be a brief visit to the Veil."

The stark reminder that he's no longer illusié sits heavy on his chest. "Regardless, I really don't think you're in any condition to travel. We need to stick to our original plan and get you to the infirmary."

"There was something else in Queen Tymond's speculor," she blurts out. "Something you're bound to find *very* interesting."

Rydan gives her a weary look, knowing she's only trying to delay the inevitable. Still, he plays along. "And what might that be?"

She grins. "How to wield the crescent fire."

BRAXTON HORNSBY

THE FIELD HAS mostly cleared out, save for a few mages and a couple of the Caldari. Braxton faces the Mallum, now powerless, soulless, and not the least bit ominous as it was before. Even with the staff strapped to his back and the amethyst ring on his finger, he's still at a loss—because Lane isn't here.

Knots form in his stomach as he replays the events from the watchtower in his mind—the way she'd so selflessly flung herself into the Void to save his life . . . and ensure his father would no longer have one.

"You've caused me a world of trouble," he says to the entity, knowing he may as well be talking to a wall. "What am I to do with you now?"

In the distance, he can see Arden stumbling up the steps to Sardoria castle with Rydan by her side. He isn't the only one who's lost someone. Arden has, too, but they certainly won't be the last . . .

His heart shatters as he spots Estelle approaching him, her midnight hair whipping in the wind. He straightens, readying himself to deliver the news no one ever hopes or expects to hear. She spares him the words, however, as she draws closer, eyes searching for his counterpart . . . who isn't there.

"Lane?" She halts more than a few steps from him, hand covering her mouth. "No."

He opens his mouth to speak, but suitable words escape him. How can he tell her that her cousin may or may not be dead? That she was alive when he last saw her but that she may as well be dead having ended up in the Void?

"I'm sorry." The words don't even begin to convey the depth of what he's feeling, but he has to say *something*.

A sob wrenches free as Estelle clutches her chest. A swift decision has Braxton moving toward her and taking her into his arms, her entire body shuddering as she weeps into his blood-stained shoulder.

"She saved me," Braxton whispers into her ear. "Your cousin is the bravest, most selfless person I know."

The sentiment only makes her cry harder. Braxton clamps his mouth shut, continuing to hold her until she calms. When she finally pulls away from him, eyes puffy and rimmed with red, she says, "Can you take me to her body?" She sniffles. "I'd like to give Lane a proper burial."

The request nearly splits his heart in two. "I'm afraid I can't."

She looks at him in confusion. "Why not? She's just lying out there on the field somewhere—" Her eyes narrow. "Or are you saying you won't?"

"Neither. Because Lane isn't here." There. He said it.

"What do you mean she isn't *here*?" Estelle presses. "If she isn't here, then where is she?"

Braxton braces himself for what is sure to be an unpleasant reaction. "We were on the watchtower when the Mallum took her abilities. My father was going to kill us both when Lane . . . used her pocket watch."

Estelle blanches. "She's in the Void?"

Braxton grimaces, then nods. "Along with my father."

"Fuck," Estelle whispers, jaw working. "This is bad."

No argument there.

"But you've been there, haven't you? In the Void?" The look on her face is so hopeful, it borders on desperation. "If you were able to make it out, there has to be a way out for her as well."

He'd thought the same thing . . . until he'd recalled the one differentiating factor that had determined his fate. "It might be possible, but when I was caught in the Void, I had something that she doesn't: the crescent fire. It helped guide me to the Medial, the place in between the Veil and the Void. That's where I found Stanton. And Hanslow."

Estelle chews on her lower lip, deep in thought. "But we have the crescent fire, don't we? I can go and bring it with me. Without my abilities, I'll land in the Void, just like Lane. I'll find her and we'll use the crescent fire to get to the Medial and—"

"Wait." Braxton shakes his head as another thought occurs to him. "We must also consider the disruption in the Veil's power source after the Savant got ahold of it. Because of that, who knows if the Medial still even exists? Not to mention, the only reason Hanslow and Stanton were able to escape the Medial was *because* the Veil went down."

Estelle opens her mouth to counter, but ultimately stops herself. Her shoulders drop in defeat.

Braxton hates that she's just come to the same realization he has because it's a hopeless one. "Even so," he says, trying to lighten the mood, "because it's Lane we're talking about, I'd take the risk."

Estelle's voice hitches. "I can't ask you to do that."

"You don't have to," Braxton assures her. "I'm offering."

He can tell how much she wants to accept his offer. But, if there's one thing he's learned about Estelle, it's that she respects others' decisions even if she disagrees with them. Glassy-eyed, she shakes her head. "If there's no way out—and it sounds like there isn't—Lane wouldn't want you to risk your life to save hers. Not when she's already made the decision knowing she wouldn't be coming back." Estelle sniffles, coming to terms with the loss.

Her response weighs heavy on his heart. "Just . . . say the word if you change your mind."

She brushes a tear from her cheek. "My conscience would never rest if you left and didn't return." She heaves a loud sigh. "I wouldn't be able to live with myself."

Braxton nods in understanding. "I can help make arrangements in her honor. She'll go out just how she should, how we'll always remember her. With dignity and grace."

Estelle takes his hand, giving it a light squeeze as she echoes the words back to him. "With dignity and grace."

RYDAN HELSTROM

Arden had agreed to visit the infirmary at his request, but what they *hadn't* covered was for how long. One look at the room full of wounded soldiers and woefully understaffed Healers and she'd turned on her heel to head elsewhere. Seeing no choice but to follow her, they arrive at the Sardoria library, which, thankfully, hadn't been tainted by the battle that'd just waged outside.

Arden's chatting with his cousin, Andri, after Rydan had briefly introduced them on the field. He has no idea what could have them so engrossed in conversation, but he's thankful for the exclusion. It's giving him time to gather his thoughts.

When they finally arrive at the hearth in the back of the room, Rydan's glad to see it's already burning brightly. He looks at his hands, once again trying not to be reminded of the fact that he's no longer an Ignitor. His cousin seems to pick up on his line of thought.

"We'll get them back," Andri says cheerfully. "Your abilities are literally a hands-reach away."

Rydan forces a smile, but neither that nor the sentiment make him feel any better. "What have you two been so busy discussing?"

Arden takes a seat near the fire, gesturing for Rydan and Andri to do the same. "I wanted to make sure that what I saw in Aldreda's speculor was accurate. It seems Andri, here, already knows how to wield the crescent fire."

"Grandpa Erle was always willing to teach me anything I wanted to know about illusié," Andri says, taking the seat across from her. "But when it came to the crescent fire, it was Grandma Radelle who taught me everything I know." He blinks back a tear. "I just never thought I'd be in a position to use it."

"None of us did," Rydan says. "And yet . . . here we are."

Andri clears his throat. "I wasn't there for the memory Arden shared with me, so I think it's best that she recount what she witnessed." He pauses. "If that's all right with you?"

"Why wouldn't it be?" Rydan says, suddenly disliking the exclusion he'd felt earlier. Of course they'd been talking about the crescent fire. What else would the two of them have in common?

Arden nods, readying herself to reveal what she knows.

❧ ❧ ❧

Rydan listens intently as Arden sets the scene some odd years ago back in Midvale. Archmage Galdor is in her prime, standing behind her desk as Queen Aldreda Tymond approaches. She's flanked by two others, Radelle and Erle Soames.

"So," Archmage Galdor says flatly, "you're one of us. Does your husband know?"

"Do you really think I would risk the only power I have?" Queen Tymond retorts.

"Fair point." Her gaze shifts to Radelle and Erle. "There must be a reason you've gone through all this trouble to apprehend the Queen of Trendalath and bring her to me."

"She knows where the crescent fire is located," Erle answers, clearly not one for beating around the bush.

The Archmage raises a brow at their captive. "Is this true?"

Aldreda nods. "It is."

"Pray tell, where *is* the crescent fire?"

Aldreda lifts her chin. "An answer for an answer."

The Archmage purses her lips. "And what is it you seek?"

A simple response, the queen says, "Knowledge."

Archmage Galdor laughs. "Well, you've come to the right place." She gestures to her office and the doors beyond. "The collections in our libraries are rather extensive. If we deem you trustworthy, you can take your pick—"

"The knowledge I seek cannot be found in books," Aldreda remarks. "I'm afraid your *extensive libraries* are of no use to me."

The Archmage bristles at her tone.

"However," the queen says, turning to face Radelle and Erle, "the knowledge I seek can be found within these two."

Radelle exchanges a glance with her husband. "Us?"

"Yes," Aldreda says, a touch harshly. "You're in search of the crescent fire because it's your family crest, is it not? A worthwhile endeavor, I might add. One that I can help with—in exchange for knowledge on how to wield it."

Erle scoffs at the sheer audacity of her request. "That knowledge is reserved only for those of Draconian blood."

Aldreda is quick to respond. "As it should be. However, I feel I must implore you to make an exception."

"For a *Tymond*?" Radelle says the name as if poison has touched her tongue. "You may as well just kill us now."

The queen lifts her hands in the air in a show of solidarity. "My husband wears the ring. The staff is also in his possession. The Mallum is at *his* disposal." She arches a brow. "However, it's my understanding that the crescent fire has the capability to destroy items of illusié origin, including the ring and the staff."

"She speaks the truth," the Archmage interjects. Aldreda glances over her shoulder at her. "And your assumption regarding the crescent fire happens to be correct."

"If you can show me how to wield it, perhaps we can stop my husband before he ravages what remains of illusié from our lands."

"And why would you want to stop him? You swore fealty to him, to Trendalath—"

"Because I'm one of you." There's an edge to the queen's voice. "And because I believe one of our Cruex is of Draconian blood and will one day require this knowledge to do the very thing I've just described." She goes on to say, "I'm not asking for me. I'm asking for all of Aeridon."

The Archmage walks around her desk, passing by the queen until she's standing directly in front of her. "How do you know this?"

"Because of my illusié ability."

The Archmage studies her closely. "Which is?"

Aldreda straightens, looking each of them dead in the eye. "I'm a Diviner."

ARDEN ELIRI

I HADN'T CAUGHT it the first time around since I'd been so focused on the crescent fire, but there's no denying it now. "Queen Tymond *knew*. She knew that all of this was going to happen."

Rydan continues to stare at her, brows furrowed as he's clearly still processing the fact that, much like a dragon, he can *breathe* fire. "How do you figure that?"

"A Diviner is another name for a Seer," Andri answers for me. "Meaning she could foretell events before they occurred."

Rydan blanches. "In that case, do you think she knew all along that the Soames would be a target? That Darius would send the both of us on that mission?"

"More likely than not," I say glumly. "Depending on how far she could see into the future, it's possible she knew that, eventually, we'd discover it was Dane who was actually behind everything." Just speaking his name causes my stomach to turn.

A muscle ticks along Rydan's jaw as he rises from his seat. "Do you think Darius knew that his wife was illusié? Or somehow found out?"

"It's entirely possible. It would certainly explain a lot."

"Then why not use her to his advantage?" he questions.

"Maybe he tried only for her to refuse," Andri points out.

"But why?" Rydan presses. "Why would she refuse to help her husband, their kingdom? Furthermore, why wouldn't she intervene if she knew the outcome?"

He raises a valid point, one that has me pondering in silence for more than a few minutes. The conversation feels familiar and that's because I've heard a similar one before.

"It's like Opal used to say . . . intervening with time can change its entire trajectory. She may have been traversing memories, veiled or not, but, as an Inverter, she *never* risked changing one."

Rydan begins to pace in front of the hearth. "Are you saying that Queen Tymond abided by that same code?"

"She must have. She wasn't exactly fond of the idea of her husband being in possession of the ring, the staff, *and* the Mallum because she knew it would cause an imbalance of power." I pause, then add, "Why would she go through the trouble of risking her own safety to ensure that you would one day know how to wield the crescent fire?"

Rydan stops pacing. He runs a hand through his mud-splattered hair. "She was on our side this whole time." His voice is barely above a whisper. "This must have been her only way of intervening without upsetting the natural order and progression of things. With the speculor."

I nod, having come to the same conclusion, but Rydan seems to have picked up on something else I haven't.

"Can the Mallum take a Diviner's power?"

"As far as I know, yes. The only illusié not at risk are Channelers, Extractors, and Rescinders. The Sacred Trinity."

"Then it wasn't your healing ability in question, having gone bad or not, that killed Queen Tymond." He gives me a warm smile. "It *was* the Mallum."

Although I'd already convinced myself of this—and with evidence to back it up, no less—there's still a part of me that's feared I'd somehow added to the queen's death by attempting to heal her.

"Whether Darius knew Aldreda was illusié or not is irrelevant," Rydan continues, further bolstering his stance. "When he summoned the Mallum that day, it absorbed her ability. And then it took her soul."

I stumble over my words. "But my mother . . . she was bound to the Mallum when that happened. She wouldn't do that to her sister—"

"But Darius would, seeing as your mother was the object of his affection. And, since he controlled the Mallum, what a convenient way to rid himself of the sister he didn't actually love *and* absorb the ability she'd kept hidden from him."

"Then why not kill me?" I challenge. "I came across the Mallum numerous times. There was every chance to—"

"—kill the daughter of the woman he loves?" Rydan finishes. "He wouldn't dare."

My mind races to try and poke holes in his logic, but, of course, there aren't any. As if echoing my very thoughts, Andri lets out a long whistle. "That's some twisted shit right there."

"More twisted than me being able to breathe fucking fire without knowing it?" Rydan shakes his head. "Seriously, how many times could I have decimated everything and everyone around me?"

"With that temper?" I tease. "It's a miracle we're all still standing." Happy to be on a topic other than the unnerving Eliri-Tymond love triangle, I ask, "Did you even have the slightest inkling?"

Rydan shakes his head. "I always assumed the heat rising in my body would be transmuted through my hands."

"It's good you chose to direct it there, then."

"I wasn't aware I could choose differently." There's no mistaking the despondence in his voice.

"So, what now?" Andri asks.

"Well, the good news is we've got two people of Draconian blood *and* the knowledge we need to destroy the very thing that threatens to tear Aeridon apart," I reply. "The bad news is neither of you are illusié so wielding the crescent fire is an impossibility at present."

"The irony isn't lost on us," Rydan retorts. "Believe me."

"Maybe that asshole *will* end up getting what he always wanted," Andri murmurs.

"No," I say firmly, refusing to let their low morale get to me. "Dane is long gone. And so is his ill-fated legacy. As one of the last-standing Eliris, it's up to me to restore my family's name."

Even if it kills me.

CERYLIA JARETH

IT'S UNLIKE HER niece to just disappear without notice, but after what's just transpired, she's choosing to trust that Arden has a reason.

"No luck?" she asks Estelle as she enters through the doors to the White Room.

Estelle shakes her head. "They're not in the north wing of the castle."

"Nor the east," Haskell echoes, trailing behind her.

"I just checked the west chambers and no luck there," Avery says, falling in line next to the others.

Cerylia turns to the last Caldari in the room.

"The south wing is also a dead end," Vira remarks. "Although I didn't think to check the library. I would be remiss to mention that Arden isn't the only one missing. Rydan and his cousin are as well."

"Chances are, they're all together," Haskell comments. "I doubt they'd leave the castle after everything we've just had to endure."

Cerylia sighs. "Has anyone seen Braxton?"

His ears must have been burning because he waltzes into the White Room not a second later, the Mallum floating behind him. The sight is disconcerting. "Here and accounted for," he says wearily, motioning to the black mist. "The both of us, if you can even count such a thing."

Cerylia observes the entity with due scrutiny. "Seeing as there's no longer a soul attached to it, the Mallum is more like a shadow than a being,"

Braxton sighs. "A shadow I never asked for."

"But an important one, nonetheless," Cerylia counters. "Keeping the Mallum in our sights, under a watchful eye, is the best case scenario at the moment. At least, until Arden is able to redistribute the abilities back to illusié, at which point Rydan—"

"—*or* Andri can wield the crescent fire to ensure nothing like this ever happens again," Rydan finishes as he strides into the room with Arden and his cousin flanking him on either side.

"Precisely," Cerylia says, relieved to see that they're still in one piece. "I'm pleased to report that I was able to retrieve the remaining crests from Dane before the dragon . . ." Her voice trails off as the unpleasant memory of her husband being brutally devoured surfaces.

"Thank you," Rydan says as he approaches the dais to retrieve his family's crest. "I'm pleased to report that I now know how to wield it."

The news shakes Cerylia from her daze. "Is that so?"

"Thanks to Andri. And Queen Tymond, of all people." Arden directs a smile at Braxton, her eyes brimming with appreciation. "It seems the speculor she left behind contains nearly all the answers we've been searching for."

An invisible weight seems to lift off his shoulders. "At least there's one Tymond we were able to count on."

"*Two* Tymonds," Cerylia corrects. "Don't diminish your importance to our cause. Your accomplishments are greater than you realize."

"Not when it cost one of our own her life," he whispers.

Estelle clears her throat before averting her gaze to the domed ceiling, blinking back tears.

"It fills me with great remorse to hear about Lane," Cerylia says softly, sensing the undeniable grief rippling across the room. "You have my deepest condolences." She looks between Braxton and Estelle. "Both of you."

"In Lane's honor, we'd like to give her a proper ceremony—" Estelle starts.

"Say no more," Cerylia interjects. "Whatever you need, Delwynn will arrange for you."

Estelle bows her head. "Thank you, Queen Jareth."

Cerylia returns the gesture before turning her attention to her niece. "How are you holding up?"

Wearing a perplexed expression, Arden breaks her focus from Estelle. Cerylia can only assume that, because she was at the heart of the incident with Dane, she's still catching up on the events from the day. She shoots her niece a stern look to not stray from the question. Thankfully, Arden seems to take the hint.

"All things considered, I'm doing well," she replies, although there's a trace of confusion underlying her tone.

"No side effects from channeling?"

Arden shakes her head. "I think it goes without saying that I'm tired, but that's about it."

Her response garners a heavy laugh from the group.

"Aren't we all?" Cerylia concurs. "It's been quite the day."

"Quite the year is more like it," Rydan challenges.

"Really?" Arden quips. "I was going to go with *decade*, but—"

Cerylia leans back in her throne, unable to hide her smile at the lightheartedness filling the room. There may be fewer Caldari than when this all began, but that hasn't diminished the love and respect they have for each other. They're certainly going to need it for whatever future trials await.

❧ ❧ ❧

Though victorious in their endeavors, dinner amongst the Caldari is unseasonably quiet. Perhaps the weight of battle and bloodshed is taking its toll. Perhaps the reality of all that's occurred is finally sinking in. Or, perhaps they're all just exhausted from the day. Cerylia chooses to believe it's the latter, if only to keep her conscience clear.

She rises from the head of the table, lifting her glass as she taps her dinner knife against it. A hush falls over the room as all eyes turn toward her. "I trust you're finding tonight's menu satisfactory," she remarks, taking note of the near empty plates on the table. "I'm pleased to see the events of the day haven't diminished your appetites."

"Not in the slightest," Haskell says as he sinks his teeth into a chicken thigh, ripping the tender meat straight from the bone. "In fact, I've never been hungrier."

Cerylia smiles, motioning to Delwynn to have the kitchen prepare another serving. He nods as he scurries to the scullery. "Seeing as we're all gathered here this evening, I'd like to discuss what comes next."

"Speaking of," Arden says as she raises a hand and looks around the table, "if anyone has any idea as to how I can redistribute all of *this*"—she motions to her body as if it isn't her own—"please take it upon yourself to enlighten me."

"To enlighten us all," Estelle corrects.

"I second that," Andri adds.

"Hear, hear!" Rydan says, lifting his glass.

The rest of the group moves to imitate the motion, except for one person. "What is it, Avery?" Cerylia asks.

Deep in thought, he doesn't seem to hear her at first. Only when the room goes completely silent does he break out of his trance. "Oh. Well, it's probably nothing, but I—I might have an idea," he stammers, the thought only half-formed.

"Let's hear it," Vira encourages.

Avery shrugs before saying, rather simply, "Water."

When he doesn't elaborate, Cerylia considers reaching for the pitcher to refill his glass, but a follow up question stops her.

"Water?" Vira repeats. "Care to explain?"

"I would indeed," Avery says as he pushes back from the table and begins to pace. He stops, mid-stride, looking at the queen apologetically. "It helps me think—the pacing."

Cerylia makes a sweeping gesture with her hand. "By all means."

Avery nods in appreciation. "Correct me if I'm wrong, but most of us are aware of the natural elements and their basic properties," he says, rattling off earth, fire, air, and water. "But what only those illusié who study herbal alchemy know is that water has the capability to hold energy." He pauses, noting their dubious expressions. "Try to stay with me."

"Try we will, mate," Haskell offers with a small laugh.

Avery laughs nervously. "If water can hold energy—and can also act as a conduit—all we'd need to do is find a body of water that's easily accessible to illusié and have Arden immerse herself in it. She can then channel the abilities into the water, at which point illusié can travel, as needed, to regain their abilities by immersing themselves in said body of water."

A stunned silence fills the room. Avery looks as though he's about to slink away in embarrassment when Haskell boasts, "Bloody brilliant, you are!" He tips a faux hat in his direction. "Leave it to the Alchemist to save us all."

Avery sighs in relief, grinning at the compliment.

"What about the spring in Volkharn?" Arden suggests.

"It was bone dry the last time we visited," Braxton points out.

"Nothing an Elemental can't solve," Andri chimes in. "They can easily invoke water to refill the spring."

Impressed, Avery arches a brow at the newcomer. "Now that you mention it, it might be worth having an Elemental there to stabilize the mix of energies." He chews on his lower lip. "It's too bad we don't have one in our ranks."

"Maybe not here with us right now," Braxton says, perking up. "But I know where we can find one."

BRAXTON HORNSBY

GRATEFUL FOR THE distraction, Braxton finishes his plate, then heads for his chambers to pack for the long trip ahead. He'd nearly asked Haskell to join him so they could transport when he realized . . . he's no longer able to. And while Arden *could* wield the ability to transport, the learning curve would be far too great. Not to mention, her safety is of the utmost priority if there's any hope of restoring all their abilities.

Horseback it is.

He's nearly packed when there's a loud knock at his door. "Braxton? Are you in there?"

Braxton lugs the heavy bag over his shoulder before greeting Arden at the door. "I was just about to leave," he says, moving to squeeze by her.

She positions her hand on the doorframe so that it blocks his exit. "I know I can't help you transport, but what about flying by dragon?" She waggles her eyebrows.

"Let me guess . . . Vira taught you?"

"What can I say, I'm a fast learner."

"It's a good thing, too. I would've frozen my tail off."

"And you'd rather not brave the seas?"

"With dragons burning every ship in sight, Crostan or otherwise?" He shakes his head. "No thank you."

"I'm happy I caught you, then."

He gives his cousin a sincere smile. "Me, too."

❧ ❧ ❧

The first leg of the trip through the skies was frigid beyond comprehension, but thankfully hadn't lasted long. While flying dragon-back over the windy seas had its disadvantages, he must admit it was infinitely more comfortable than freezing his ass off on horseback—and a lot quicker, too.

Hanslow hadn't told him where he was headed but, creature of habit that he is, Athia is probably his best bet. It dawns on Braxton that he hasn't been back to the small seaside village since the Savant came looking for him, forcing him to flee the very place he'd made his home. Days spent working at the inn and nights stargazing at Lake Ipcea seem distant and foreign—like it'd been a lifetime ago.

In some ways, he supposes it has.

The second leg of the trip is much smoother and noticeably warmer. He's surprised at how familiar the terrain looks from overhead even though it's his first time flying over it. He's instantly reminded of why he'd first fallen in love with this place—the undeniable feel of a small town without actually being one, which is rare to come by in Aeridon.

Before he'd left Sardoria, Vira had instructed him to pat the dragon's neck twice to signal when it's time to land. Recognizing Lake Ipcea in the distance, he gives the dragon two pats, bracing himself at the swift and sudden change in their trajectory. He clutches onto the dragon's raised scales, eyes watering as they dive, headfirst, straight for the ground. If the dragon doesn't slow soon, they're bound to crash. As the wind lashes his face, he squeezes his eyes shut, mumbling a quick prayer to the lords above for a safe landing.

Thankfully, the wind comes to a screeching halt as the dragon evens out its flight path, just in time to avoid hurtling into the ground. Its claws touch down, talons dragging dirt, rock, and gravel behind them. Braxton inhales a sharp breath at the bumpy landing, hanging on for dear life until they've stopped all together.

Eager to get the hell off the beast, Braxton slides down its side with his pack in hand. Taking Vira's advice to heart, he moves into the dragon's eyeline and bows his head in thanks. The dragon huffs in clear annoyance but still lowers its massive head in a show of respect. A roar rattles his bones, reverberating through the trees and the very ground he stands on. He watches as the dragon lifts off into the sky with stunning ease.

Braxton sighs, spotting the path that'll take him into town—and the inn. He can only hope Hanslow *is* in Athia after all and, if not, that he finds another means of transportation. Because if its departure was any indication, that dragon certainly isn't headed back this way anytime soon.

❧ ❧ ❧

The inn looks just as he remembers it, if not better. The upkeep is noticeable, which makes him wonder who had taken over after the old man had left . . . and ended up in the Medial. Little does he realize, his question is about to be answered.

He pushes the door open. A little bell from above that wasn't there before jingles to signal his arrival. A light head of hair pops up from behind the bar, russet eyes crinkling at the corners. "May I help you?" she asks as she takes a damp rag to wipe down the counter.

"Hi," Braxton says with a small wave, suddenly feeling awkward. "I'm looking for someone and was hoping you might be able to help."

"I can certainly do my best." She smiles, nodding. "Are they a guest here?"

"Not exactly," Braxton says as he walks over to the bar. "Actually, the person I'm looking for used to own this inn—"

Her eyes grow wide with recognition as she takes in his features. "You're Prince Tymond, aren't you?"

"Uh, technically, I suppose so, but I'm not exactly one for titles." He chuckles nervously. "You can call me Braxton."

"How wonderful. Hanslow has told me so much about you," she boasts, coming around the counter for a better look. "I was so relieved when he finally returned—"

"My apologies, at the risk of sounding rude, you seem to know me but I don't know you."

She smacks her palm against her head before extending it for a handshake. "Please forgive my insolence. I'm Diera, Hanslow's younger sister."

Braxton tries to keep his mouth from dropping open in shock. "Hanslow never told me he had a sister." He studies her for a moment, the similarities becoming apparent. "I'm delighted to meet you. Truly."

"Likewise," she says, returning behind the counter to pour them both some ale. "It was so kind of you to help Hanslow with the inn. It's always been a challenge for him to take care of all the duties that come along with it, so having someone like you around surely made his life much easier." She slides the mug of frothy ale across the counter.

"Your brother's the one who deserves all the credit," Braxton says, taking a sip. "He took a chance on me when no one else would. Saved me from what could have been a terrible fate."

She sighs. "Admittedly, the Tymonds aren't too popular around here."

"And for good reason," he scoffs. "Why do you think I fled?"

"Right. Well, at least you still had your illusié ability," she murmurs. "Unlike so many of us." Her somber tone causes the atmosphere to shift.

Braxton sets his mug down. "You're illusié?"

"I *was*," she emphasizes, blowing a stray tendril of wavy hair out of her face. "Sadly, I happened to be one of the Mallum's early victims. I haven't been illusié in quite some time."

Having been through it himself, Braxton's heart cracks a little. "I lost my ability to deviate pretty early on as well."

"A Deviator, huh?" she says, impressed. "You're the first one I've met."

"How about you?" he inquires, genuinely curious. "What is—*was* your ability?"

She hesitates before saying, "My ability wasn't for the faint of heart. In fact, there were times I wished I never had it to begin with. But the more I studied and practiced, the more comfortable I became. Well, as comfortable as you can get working with the dead. I actually got pretty good at it."

"Your ability was necromancy?" he confirms.

Her brows raise. "You sound surprised, but not the least bit uneasy."

"Should I be?" He angles his head at her. "Uneasy?"

"Most people would be, seeing as soul magick is a bit taboo, even among the highest of illusié ranks."

"Hard to understand why," he says, leaning back from the counter. "Well, Diera, it seems we're in the same boat because you're the first Necromancer I've met. I hope you don't mind my asking . . . just how practiced are you at soul magick?"

Diera's grin stretches from ear to ear. "Quite familiar. Not to boast, but I'm somewhat of an expert, if I do say so myself."

"That's great to hear," Braxton says, a plan forming in his mind.

"It probably would be . . . if I were still capable," she remarks glumly as she grabs her mug for another round. "Damn Mallum. And just when I'd started to accept what I was—"

"What you *are*," Braxton corrects before finishing the last of his ale. "What if I told you that the reason I'm here is because you, and any other illusié who's lost their abilities to the Mallum, can now get them back?"

She nearly drops her mug. "Is this theoretical or . . .?"

"No," Braxton says with a chuckle. "I assure you it's very much real."

"Well, this is quite unexpected," she says, clearly thinking it over. After a few moments, her brows furrow. "I just realized I never answered your original question."

"Hmm? And what's that?"

"I thought the reason you came here was to find my brother."

"Right," Braxton affirms, "because we're going to need an Elemental if we have any chance of this working."

"Any chance of what working?" a male voice echoes from behind him.

Braxton swivels to find his old friend standing in the doorway of the inn.

Hanslow's gaze shifts to the back of the bar. "I see you've met my sister," he remarks. "Dee, be a dear and pour me a glass," he says before joining Braxton at the countertop.

"Coming right up," she says as she grabs a clean mug from one of the shelves. "You're going to need it once you hear the news."

Hanslow turns his curious stare from her to Braxton.

"She isn't wrong," Braxton says with a shrug.

"Do tell," Hanslow says, eyes glinting. "And don't leave out a single detail."

ARDEN ELIRI

AWARE OF THE treacherous climb ahead, I follow Braxton's instructions to the best of my ability and find a nearby tree to tie off my horse. The other Caldari do the same, their gazes tracking the steep incline that leads to Volkharn and the jaded spring.

"I thought we agreed on the location being easily accessible," Rydan grunts as he tightens the knot on his rope.

"This climb looks daunting as hell," Andri points out.

"After what we've just been through, I'm sure it'll feel like a breeze," Vira says as she adjusts the bandage on her arm.

"I'm inclined to agree with Vira. We've been through much worse," I assure them. "The climb only *looks* daunting, At least, that's what I was told." I swallow the knot that's forming in my throat, wishing my cousin were here to show us the most direct path, if such a thing even exists.

"You're absolutely certain Braxton is going to meet us here?" the queen asks. She gathers her robes, tightening them around herself.

"Yes, Aunt Cerylia. With the ring and the staff. And hopefully Hanslow won't be far behind."

"What do we do once we get to the gate?" Estelle asks as she joins me at the bottom of the hill. "What if it's locked?"

"Have we all forgotten that I currently have the option to wield *all* illusié abilities? Getting through the gate should be the least of our problems."

"Spoken like a true Eliri," Haskell says with a huff.

I roll my eyes. "Now, if you'll all follow me," I say, motioning to the climb ahead. "Don't stray from the path. If you follow my exact footwork, you'll be just fine." I can only hope I sound more confident than I feel.

"And if we don't?" Avery asks.

I shrug my shoulders. "It's your funeral."

෴ ෴ ෴

The climb is longer than Braxton had let on—and way more exhausting. Rydan and his cousin are the only ones who seem to be able to keep up with my pace, which serves as a stark reminder that, having gone through rigorous strength and endurance trials, not everyone was raised to be an assassin. It makes me wonder what Andri was involved in before sailing to Sardoria with the Crostan warriors, but I don't get the chance to ask as someone shouts from behind me.

"You might want to slow down some," Haskell calls out. "Our aunt's falling behind."

I stop, turning around. "Is she alone?"

"Of course not. Estelle's with her."

"At this rate, it's going to take all day for us to get there," Rydan mumbles.

"All day and all night," Andri quips.

"Believe me, no one wants to get there as quickly as I do, hence the freakishly abnormal pace."

Rydan lifts a brow. "Seems perfectly normal to me."

"Yeah? Well, apparently, we three are the anomaly."

Rydan sighs. "It would have been so much easier if we could have transported—"

"Don't remind me," I say, trudging along. "It's bad enough that you all lost your abilities. Even worse that I have complete access to them with limited knowledge on how to wield them."

Andri has the nerve to scoff. "How is that worse? At least you're still illusié."

Like I need the reminder.

"Let's just get up this damn hill."

"Mountain," Rydan corrects. "This is definitely a *mountain*, Arden."

❧   ❧   ❧

Although it takes longer than I'd hoped, we finally arrive at the gates of Volkharn. I'm somewhat dismayed to discover that Braxton hasn't arrived yet because I was counting on him to unlock them. Now it's up to me to channel *something* to get through them. And, if I'm being honest, that climb has me spent.

"Here, everyone, drink up," Avery says as he passes around some canisters of water and forest-green vials. "Something to replenish our stores."

We each take a vial and guzzle it without a second thought. Haskell's the first one to make a face, and I follow shortly after.

"I have to admit, it isn't your best work, mate," he says with a cough. "I feel like I just swallowed some leaves and dirt. Some *spicy* leaves and dirt."

"That would be the ginger," Avery replies, taking the empty vials and placing them back in his knapsack. "And I know it doesn't taste all that great—"

"All that great?" Vira teases. "Try atrocious."

Avery rolls his eyes. "You'll be thanking me in a few minutes. You'll see."

Haskell guffaws. "It'll be a miracle if I can keep it down for *more* than a minute."

I elbow my brother in the side, hoping it'll be enough to silence him. "Thank you, Avery. We're going to need all the strength we can muster."

He gives me a small nod. "I'm glad at least one of you appreciates the art of alchemy," he mumbles.

Needing to diffuse the tension, I say, "Right, now that that's sorted, let's talk about this gate." I take a step toward it, eyeing the monstrosity as if it were a living, breathing foe.

"Practiced or not, you're going to have to try to wield *something*," Rydan says in my ear. "Any ideas?"

Having overheard us, Andri suggests, "Perhaps she can melt it."

I turn to face him. "You want me to *ignite* the gates?"

He shrugs. "Why not?"

Rydan tilts his head from side to side as he considers his cousin's proposal. "You *were* able to channel it that night in the library at Midvale. Rather easily, I might add."

"True, but—"

"Unless you have a better idea," Andri challenges.

I don't. And the clock is ticking.

"All right," I agree somewhat hesitantly. "But if this doesn't work, at least we'll know who's to blame."

RYDAN HELSTROM

HIS NERVES THREATEN to get the better of him as he positions Arden slightly away from the gates. He'd never forgive himself for allowing her to ignite too close and join the wreckage of the aftermath.

"Igniting is attached to emotion," Rydan explains, recalling his lessons with Avery. "The quickest way to get a blaze going is to think of something that makes you angry."

She glances in his direction, the concern apparent in her gaze. "Sounds dangerous."

"As long as you direct it at the proper target, you should be just fine." He squeezes the sides of her shoulders before backing away a step. "You remember what it feels like? The rising heat? The inexplicable pins and needles?"

She raises a hand to silence him. "Yes. I remember."

"Okay. Stand back everyone," Rydan instructs, leading the rest of the group slightly down the hill. "Just in case something unexpectedly blows up—"

"You can stop talking. It's already done," Vira says.

"She did it," Haskell affirms, pride gleaming in his eyes.

"A born natural," Avery remarks.

Rydan whirls around to find Arden exactly where he'd left her, molten metal oozing where the gates once stood. It'd taken him an almost embarrassing number of attempts to be able to control his igniting ability—and yet, she'd done it on her very first try? He tries to ignore the sting of envy as he retraces his steps back to her. "That was . . . fast."

"Don't sound so surprised," she says. "I mean, I did have a great teacher and all . . ."

"I told you *one* thing." He tries to rein in his budding anger. "It would have taken me days, *weeks*, to be able to pull something like this off."

She angles her head, studying him. "Well, we don't have days. Or weeks. So, it's a good thing it worked as quickly as it did." There's an air of annoyance in her tone as she turns away from him, motioning to the others to head back up the hill. "Not to mention, now that the gates are gone, all illusié will be able to enter the spring without difficulty."

They remain standing across from one another as the Caldari pass by, stepping over and around the piles of molten metal. When he's sure they're out of earshot, he bows somewhat mockingly, gesturing for her to go first. "After you, Lady Eliri."

But she doesn't walk in the direction of the others. Instead, she walks right up to him, her mouth just inches from his. "If it's any consolation, the memory I recalled before igniting the gates was that night with you. In the Midvale library." She pauses, lifting her hand before gently resting it on his cheek. "Perhaps there's another emotion you haven't considered that burns just as brightly as anger."

His breath hitches. "And what emotion would that be?"

She plants a soft kiss on his other cheek. "Passion."

CERYLIA JARETH

THE SPRING IS desolate, barren—far from what she'd expected. She's the last to join the Caldari around the edge of the pit, seeing as she's still recovering from the climb. It'd been ruthless and, if it weren't for Avery's tonic, she likely would have collapsed upon arriving at the gates.

"It's so . . . empty," Estelle comments as she takes in the vast nothingness around them. "Dare I say, it's almost in worse condition than the way we left Midvale."

The mention of the institution weighs heavy on the queen's heart. Although they'd never quite seen eye to eye,

Cyfrin Galdor was not only essential to their illusié ranks, but the very reason any of them are still standing here now. Her death had been a monumental loss for them all.

Cerylia shakes the memory away, having to clear her throat as she says, "Shall we discuss our options?"

The question is pointed at the only two remaining illusié, other than herself. Arden and Nevaeh both nod, walking along the crater's edge toward the queen. Cerylia pulls them aside, casting an apologetic glance toward the rest of the group.

"As if we didn't already feel like shit," Rydan murmurs.

Having caught wind of the comment, Arden turns over her shoulder. "Let's not make this any harder than it has to be. The fact of the matter is, if something goes awry when I attempt to channel all this energy into the spring, it'll be up to illusié to make things right." She pauses, turning her gaze on all of them. "Given a situation as risky as this one, there must be contingencies. I will do everything in my power to ensure each and every wielder of illusié gets their abilities back."

Thankfully, the group nods in understanding before turning away to let the three of them discuss. Cerylia gives her niece a proud smile. "You have the makings of a queen."

Much to her surprise, Arden scoffs. "Believe me, that is the last thing I'd ever want."

Cerylia doesn't know whether to be offended or relieved. Perhaps it's a little of both. "What makes you say that?"

Arden narrows her eyes. "If I'd had even the slightest desire to be queen, I would have just followed in your husband's footsteps," she says coolly. "Need I remind you that I have access to every single illusié ability on the continent. And yet, here I am, desperate to give it all back. Even if it costs me my life."

Stunned by her niece's response, Cerylia retreats a step. "Who said anything about it costing you your life?"

Nevaeh raises a shy hand. "Unfortunately, a process such as this doesn't come without its fair share of warnings."

"Especially since it's never been done before," Arden adds. "If you think about it, we're essentially walking into this blind."

Cerylia falls silent for a moment. "The contingencies you spoke of," she says quietly, "what are they?"

Arden looks to Nevaeh. "All yours."

Nevaeh sighs as she runs a hand through her hair. "For starters, we should discuss our expected outcome. Which is for Arden to successfully channel all abilities into the spring, at which point it will be stabilized by the Elemental."

"Hanslow," Arden interjects. "His name is Hanslow."

"Right," Nevaeh says with a nod. "Now, if there's any sign of the water not taking to the abilities or rejecting them in any way, that's where I come in. To reverse the process."

Cerylia looks between them, mouth agape. "*Back* to Arden?"

Nevaeh nods. "That is correct."

Cerylia gives an adamant shake of her head. "It nearly killed her the first time around. You'd really want to risk a second?"

"If it means saving illusié," Arden intervenes, "then yes."

Cerylia huffs her disagreement but doesn't dare argue further. It's quite clear that Arden's mind is made up, and if there's one thing she knows about her niece, it's that there's no changing it. For anything. Or any reason.

Sensing the tension, Nevaeh continues, "The second contingency is where you would come in, Queen Jareth. And, I must warn you, if you're not fond of the first scenario, you'll likely despise what I'm about to suggest next even more."

Cerylia's stomach drops.

"In the event that Arden doesn't make it, for any reason, we would then rely on your capabilities to extract."

Cerylia nearly laughs out of shock. "You want me to extract my niece's soul?"

"You've done it before," Arden whispers. "With Felix."

"Because it was the only option!" she exclaims, her temper getting the better of her.

"Well," Arden says pointedly, "it might end up being *our* only option as well. I know you have an extra soul gem on you. I saw the exchange between you and my father on the field. One was used for my mother, but the other is empty."

Cerylia's about to argue her point further when the sound of footsteps draws her attention. She turns around to find a woman approaching that she's never seen before, flanked by two others. As the men come into view, she recognizes them instantly. "Impeccable timing," she says, rushing over to greet Hanslow and Braxton.

The woman stops her, taking the queen's arm gently. "I didn't mean to eavesdrop, Your Greatness, but did I overhear you discussing soul magick and extraction?"

Cerylia gives the woman a wary look. "You did."

Her face falls. "I would advise against it."

"And why is that?" Nevaeh challenges as she saunters over. "Under what authority?"

"If you plan to use a soul gem on your dear friend, here, it won't work. In fact, after all is said and done, you'll only ensure her death."

Hanslow scurries forward and takes his sister's arm, bowing before the queen. "Forgive us, Your Greatness. This is my sister, Diera."

Cerylia ignores the nicety and locks eyes with the woman. "What do you mean it'll only ensure Arden's death?"

Diera sighs. "If what Braxton's shared with me is correct, you plan to destroy the Mallum, yes?"

"Of course," Arden says. "We want absolute certainty that nothing like this can happen to the people of Aeridon ever again."

"A noble cause," she says softly. "And one that requires substantial sacrifice, I'm afraid."

"We've already cut our losses," Nevaeh counters. "Now there's only gain."

"Not if you plan to destroy the Mallum," Diera says, "seeing as the creation of the soul gems are inextricably linked to the existence of the Mallum itself."

Arden holds up a hand. "Wait. What exactly are you saying?"

"If you choose to destroy the Mallum, the soul gems will be destroyed along with it." Shadows darken the woman's eyes. "The souls will be set free, of course. But any chance of bringing your loved ones back in this lifetime will be forcibly and permanently withdrawn."

"Again, I must ask, under *what* authority do you speak?" Nevaeh presses.

As an older brother would come to a younger sibling's defense, Hanslow opens his mouth to respond, but Diera speaks first. "Why, under the authority of Necromancy." Her tone falls flat. "My illusié ability."

"You'd be wise to listen to her," Braxton says.

Nevaeh folds her arms over her chest. "And why is that?"

"Because, unlike you, or anyone else here, I was there," Diera answers. "I was there when the Mallum was created."

BRAXTON HORNSBY

THERE'S ONLY ONE word to describe the look on his cousin's face: devastation.

"Well," Arden murmurs, "that changes things a bit."

She doesn't have to say what she's thinking. It's obvious, at least to him. With Felix's soul tied up in a soul gem, as well as her mother's, there's a lot at stake. But after wearing the amethyst ring and being able to summon the Mallum at will, there's just as much, if not more, at stake.

It shouldn't be his job to convince her of that, but it might be the only way to keep the past from repeating itself.

Cerylia exhales a long sigh. "That certainly isn't the news we'd hoped to hear." She removes a grand total of four soul gems from her left pocket. "Because we have three very deserving souls who, in my opinion, should be able to see the light of day again, if at all possible."

Arden gapes at her. "I know that one of those is empty and that my mother's soul resides in another, but the other two?"

"Xerin Grey and Felix Barlow," Diera affirms. "At least, the imprint signatures on the gems say as much."

"When did you retrieve them?" Arden presses.

"One from Dane's study, one from Dane himself."

"Before the dragons made a meal out of him," Vira murmurs, anger simmering beneath her gaze.

Arden turns to Diera. "Is that why you've come? To help us?"

"I'm afraid I'm of little use at the moment," Diera says glumly. "Allow me to clarify. I *was* a Necromancer. Until my altercation with the Mallum."

"You're here to get your abilities back."

She nods. "Something I've been told you can provide."

"We can discuss the soul gems at a later time," Cerylia says, placing them back in her pocket. "For now, our focus should be on the spring."

Hanslow steps forward. "I suppose that's my cue." He walks to the edge of the spring, then rubs his hands together and places them on the ground. Head lowered, he begins to mumble incoherently.

Braxton nudges Diera in the side before asking, "Is that normal?"

"For Hanslow?" She chuckles. "More than you might think."

Braxton joins the innkeeper at the edge of the spring, watching in awe as water appears from nowhere, spilling in from all sides. It takes mere minutes for the entire pit to return to its original state full of crystal clear water. He pats Hanslow on the back, then helps him to his feet. "Well done."

He grins, motioning for Arden to come forward. "This area here is quite shallow. Perfect for wading in to do . . . well, whatever it is that comes next."

Arden peers over the edge. "And you're sure, even with all this energy, that you can stabilize the spring?"

Hanslow nods. "Once you've completed channeling the energy *into* the water, then yes."

Something in his tone must come across as rather convincing because Arden doesn't hesitate to remove her cloak. She hands it to Braxton.

"We're right here," he whispers.

She forces a smile as she squeezes his arm, then, still clothed, wades into the water. She doesn't stop until it covers her shoulders. Even from where he stands, he can hear the lengthy inhale before she plunges underwater and disappears from view.

Braxton inches forward, getting as close as he can to the water's edge without actually touching it. Ripples form at the very spot she'd ducked under, spreading outward like wildfire. When they reach the perimeter, the color has shifted, from a clear blue to muted purple to hazy green to bright orange, until the entire spring mimics the effects of a kaleidoscope. The process is mostly silent, save for the water lapping at the bank, and just when he realizes that Arden probably can't hold her breath for much longer, her head pops up. Gasping for air, she wades back to the edge of the spring, each current she creates electrified with energy.

Hanslow readies himself before creating what looks like a small tornado between his hands. Upon releasing it, however, it flattens out over the spring's surface, as if he's just cast a wide net to contain all that lies in the depths below.

Arden climbs out of the water, teeth chattering as Braxton wraps her cloak back around her. When it doesn't seem to do much in the way of warmth, he strips off his own to provide an extra layer. He waves at Avery to get his attention, hoping he's got a tonic in his pack to help her restore the body heat she's just lost.

"Did . . . it . . . work?" Arden stutters, her lips a pale shade of blue.

"It looks like it," Braxton answers. "But, to be sure . . ."

He takes his leave as he nods at Avery, who's already rifling through his bag for the proper vial. The pop of a cork follows Braxton to the spring. He can hear Arden trying to beckon him back over, her voice already hoarse from her previous efforts.

Braxton looks to Hanslow.

He nods in confirmation. "It's ready."

Braxton returns the gesture, then closes his eyes. "For you, mother," he whispers as he puts one foot in the spring, followed by the other. "And for all fallen illusié who will never have the opportunity to make it this far."

He blocks out the cries of concern as he swims to the center of the spring and dives under. He waits, not knowing how much time needs to pass in order for the spring's energies to take effect, only coming up for air when he can't hold his breath any longer. The group has gone silent as everyone waits for his return with bated breath. Braxton takes his time, wondering if he's supposed to feel something, but there's no noticeable difference.

Trying not to be disheartened, he swims back to the water's edge, the anticipation building around him as he exits the spring.

"Well?" Avery asks, looking him up and down. "What's the verdict?"

"There's only one way to find out if it worked," he replies, setting his sights on the person farthest away from him. "Throw a rock at me," he directs Haskell. "And throw it like you mean it."

Wide-eyed, Haskell looks around at the group. When no one objects, he shrugs and picks up one of the palm-sized rocks at his feet. "Fine. But if you get a black eye, that's on you."

"Deal," Braxton says, readying himself to do something he hasn't done in what feels like ages: deviate.

"Here goes nothing," Haskell rears back in preparation, but doesn't release the rock. "Are you ready?"

"Waiting on you."

"Incoming!" Haskell's arm flings forward as the rock leaves his hand and sails in Braxton's direction. He only has a split second before he gets pelted in the face to recall how to do this. It dawns on him that muscle memory may not be enough. He brings his hands in front of him, forming a triangle as the rock inches closer. And closer. And closer.

His heart sinks. *It didn't work.*

He's about to throw his arms over his head to minimize both the damage and impact to his face when, finally, he feels something.

It.

Illusié.

Braxton grins as the rock suddenly halts in mid-air, as if someone's planning to pluck it out of space and time. It worked. Holy lords, it *actually* worked. He's illusié again.

Back to which it came, he says to himself, feeling overjoyed when the rock suddenly appears to backtrack, heading straight for Haskell's head. Thankfully, his assailant catches it just in time. Having witnessed an illusié miracle, the group shouts and hollers as they all rush forward to congratulate him.

After numerous pats on the shoulder, Braxton says, "All right, all right. Who's next?"

Haskell scrambles to the front of the line, followed by the rest of the Caldari. Diera takes her place at the back, waiting patiently for the others to take their turn, even though she's undoubtedly been waiting the longest.

Braxton joins Arden, who's still shivering despite wearing two layers of cloaks. "Once Avery and Rydan get their igniting abilities back, we'll have them light a fire."

She gives him a brief smile, but it doesn't reach her eyes. "I'm glad you can deviate again, cousin."

"Thanks to you," he says, meaning every word. "You should feel proud of what you've accomplished here, what you *chose* to do. Not many people with that much power available to them would have chosen to do the same thing."

"I suppose not." A muscle flexes in her cheek. "I can only hope it makes what needs to happen next a little easier."

He looks to the amethyst ring. "The Mallum?"

She doesn't look at him. Just sighs.

"We have everything we need to destroy it."

"I know," Arden says half-heartedly, "and, in turn, lose the very people I've been trying so hard to save."

"You heard Diera, didn't you? Their souls will be set free," Braxton reminds her. "No longer tethered to this world through the soul gems or the Mallum."

"No longer existing at all," Arden whispers.

Suddenly at a loss for words, Braxton sits alongside her in complete silence. The tension is palpable as he can only imagine the thoughts running through her head. He wants to comfort her, but what can he say? What could even *be* said to make the situation less tragic?

Relief washes over him as Rydan emerges from the spring, flames dancing at his fingertips. Braxton motions the Ignitor over, and they switch places as he takes his leave, heading for the group to offer his congratulations on the successful restoration of their abilities.

Impulsivity gets the better of him as Braxton dares a glance over his shoulder, mistakenly catching Arden's glare. The intensity of it chills him to the bone. He tries to ignore the knot forming in his stomach, but, truth be told, he has every right to be worried—because he's the one thing standing in the way of Arden seeing her mother and Felix again.

ARDEN ELIRI

I ALREADY KNOW what Rydan's about to ask me before he even opens his mouth.

"Are you ready to finish this?"

I lower my gaze. I don't have the heart to tell him I'm having second thoughts. We've come this far *and* have a Necromancer among our ranks—the thought of never seeing Felix again or meeting my mother feels too great a burden to carry for the rest of my life, especially knowing that it's completely possible.

But what it'll cost . . .

I exhale a shaky breath, then bury my head in my hands.

"Hey," Rydan whispers as he scoots closer. "Tell me what's going on."

I squeeze my eyes shut, wishing that what I'm about to say isn't true. "When we destroy the Mallum, the soul gems go along with it."

He lets out a low whistle before leaning back. "Shit."

His reaction makes me feel a little better, knowing that he'd be at war with the concept if he were in my shoes. "It's so selfish of me to even consider keeping the Mallum in existence but . . ."

"The people you love are within arm's reach," he finishes quietly, deep in thought. "There has to be something we can do, another way to—"

I shake my head. "There isn't."

"How do you know?"

I angle my head toward where Diera is standing.

He tracks the movement. "The Necromancer?"

"If there *was* another way, she'd know about it. And I'm sure she would have shared it. But she was there when the Mallum was created." I blink back a tear. "This is the end of the road."

Rydan chews on his lower lip as he takes in everything I've just said. A long silence stretches between us until, finally, he turns back toward me. "Tell me what you want to do, Arden." Shadows darken his gaze. "Not what everyone else wants you to do or expects of you . . . what do *you* want to do?"

A sob breaks free from my chest as do my desires. "I want to see Felix again. I want to meet my mother." The tears feel uncontrollable as they stream down my cheeks. "Otherwise, my father died for nothing! And I'll be left with no one, alone all over again. All because his fucking brother—" I suck in a sharp breath, unable to finish the thought as my rage builds.

"Listen to me. You are *not* alone, all right?" Rydan takes my face in his hands, gently brushing the tears away. "You have me. You have your brother. And your aunt. And all the Caldari."

"I know." I raise my hands so that they're covering his. "Which is why it's selfish to want more. Especially when we've all lost so much."

Only when I say the words does it fully sink in just how much everyone here has sacrificed. Estelle's lost Lane to the Void. Braxton's lost his mother *and* his father. Vira's lost her brother twice, in a way—first, when they were separated, and again when Dane had the gall to parade around as Xerin. Rydan may have gained a cousin, but it was at the expense of his relatives, having murdered them with his own two hands. Cerylia's lost her husband—beyond that, she had to make the impossible decision to end his life.

And then there's my brother. Who'd gotten his father back only to lose him again . . . because of me and this damn illusié ability we were destined to share. I look around the spring at the Caldari, at my chosen family. We've all lost people we love. But just because of opportune timing and the existence of soul gems, I get another chance?

It doesn't sit right. At all. The guilt I would carry . . .

When I thought I'd killed Aldreda, my conscience was heavier than I ever could have imagined. If the Mallum were to somehow get into the wrong hands, everything we've just fought for and the sacrifices we've made would be erased.

Rydan squeezes my hand, pulling me from my internal dilemma. "Is that it? There's nothing else you want?"

I draw in a breath to steady my nerves. "I already told you. What I *want* is to see Felix again, to meet my mother—"

"Then consider it done. We'll find some way to contain the Mallum—"

"Let me finish," I interrupt, breaking our grip. "Yes, that's absolutely what I want. But often what we *want* to do is at odds with what we *need* to do."

Rydan waits a beat but when I don't continue, he says, "I suppose I should rephrase my question, then. What is it that you *need* to do, Arden?"

"I need to destroy the Mallum," I say, feeling surprised when my voice doesn't crack. "Even if it means the soul gems have to go along with it."

He studies me for a long moment. "You're certain?"

I heave a loud sigh. "Yes."

"Okay, then that's what we'll do." He pushes himself to his feet, then extends a hand to help me up.

I take it, still shivering from the cold.

He wraps an arm around my shoulder, guiding me toward the spring where Braxton awaits, the Mallum drifting behind him like a shadow.

"Let's finish this," Rydan whispers. "For the land we took an oath to protect. For Aeridon."

"For Aeridon," I agree, matching his stride.

When I look up, the relieved expression on Braxton's face is all I need to see—to know that, while my heart is currently shattering, I'm making the right decision by us all.

RYDAN HELSTROM

RYDAN STANDS AT the molten gates with Braxton and Andri, crescent fire in hand. "The Mallum will never see outside this place again."

"Let's make sure of it." Braxton steps forward to place his father's staff on the ground. "We'll start with this."

Rydan can feel the presence of the Caldari behind him as he raises the crescent fire to his mouth, just as Arden and Andri had told him to do. Hoping his memory will serve him well, he replicates the process as best he can, step by step, until he feels an acrid burn climb up his throat.

Knowing what to expect, Arden warns the group to stand back. It's a good thing, too, because the blast that's emitted from his lungs is so powerful, it nearly takes his cousin and Braxton out. Fortunately, Braxton's able to deviate the blast to its intended spot, the draconian fire burning straight through the staff as if it were merely kindling. Rydan coughs, sputtering at the sheer temperature overtaking him. As a precautionary measure, Andri stands firm as ice crystallizes along his fingers—a failsafe if things go sideways.

"Since we know it works, the Mallum should be next," Braxton says, guiding the entity to the scorched ground.

"What about the ring?" Rydan asks. "I've likely only got one more go left in me." He claws at his throat. "I've never been so thirsty in my life."

"It's a good thing there's two of us that bear draconian blood, then," Andri points out. "I'd be honored to do my part."

Rydan glances at Arden before handing the crescent fire over to his cousin. "It's decided," he says, wanting to destroy the Mallum himself. "The ring will be next."

Braxton nods as he removes the amethyst ring from his finger and places it on the ground. "Whenever you're ready."

Andri grins before bringing the crescent fire to his mouth. Unlike Rydan's, which had been green in color, blue flame travels across the ground, wrapping itself around the ring until not even the amethyst remains.

Andri coughs, patting his chest as he hands the crescent fire back to Rydan. "You weren't kidding about the aftershock." He scans the area around him, looking for somewhere to sit. "I'm going to need a minute."

Rydan grips the crescent fire somewhat reluctantly, reminding himself that the worst of it is almost over. There's only one more thing to destroy . . . one more thing standing in the way of a peaceful Aeridon. He turns to face the entity, as well as the rest of the Caldari.

With the Mallum floating aimlessly near Braxton, the Deviator has no choice but to slowly inch away. Without the ring to control it, the entity shouldn't follow him—or do anything, for that matter. Thankfully, it doesn't.

"This is it," Braxton whispers as he readies himself beside Rydan. "On my count."

Rydan nods, unable to peel his eyes from Arden as he lifts the crescent fire to his mouth. After all is said and done, how will he be able to look at her knowing what he's done? That *he* was the one who took the opportunity away from her to see her loved ones again?

"Three," Braxton starts.

Furthermore, how would *she* look at him? Would she even be able to? Things would never be the same between them. How could they be?

"Two," Braxton continues.

His eyes blur at the sheer devastation on her face. Can he really go through with this?

"One!"

Arden buries her face in her hands before buckling at the knees. Haskell manages to catch her before she hits the ground, but the sight alone is enough to change Rydan's mind. He lowers the crescent fire from his mouth before gently tossing it to the ground. He rushes over to the group, his own eyes brimming with tears. Shock is written all over their faces, but he doesn't care. Let them think what they will. Let them think it's a betrayal on his part. He's been with Arden since the very beginning—going through with this would be the most vile betrayal of all.

He can't stomach it.

He grips Arden's arms, steadying her as Haskell slowly releases her. "I'm here," he says into her ear. "I've always been here. You're not alone."

Arden heaves a sob before lifting her head to look at him. Her eyes flit to the Mallum, to where it still stands. She won't say it out loud, but her eyes thank him in ways words never could. Her expression is quick to change, however, as rapid footsteps climb to where he'd just stood.

Stomach sinking, Rydan whirls around to find Andri picking up the crescent fire. He doesn't hesitate as he brings it to his mouth.

"Andri, wait!" Rydan shouts as he breaks into a sprint.

But he isn't fast enough. Rydan can feel his eyes bulge as Andri sends the final blast, this one larger and more harrowing than the last, directly at the Mallum. Blue flames dance around the black mist before swallowing it entirely.

Having arrived a second too late, Rydan grabs Andri by the shoulder, ripping the crescent fire from his hand and throwing it to the ground. "I told you to wait!"

"For what?" Andri gives him a sad look. "Haven't you all waited long enough?"

Rydan lowers his head as his cousin retrieves the crest and brings it back to him. Andri pats him on the shoulder before walking back toward the group. Rydan can only stand there, simultaneously devastated and relieved, as the blue flames die out until all that remains of the Mallum is a singed crimson cloak. He draws closer, gripping the crest until his knuckles turn white. Thread by thread, the cloak is reduced to ash.

It's done.

The Mallum is gone.

Its midnight reign is over.

He turns to find Cerylia handing the soul gems to Arden, knowing that she'd want to be the final tether for Felix and her mother before they take their leave indefinitely.

Arden brings the soul gems close to her heart, tears splattering onto the surface as she whispers something inaudible. The gems glow, one green, one purple, as if in response to whatever she's just said. The group waits in crestfallen silence as the glow emanating from each gem grows brighter and brighter—near blinding—before they finally wink out. Whispers begin to fill the space around them, but the words are muted, at least to his ears. From the sudden shift in Arden's demeanor, however, it seems she's perfectly aware of what the voices are saying. To his surprise, she actually musters a smile.

Once the whispers cease, the gems turn to ash in Arden's palms. She purses her lips, gently blowing on the remnants until the wind takes them away. She lifts a teary gaze to the group, wiping her eyes with the back of her hand.

There are no celebratory shouts. No whoops of joy. Just solemn solidarity. In grief. In love. In reverence.

Cerylia drifts from the group, embracing her niece as she whispers, "We're so proud of you."

Arden nods, voice hoarse as she says, "Those were their final words to me, too."

There's a flicker of guilt in her expression—one that tells Rydan she isn't sharing the whole truth—but before he can analyze it further, she breaks, lowering her head into her aunt's shoulder to cry.

FELIX BARLOW

HE MUST ADMIT, it wasn't necessarily the outcome he'd hoped for, but he's proud of Arden, nonetheless. The restraint she'd shown in pursuing her own desires is something he wasn't sure he'd bear witness to, but, when it mattered most, she'd done right by them all. Yes, she'd faltered ever so slightly, but her decision had ultimately been a selfless one. Even as her heart had fractured and shattered beyond repair, she'd chosen to rid Aeridon of its darkness—and, in turn, liberate the souls of so many who had been afflicted by the entity.

It hadn't been difficult for Felix to reach her once the Mallum had met its end. With the tether that binds them somehow as strong as ever, it'd been rather simple to impress upon her his final thoughts.

The surprise.

The pride.

The devastation.

The longing.

The love.

He may have deserved his fate, having conspired with Xerin who he now knows was Dane all along, but Arden certainly does not. Must life always be so callous and cruel?

So tragically unexpected?

He'll never forget how tightly she'd held on to that tether before his gem's light had winked out. How desperately she'd wanted him back. How much she'd give in that moment to make it happen. Her grief had nearly suffocated him.

But just as she'd made a selfless choice, so must he.

Alas, his final parting gift to her. One she likely won't want, nor even accept, but one she wholly deserves. He'd promised he'd never direct his abilities at her. Not to sway her in any one direction. Not to dredge up the repressed feelings she's been so desperate to conceal. Not even to force her hand when doing so would undeniably be to his benefit.

No, he'd stayed true to his word. Loyal and steadfast.

But all that had changed at the Volkharn spring the moment he'd been presented with an opportunity so grand, he would've been foolish not to act on it—even if it meant going against his word. Surely, one day, Arden will come to understand. What other choice would she have?

And so, out of his love, respect, and admiration for Arden Eliri, Felix had amplified, giving every last ounce of magick he had left. Not for his gain, but for hers. Because, without her, who knows what Aeridon might become?

BRAXTON HORNSBY

CANISTER OF SPRING water in hand, Braxton circles Trendalath castle until he finds what he's looking for. The grate leading to the underground tunnels.

"This is it?" Haskell whistles. "I don't know, mate. It looks pretty ordinary to me."

Braxton pays him no mind. "Hold this," he says, shoving the canister into the Transporter's grip. "And don't you dare spill a drop."

Haskell huffs but doesn't argue, standing back as Braxton pops the grate open with a fallen branch. He brushes his hands together, then retrieves the canister from

Haskell. "I must warn you, what you're about to witness is rather grim."

"If the mention of corpses is some ploy to deter me, consider the effort on your part futile." Haskell skims a hand along his jaw. "In case you've forgotten, we just came from a war in Sardoria—bloodshed and corpses included."

"Thanks for the reminder," Braxton retorts as he lowers himself into the ground. "Just . . . do me a favor and stay close. I'd rather not face Arden's wrath if you happen to disappear on us."

Haskell chortles. "Nothing we haven't faced before, I'm sure."

"You have no idea," Braxton mutters under his breath as he makes the drop into the tunnel.

❧ ❧ ❧

The sight just ahead isn't grim at all. In fact, it has him questioning whether he's even in the right place. Braxton sprints into the underground chamber, head swiveling as he takes in the vast nothingness surrounding him.

No stockpile of bodies exists.

No trace of death lingers.

Nothing but damp dirt and stray gravel lay before him.

"I don't understand," Braxton mumurs. He grips the canister so tightly, his knuckles turn white. After confirming that the spring did indeed work, not only for him, but for the rest of the Caldari, he'd pulled Haskell aside for an undisclosed trip, mostly in Lane's honor. His plan had been to come here, to the tunnels under Trendalath Kingdom, and administer the water from the spring to see if its properties would at least wake the victims from whatever illusié-induced daze they'd been put under—assuming their souls had returned after the Mallum's destruction, of course. Haskell could then transport whoever awoke back to the spring, one by one if needed, to help them restore their abilities fully. It'd seemed simple enough to execute . . . until they'd arrived to find nothing and no one.

"So, are we just going to stare into empty space all day or can we go?" Haskell glances behind him as if he has somewhere to be. "Vira's taking the brunt of the legwork summoning dragons to carry our soon-to-be-illusié-again brethren to Volkharn and, as one of the only Caldari with a movement-based ability, I feel like I'm wasting mine."

"This isn't a waste," Braxton says flatly. "They were here. I know they were. Lane saw them, too."

"Well, she isn't here to back you up, now is she?"

Braxton glares at him. "That was entirely uncalled for."

Haskell sighs, his defensive walls crumbling. "You're right. But . . . look around. There's nothing here for us to do."

Braxton drops his shoulders, defeated. "How could hundreds, if not thousands, of bodies just disappear?"

Out of the corner of his eye, a shadow appears from behind a pillar. Keen as he is, Haskell notices the movement and unsheathes his sword. "Announce yourself at once!"

"There will be no need for that," says a familiar voice. As the figure draws closer, it becomes clear who it is.

"Cyrus," Braxton says, rushing past Haskell to greet him. "What are you doing here?"

"I should ask the same of you, although you never were one to leave unfinished business in your midst." Cyrus smiles. "I suppose we have that in common."

Haskell looks between them in disbelief. "So, the king really *was* stockpiling bodies underneath Trendalath castle?"

"I'm afraid so," Cyrus confirms. "It seems I'm the only one left who can confirm what Braxton and Lane saw." At the mention of her, he bows his head and whispers, "My deepest condolences."

"Where are they now? The bodies?" Haskell asks.

"You were correct in your assumption. The bodies are indeed gone, as is further evidenced by this empty chamber."

Haskell furrows his brows. "They were connected to the Mallum in some way, right?"

"Only in that their souls were absorbed to strengthen the Mallum's resolve." Cyrus sighs. "What the king did not know, however, was that the ward I'd placed over the bodies would expire."

"Expire?" Braxton echoes. "How?"

"Through my work with someone you've only just met." The corners of his eyes crinkle. "Diera."

Braxton can only stand there, speechless.

Cyrus lays a firm hand on his shoulder and squeezes before continuing, "Although you may find it hard to believe, your mother kept close tabs on you. Even when you fled to Athia, she knew. She asked Hanslow to take you in, knowing that he would protect you when the time came."

Braxton shudders, distinctly recalling when he'd fled the inn to avoid capture by his father's Savant—when he thought he'd left Hanslow for dead.

"As a Diviner, or a Seer in the common tongue, your mother tried to curtail as much violence, chaos, and bloodshed as she could *without* intervening with the larger plan: Aeridon's fate. Which is no easy feat, mind you." Cyrus clears his throat as he adjusts his stance, clasping his hands behind his back. "She foresaw what Darius was capable of, what he'd do underneath this very castle, and tasked me with warding the bodies. To preserve them until the Mallum met its end."

"She knew all along," Braxton whispers.

"And what if we had failed?" Haskell challenges. "Do you mean to say that the bodies would still be here at the king's disposal, had he not been banished to the Void? At *Dane's* disposal?"

"Yes," Cyrus admits. "Because, as I said before, there's only so much we could do to circumvent the ill fate of so many—what was already destined to occur." He pauses. "If things *had* gone sideways, alternative measures would have been taken to dispose of the bodies."

"Like what?" Haskell presses.

"The reversal of the very ward I'd put into place," he answers, "through the use of a Rescinder. The process of decay would be slow, but they'd be of no use then."

"Is that all?" Haskell asks, clearly unimpressed.

Cyrus gives him a pointed look. "We could have buried them, burned them, brought dragons to feast on them—"

"Or perhaps worked to avoid the countless deaths of illusié all together," Braxton interrupts.

Cyrus shakes his head. "I wouldn't expect either of you to understand—but I trusted in Queen Tymond's foresight. I trusted her to do right by her kingdom, by illusié, by all of Aeridon. And, for all intents and purposes, she did. Even though she isn't here to see it. She gave her life for the cause." He brushes away a tear. "The Mallum needed the strength of the souls it took to be able to hold as much magick as it did. The very magick Arden was able to channel and return to our people. Aldreda knew this and did everything in her power to ensure illusié would not be lost to the likes of an ill-fought war." He looks to Haskell. "And by an Eliri, no less."

Haskell blanches at the mention of his uncle.

"It may have been an Eliri pulling the strings, but the Tymonds were no better," Braxton says. "My father is a shining example of that."

Cyrus gives a grim nod. "The important thing is we succeeded in our endeavors. The Mallum is gone. Illusié did not perish and has been restored. And the souls of those unfortunate enough to be caught in the midst of it all have been set free. Your mother would be proud." He looks between the Deviator and the Transporter. "Both of them."

Haskell looks to his cousin. "I suppose we should leave it at that."

Braxton nods in agreement, although the guilt of what his father had done still gnaws at him.

Sensing his distress, the Transporter places a hand on his shoulder, his expression softening. "Let it go, cousin. Try as we might, it's impossible to save everyone. And this . . . whatever your father did or didn't do—well, it isn't your burden to bear." With a quick pat, he turns and starts walking back toward the tunnel.

Braxton sighs, wishing that were true; but if he's learned anything about being a Tymond, it's that past mistakes are destined to haunt him, even if he wasn't the one who made them.

CERYLIA JARETH

Although it's expected, the knock on the doors to the White Room have Cerylia straightening in her seat. "You may enter," she says a touch harshly.

Delwynn is the first to enter the room, followed by four guards who currently have her visitor surrounded, blocking him from view.

"Leave us," she orders without further explanation.

The guards glance at one another with brief hesitation but retreat without a word. Delwynn opens his mouth in protest, but Cerylia raises a hand before he can speak. "That'll be all, Delwynn."

At the rather abrupt dismissal, her advisor turns toward the doors, leaving her alone with none other than Clive Ridley, the Savant's esteemed Caster.

Clive approaches the throne slowly. "Queen Jareth." Much to her surprise, he bends into a low bow. "Your summons was the last thing I expected to receive."

"Come now." She arches a brow. "Certainly not the last?"

He shrugs. "Dangerously close to it."

Cerylia smirks, placing her hands in her lap. "You may find it rather surprising, then, when I tell you that you've been summoned here for an apology. One that needs to be made on my behalf." She pauses, if only to steady her pounding heart. "For it was not you I should have relentlessly pursued over the past decade, nor Aldreda Tymond, but my own husband." Admitting the fault out loud nearly causes her voice to break. "Please accept my deepest apologies for any trouble I have caused you."

Astonishment crosses the Caster's face. "With all due respect, Your Greatness, such an apology may as well have been preconceived. Your husband *was* my intended target."

"As he should have been. I was too blind to see it."

"To no fault of your own. We all were—blind, that is."

Cerylia drops her gaze. "I only wish your counterpart were here to receive my apology as well."

"I can assure you, being a Diviner and all, Aldreda already knows. And just as I forgive you, she undoubtedly would as well."

Cerylia looks up, the sadness on his face mirroring her own. "What went wrong all those years ago?"

Clive skims a hand across his stubble, jaw working. "I honestly couldn't say. Although I was a sworn member of the Savant, my ties to Aldreda ran much deeper, especially when I learned she was illusié. Darius's intentions were misguided and wrought with greed, but Aldreda's were pure—" Unable to finish the thought, his voice cracks. Only when he's composed himself does he continue. "My involvement with the queen and my affections toward her may have been unsavory to those who became aware of our indiscretions, but who am I to fight the tides of fate? Darius would have exiled her—or worse—had he known of her abilities. He certainly would have used them to his advantage," he scoffs. "Knowing what Aldreda knew about Dane, and about Aeridon as a whole, I felt inclined to protect her. To aid her in whatever cause she deemed worthwhile."

"So, you set out to eradicate the problem," Cerylia says, "as anyone facing a threat would do."

"Yes," Clive answers, taking a step forward, "but not before attempting to eradicate the ever-present problem looming over us all."

Cerylia's eyes widen. "The Mallum?"

Clive nods. "Having learned that it was her sister's soul trapped within the entity, Aldreda attempted to reason with it in the hopes a mutual resolution might be reached. While that interaction didn't cost her her life or her abilities, it did weaken them tremendously. It seems wearing the amethyst ring, however brief a time, ended up having far greater consequences than they were worth. Her abilities as a Diviner were more or less corrupted after that. She could only trust what she'd foreseen *before* the unfortunate incident with the Mallum."

"So, Dane continued to be your target, but, ultimately, it was Xerin who paid the price," Cerylia finishes softly.

"Not to mention countless others," he admits. "It was difficult enough for Aldreda to accept her own fate, but, in the weeks leading up to her death, she expressed time and time again that her ability as a Diviner had started to feel like more of a curse than a gift."

Cerylia sighs, giving a sullen shake of her head. "I can understand why. To know of the demise that awaits but be able to do nothing."

Clive nods. "Needless to say, it ate at her, driving her to the brink of madness, until she had no choice but to welcome death with open arms . . . even if it meant her last breath was to be taken at the hands of her husband and the Mallum." The anger written across his face is palpable.

"At least Arden was there," Cerylia whispers. "I hope the late queen found some peace in her niece's presence."

"I would hope so as well." Clive clears his throat. "I will always think of Aldreda Tymond as my queen, however, given that I've been fighting for the sake of Aeridon all this time, I . . . well, I would be honored to serve the throne in any capacity." He bows his head. "That is, if you'll have me, Your Greatness."

Cerylia doesn't even try to hide the shock on her face.

"Although," he adds quickly, "I can understand if not since, in your eyes, I've been the enemy—"

"On the contrary," Cerylia interrupts, "I should like to have you as High Commander of the Queen's Guard."

Having expected a rejection, the surprise on Clive's face is apparent. "Thank you, My Queen. I graciously accept the position as High Commander of the Queen's Guard."

"Your abilities will be invaluable against any future threats we might face, although I sincerely hope conflict will not touch Aeridon as long as I sit the throne."

Clive gives her a reassuring smile, one she's inclined to believe is genuine. "If the late queen's visions are reliable, as I wholeheartedly believe they are, then I'm pleased to report that Aeridon and all its provinces will experience nothing but peace for years to come."

What a welcome relief to hear those words. Cerylia returns the smile. "For our sake and the sake of all those who reside in Aeridon, High Commander Ridley, I sincerely hope you're right."

EPILOGUE

CERYLIA JARETH

WORD SPREAD LIKE wildfire of the Sardorian King's treachery and the Queen's impossible task to choose duty over love. Her return to Sardoria had been received with an outpouring of love and admiration from not only her constituents, but those residing in the neighboring towns as well. With both the Trendalath and Sardorian Kings gone, she thought it only just to put her queenship up to a vote. It'd been unanimous, on all fronts.

Cerylia Elise Jareth, Sovereign Queen of Aeridon.

Wearing a new crown for a new beginning, she finishes pinning up her hair, dabbing some crushed berries on her lips for some color. A final look at her reflection has her making a few minor adjustments before answering the knock at her door. It's her advisor, Delwynn, carrying a round silver tray containing bundles of primrose, winterberry, and clary sage—three plants hardy enough to make it through even the harshest of Sardoria's winters. She reaches for one, her hand grazing the white ribbon holding the bundle together, and lifts it to her nose. She inhales the familiar scent, instantly feeling at home.

Nodding in approval, she carefully returns the bundle to the tray. "Everything has been arranged as I've asked?"

"Yes, Your Excellency."

Cerylia pauses, studying her advisor. "Well, that's new."

Delwynn shrugs. "A new title for a new reign. I hope you don't mind—"

"Not at all," she interjects with a smile. "In fact, I love it."

Delwynn grins. "I thought you might."

Cerylia steps out of her chambers, closing the door behind her. She straightens her robes, brushing an invisible wrinkle out of the fabric. "How do I look?"

"As a queen should," Delwynn answers. "Remarkably regal."

"I knew I kept you around for a reason," she teases, extending an arm to him. "Shall we?"

Surprised and rather pleased by the gesture, Delwynn takes her arm in his. "It would be my greatest honor, My Queen."

ॐ   ॐ   ॐ

The ceremony to honor their fallen brethren is packed to the brim with Aeridon's residents. The field had taken weeks to clean up, at which point illusié from all over had arrived to offer their help—after visiting the spring to restore their abilities, of course. The Telekinetics were of immense help, given their ability to move collapsed columns and pillars with merely their minds. Much to Cerylia's surprise and delight, those who had originally sailed from the Crostan Islands to fight against the Sardorian forces had ultimately pledged their allegiance to not only Aeridon, but to recognize her as their queen as well.

Cerylia places the final bundle of herbs on the last pyre, signaling to the Ignitors to light them. Among them are Rydan and Avery, who stand side by side, as they call their abilities forth. Cerylia climbs the steps to the dais, heat hitting the side of her face as ten pyres rise in flames, one for every major province of Aeridon. To her left, those who reside inland to the west bow their heads in reverence, banners from Miraenia, Declorath, Chialka, and Trendalath waving as one in the brisk wind. To her right, the residents of Athia, the Isle of Lonia, and the Crostan Islands lift their hands to their temples in an honorary salute. At the rear are the residents of Sardoria and the few who survived the attack at Midvale, hands pressed together in prayer for the fallen. A lone banner for Drakken Isle flutters behind them to honor the dragons who were summoned and unjustly maimed, called for a fight that was never theirs to begin with.

The last pyre, the one for Midvale, seems to burn the brightest, as if the Archmage herself had been here to light it. Cerylia sheds a single tear for Cyfrin Galdor, a woman who certainly felt like her nemesis at times, but ultimately wound up being a mentor and, dare she even say, a friend.

The Caldari stand just behind the pyres, dressed in Sardoria's royal colors of blue and silver, with their arms positioned behind their backs. They look at their queen expectantly, waiting for her to deliver the eulogy as their sovereign leader. Her gaze lands on her niece, the grief in her eyes palpable.

"It is true that we will never be the same again after a travesty such as this," she begins, keeping her gaze pinned on Arden. "But the best way we can honor the fallen is to unite as one people, one land, one mind." She pauses, finally breaking her gaze from her niece to survey those staring up at her, hope flickering in their eyes. "For as one, there will be no wars fought. Disagreements and differences of opinion are inevitable, yes, but we can honor those before us by settling them with dignity and grace."

"Hear, hear!" someone from the left shouts.

"Aye!" yells another.

A raucous echo of agreement floods the field.

Cerylia smiles, raising a hand. "Your enthusiasm is duly noted." Her grin grows wider. "And as your queen, I'm going to hold you to it."

A collective laugh ripples amongst the group.

She clears her throat, continuing, "While we're all gathered here, there are some announcements I'd like to make. The first is one I've given tremendous consideration. From this point forward, I hereby declare Midvale Arcane Haven a historic landmark, as the Veil will no longer separate those who wield illusié and those who do not. Let it serve as a reminder of all we had to endure to reach where we are today."

Less than half of the audience claps or shows any kind of interest, but the Caldari nod at each other in approval.

Cerylia goes on to say, "As you may or may not be aware, while there are many who fought this war to aid in our triumph, there are a select few who were instrumental in such a victorious outcome. I would like to honor them now." She shifts her gaze. "Braxton Hornsby and Arden Eliri." She waits for each of them to step forward, pleased to see that they do so willingly. "Without your sacrifice, we certainly would not be standing here today. With that being said, I bestow upon you the following titles as you've not only earned them, you wholeheartedly *deserve* them." She beckons them to climb the steps to the dais.

Cerylia turns behind her to where Delwynn stands, urging him to bring forth the marble tray she'd prepared earlier. From it, she removes a crown, fashioned of the same fine metals and gems as her own, and places it on Braxton's head. "People of Aeridon, I present to you Braxton Hornsby. Rightful heir to the Tymond throne. Crown Prince of Trendalath."

Clapping ensues, albeit slowly at first, given the Tymonds' history in Aeridon, but the Caldari make up for it with their generous whooping and hollering.

Cerylia winks at them, then turns behind her once more to find Delwynn at the ready with a second tray. From it, she removes a midnight blue cloak adorned with silver buttons and a satin lined hood. "People of Aeridon, may I also present to you Arden Eliri. Our very first Divine Master of Channeling. And . . . Distinguished Archmage of Aeridon."

Arden's head swivels toward her in shock.

Cerylia gives her a reassuring smile before draping the cloak around her niece's shoulders. She leans in to give her a hug, whispering in her ear, "I know it isn't exactly what we discussed, but the title is yours if you want it."

"Thank you," Arden whispers back. "I accept."

She and Braxton turn to leave, but Cerylia stops them, grabbing one last thing from behind the dais. To the eyes of an onlooker, it would appear to be an ordinary scroll of parchment, but it represents much more than that. "For my final announcement of the evening," she says with pride, "it is with great honor that I present our Prince and Archmage with the royal charter to Trendalath Kingdom, as I trust the two of them will do well by it." The surprise on their faces doesn't go unnoticed. "May you both finally have a place to call home."

ARDEN ELIRI

I THOUGHT BEING back here would dredge up the ghosts of my past but, if I'm being entirely honest, there's nothing left in Trendalath Kingdom to haunt me. Perhaps it's the complete restructuring and renovations Braxton and I had agreed upon before even stepping foot inside, but the castle feels warm and welcoming now in a way it couldn't possibly have before. A large part of that is thanks to the people residing here.

Inspired by Queen Jareth's speech, we'd decided to open the doors to all residents of Aeridon, regardless of magickal ability. As Archmage, Braxton had suggested I choose a new name for the castle to better represent what we're trying to do here. I landed on the Barlow Academy of Defense and Magick. Because if there's one person who tested me, pushed my boundaries, and challenged me from the very beginning, it was Felix. In a lot of ways, I owe him a life debt. And so, I figured if he can't live here amongst us in the flesh, then at least he can live on in the hearts of the people we teach and train.

In true Braxton-nature, he'd put me in charge of the curriculum. A solid mix of Cruex training and illusié wielding seemed appropriate. I'd appointed Rydan and Andri as two of our Guild Leaders for training in Natural Elements, although Rydan had opted for a specialty in weaponry and hand-to-hand combat. Braxton had willingly volunteered to take a similar position as Guild Leader, but with a focus on defensive reversal tactics and, surprisingly enough, healing.

It seems I've rubbed off on him after all.

The other Caldari have their roles, too. I thought it best they choose what they wanted to teach. That said, I wasn't at all surprised to learn that they each wanted to stay within their respective fields ability-wise, with Estelle teaching cloaking and Haskell teaching transporting. Vira's class on summoning and working with dragons is, by far, the most popular amongst the students, much to Avery's chagrin, but what can I say? Alchemy and herbal botany just haven't made it onto the students' radar yet.

Or so I keep reminding him.

As for those who weren't born illusié but always wanted to be, the spring's offered us an opportunity we didn't even know existed. Not all illusié who lost their abilities to the Mallum decided to travel to Volkharn to restore their magick. In fact, a staggering number decided to remain just as they were, preferring what they deem an ordinary life over that of an illusié wielder. We'd wondered what would happen to the abilities that weren't reclaimed, only to discover that they could be transferred to those worthy of having them. Their only requirement, as stipulated by Queen Jareth, is to attend the Barlow Academy of Defense and Magick so they can fully understand what it is they're voluntarily getting themselves into. Because, if the past decade is any indication, being illusié certainly comes with its own trials and tribulations.

"On your left! Your left!" Rydan shouts at one of the students, running a hand through his tousled hair. I catch his eye from across the courtyard, smiling at how worked up he's getting. "You better make me look good because the Archmage is mere steps away," he adds before throwing a wink my way.

I laugh at the remark as the students turn toward me to bow. "As you were," I say with a lighthearted wave. "Don't let my presence distract you."

Rydan blanches at the subtle double meaning in my words, even though it's the truth. A distraction is all I am for him. All I've ever been. I've told him, more times than I can count, that he and Vira are so well aligned in their values that they'd undoubtedly lead a happy life together. Even so, he resists.

I give him a polite nod, gazing at the setting sun before retiring to my chambers for the evening, hating that after everything we've been through, we're nearly strangers. But if they knew—if *any* of them knew . . . I shake away the thought, locking the double doors to my chamber behind me. I'd had the interior renovated to appear nearly identical to my room in Midvale since it was the last place I'd been with Felix—the last place I'd felt his touch, heard his voice . . .

Longing pierces my heart, careening straight into my soul.

I hastily remove the cloak that signifies my status, one I'm still convinced I don't deserve, and toss it onto the bed. I give Juniper a quick scratch behind the ears before extending my hand to the hearth, waiting for the familiar stirring in my fingertips. The kindling ignites, the warmth floating across the room to wrap itself around me like a wool blanket. After being confined all day, I sigh with relief at the chance to finally wield an ability, no matter how small.

But igniting isn't all I can do.

My parting moments with Felix—before his soul was released into the ethers—had yielded information I wasn't expecting. At all. Apparently, whilst in the Volkharn spring, Felix had chosen to surrender his amplification abilities. For good. I'd subconsciously managed to channel said abilities— and while Hanslow had worked to stabilize the surrounding energies in the spring, I, having been in the water at the same time, had unknowingly been successful at channeling them.

Ergo, all illusié abilities were stabilized *within* me, granting me access to wield whatever ability whenever and however I so choose, just like before. Hence my reason for keeping everyone at arm's length. They cannot know. This secret will live with me. And it will die with me.

Just as channeling will.

It's a stark realization, knowing I'm the anomaly in Aeridon. If I haven't already upset the balance and the natural order of things, one day, I will—whether it's intentional or not. And I say this because I *know* it.

In my attempt to heal Aldreda Tymond, I unknowingly channeled her ability as a Diviner to *see*. Felix could sense it, kept it alive by amplifying it, but never told me. He figured, one day, I would need it. And he was right.

His final parting gift to me, he'd said.

As devastating as it is, any hope of a normal future for me is impossible. I've seen the implications of my ability, of bearing a child with the ability to channel, of having to say good-bye to her just as my father had to say good-bye to me.

It's bleak. It's cruel. I want no part of it.

And so, I was forced to make another impossible decision. One to ensure channeling ends with me. One that would force me to live a life of solitude, tucked away in the vision of a future I'll never get to be a part of.

But at least I got to see it, if only in glimpses.

And at least I'll know, when I take my final breaths, that the Aeridon we built and fought for all these years will stand the tests of time . . . because of me. A lords-damned Eliri.

And *that's* a legacy worth leaving.

ACKNOWLEDGMENTS

Ten straight months of tandem writing and editing the final two books in this series is no easy feat, especially with two kids under 10 and one under a year old… and another one on the way! As I write these acknowledgments, I'm 9 weeks along in my second pregnancy and we're gearing up to move our family farther north. Life doesn't slow down and often throws curveballs when you least expect them, so to my fellow aspiring authors waiting for the "perfect time"… there is only ever the time you have right now and what you choose to do with it. Don't let external circumstances define whether your book gets written or not because they will always, always be there. Our task, as creatives, is to write, regardless. Creation is our birthright. Don't you forget it!

First and foremost, I'd like to thank the Divine Mother for keeping the spark to write alive. This current season of life is beautiful and trying, fulfilling and beyond challenging as I learn to juggle the needs of a household of eight. Embracing the feminine and releasing so much undue pressure is the sole reason I'm even able to write these acknowledgments, knowing I didn't sacrifice one thing for another.

To M.O.: my husband, my soulmate, my pea—It still feels surreal being able to write you into my acknowledgments. Life has come at us so fast, in the most wonderful way, ever since we reconnected that night in May. To think that we were on completely different trajectories but *still* managed to come together is all the proof I'll ever need that fate is real. I adore our growing family, and can't wait to welcome another little one into the world together. I love you always . . . to whatever end.

To my sweet Ivy girl—You were in the womb when I finished writing the fifth book in this series, and you're about to be a year old as I make plans to publish the sixth. It feels so special knowing I got to share this chapter of my life with you, one that I built before even knowing you'd arrive. You're going to be the best big sister. I love you so much.

To L&L—While I may technically be your stepmom, you've fully embraced me as your mama and I could not be more proud. Thank you for reminding me of the importance of joy and play. You've made space for my inner child to thrive without even knowing it. I love you both immensely.

To Anna Vera, for being the first person I call (or send voice messages to) for anything and everything going on in my life. I love that I can quite literally tell you anything and be met with love, understanding, and lightheartedness. You serve as a reminder of everything good and beautiful in this world. I love you, bb!

To my sister, Erin, for being just as enthusiastic, if not more, about books and reading. Of all the things to connect with a sibling over, reading definitely tops the list. Please know that I'm living vicariously through you on all your travels. I'm so proud of you. I love you!

To my Mom, for teaching me the value of independence, freedom, and going after your dreams regardless of opinion or obstacle. No matter the era or season of life, your involvement doesn't go unnoticed. Thank you for being such a tremendous role model over the years. I love you!

To my Dad, for being such an advocate for these books. Every time you mention one of my characters or how vividly you can picture what I've written, my heart swells. Your support has had such an impact on my confidence, from kid to teenager to adult. Now that this series is complete, I say we kick back on the beach and read. I love you!

To the incredibly talented cartographer, Deven Rue, for bringing The Lands of Aeridon to life, and to the cover designers at Damonza who continuously stun me with their artistry and professionalism. Thank you for being such a pleasure to work with!

To my furbabies—I love you more than words can express. Your snuggles, sweet kisses, and zoomies bring so much joy and laughter to my life. I'm so grateful our paths crossed in this lifetime. I don't know what I'd do without you!

And finally, to my YouTube fam, readers, and fans—Thank you for being here through it all. It's been a long road with this series, but I'll never forget how it started. Your support has meant everything to me.

Looking for your next otherworldly read?
Check out this page-turning standalone:

BEYOND THE STARS AND SHADOWS

TURN THE PAGE FOR A SNEAK
PEEK OF CHAPTER ONE

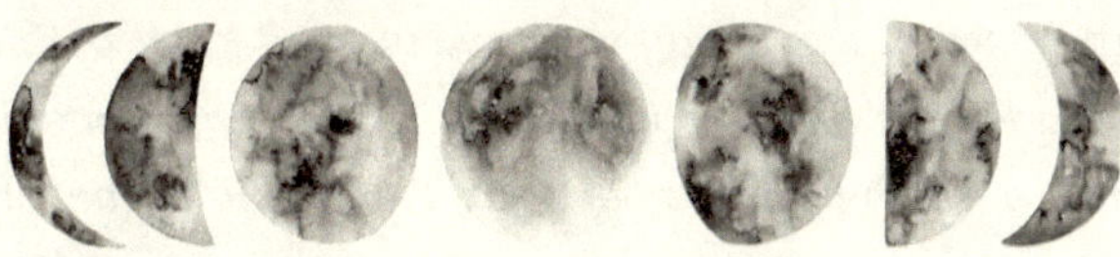

1

WHO WOULD HAVE thought it possible to
have a mid-life crisis at twenty-eight?

Such youth. Such zest. So much life yet to be lived.

Until I heard the one word that changed everything.

Pregnant.

I hadn't given much thought to this happening. I, unlike
most of the female species, did not have dreams of "the
perfect marriage" or starting a family of my own. Hell, I
wasn't even sure what was happening when my soon-to-be-
fiancé got down on one knee. It was sweet, I suppose. And
unexpected. And downright terrifying.

But *kids*? I didn't know I had a line to be drawn, but it turns out I did. It was quite a big one, too.

I know what it is I'm "supposed" to say. Something along the lines of . . . *I may not have wanted kids, but I'd do it for him. For us. For our family.* Or . . . *I never considered becoming a mother, but now that I'm about to be one, I couldn't imagine things happening any other way.*

But I'm not going to say any of that. Why? Because it's the furthest thing from the truth.

Before you go on and judge me (*yeah, I see you*), I want to preface this by saying that I had a less than traditional upbringing.

My mother? Hardly remember her.

My father? Incarcerated when I was eleven.

Why, you might ask? Because of the sudden disappearance of my mother—in which *he* was the primary suspect. So much so, they locked him up for it.

He's been behind bars ever since.

When you grow up in a dysfunctional home setting like that, it really makes you question everything. I remember hearing the girls at school talk about their "dream man" and their "dream weddings", and I honestly wanted nothing more than to punch them in the face.

I was twelve.

I was also living with my recently divorced—thrice over—harebrained aunt, whom I ran away from on a regular basis. *I mean, wouldn't you?* Between the disappearance of her sister; her brother-in-law being a total sociopath; and inheriting *me*, the irony of "coming home" was too much for me to wrap my head around, seeing as I never got to know what a "home" was in the first place. And so, the thought of providing *that*—something so foreign, so unknown—for our soon-to-be family of three scared the living shit out of me.

To make matters worse, my fiancé and I hadn't exactly had the whole "kids" discussion. After peeing on an ungodly amount of pregnancy tests, I knew it wasn't a fluke. I also knew I had to tell him.

The first words that came out of my mouth?

"I'm sorry."

How's that for a pregnancy announcement?

We're equal parts responsible, buddy, and yet here I am, apologizing for something I'm not even sure I wanted in the first place.

His response?

"How far along? Will you be showing at the wedding?"

Shallow fuck.

With all the hormones coursing through my body, I'm surprised I didn't clock him in the face right then and there. I'm also surprised that I didn't leave him. But if you've ever been engaged before—if you've ever planned a *wedding* before—then you know that once you're in, it's nearly impossible to claw your way out . . . no matter how badly you might want to.

After a tearful, hormonal, wreck-of-a-week later, I went in for an ultrasound. Alone. I was staring at that stupid ring on my finger, wondering how I'd ended up here—engaged to a man (ahem, *boy*) I couldn't stand, about to face the reality of becoming a mother when I never had the full experience of having one myself. All thanks to the one person who *vowed,* swore up and down, to protect her. Who's now rotting in jail like the prick he is.

What a fucking joke.

If I sound bitter, it's because I am. While other kids were having birthday parties and celebrating the holidays, I was in a fucking courtroom. Testifying.

Let me reiterate: I was twelve.

No kid should ever be subjected to that.

No kid should ever be subjected to *me.*

I mean, look at what I've become. You're probably thinking . . . *she's the protagonist of this story?* Damn right, I am. Don't act like you don't have shadows and baggage, too. We all do. Welcome to being human.

I digress. Where were we?

Oh, right. The doctor's office.

So I'm miserably engaged, unwillingly pregnant, and utterly alone, waiting for the doctor to return with the results of my ultrasound. I should have guessed by his abrupt exit that when he re-entered, he'd be wearing anything but a smile. I'll never forget the way his mouth pressed into a grim line. The way he spoke the words that, once again, altered my entire reality.

"There's no heartbeat."

Oh.

Based on the information I had given him, I'd only been about seven or eight weeks along, so yes, quite early for an ultrasound; but it was the blood test that sealed my fate. Urine tests are only so reliable—but blood? There's no denying the story *it* tells. And this story?

No longer pregnant.

"Most likely a miscarriage. One in eight women have them, many occurring *before* the woman is even aware she's pregnant."

Hmm.

As much as I'd like to describe the tidal wave of emotions that washed over me in that moment, I can't. To this day, they still confuse me. There was relief, yes. But there was also a lingering sense of failure. Betrayal. And *sadness.* It's strange how even when it's something you thought you didn't want, the feeling of *loss* is right there to remind you of what *could have been . . .* how things *might* have played out differently had life's circumstances been different.

It's cruel. Palpable. Unrelenting.

I wouldn't wish that feeling upon anybody.

That was in October. I'll never forget it—the changing of the leaves as I pushed the hospital doors open, a paper bag in one hand with a free month of birth control (ha!), a prescription in the other, and tears streaming down my face from behind my sunglasses.

If you're assuming my fiancé and I are no longer together, you would be correct. That was the first thing I did when I got home. Threw the birth control in his face and told him to give it to his next girlfriend. Left the ring on the counter. Stormed into the bedroom and started packing a bag . . . when I realized that it's *my* house. So I grabbed *his* suitcase instead and told him to pack his shit and get out of my life. He didn't say anything. Didn't so much as flinch. Didn't yell. Didn't cry. Didn't even fucking apologize. His silence spoke volumes as he rolled his suitcase out the door, started up his truck, and drove off.

I haven't heard from him since.

And I wouldn't hear from him ever again after the news reported a tragic accident involving him flipping his truck into a ditch, just four months after we'd split. Two unexpected losses within one year, both involving what could have been my potential "future". *Chaos theory at its finest,* my mother would have said.

It was brutal in the most incomprehensible way.

Because I'd felt truly and completely . . . alone.

With my dysfunctional family situation, I'd had no one to tell the engagement was off. No one to tell that my ex-fiancé had *died.* No one to give a damn about my life except for me. Call me cruel and heartless, but at that point, as far as I was concerned, it'd never even happened. None of it. Best to just forget and move on.

Believe me, I've tried.

It wasn't until later that next year, after I'd rid myself of everything that reminded me of him—including that house—that I was (apparently) due for a reminder. I had just slid into a relaxing bubble bath after a long day of working at the university library, when the strangest sensation came over me. I remember clenching my jaw as the entire lower half of my body contracted . . . and released. I figured it was just due to cramping—I've been known to have severe cycles a time or two—but my diagnosis changed *real* quick when it happened again.

And again.

Shorter bursts.

Immense pain.

Accelerated breathing.

I sound like I'm about to go into labor.

Sharp stabbing. Squeezing. Tension.

Wanting to hold my breath but realizing it's too painful.

Unusual breathing patterns.

*I **feel** like I'm about to go into labor.*

I reached across the ledge of the tub for my phone. Checked the date. July 17, 2029. Did a quick count on my fingers. And lo and behold, it had been nine months.

Another contraction, this one *brutal.*

I made a sound that I've never made before.

It sounded—and felt—like a *push.*

How? Why? This is impossible.

Jaw clenched, I gripped the edges of the porcelain tub, my knuckles turning white. A grunt.

Another push.

And another.

Zero possibility of it being menstrual cramps.

And on and on it went.

Until the water turned lukewarm.

Until it lost its heat entirely.

Sweating. Shaking, Stuck between hot and cold.

Confused at the impossibility of this moment.

It felt like *hours* had passed until my gut-wrenching cry.

And then, *finally* . . . sweet, sweet release.

Misty-eyed, I looked down at the water, at the crystal-clear surface. Just as it'd been before. As if nothing had even happened.

And that's when I knew . . .

That there are far more realities that exist beyond this one.

Kristen Martin is the International Amazon Bestselling Indie Author of the YA science fiction trilogy, THE ALPHA DRIVE, the YA dark fantasy series, SHADOW CROWN, the metaphysical standalone, BEYOND THE STARS AND SHADOWS, and personal development books SOULFLOW and BE YOUR OWN #GOALS. A writing coach and creative entrepreneur, Kristen is also an avid YouTuber with hundreds of videos offering writing advice and inspiration for creatives and aspiring authors everywhere. She currently lives in Texas with her husband and their six kids.

STAY CONNECTED:
www.kristenmartinbooks.com
www.youtube.com/authorkristenmartinbooks
www.facebook.com/authorkristenmartin
Instagram @authorkristenmartin
TikTok @authorkristenmartin